"A fun read. Delightful, engaging, charming, and yes, funny. Humor in the characters, and humor in the events. I thoroughly enjoyed this romp of a read."

    —LAURAINE SNELLING, author of the Red River series, Daughters of Blessing series, and *One Perfect Day*, commenting on *The Confidential Life of Eugenia Cooper*

Anna Finch and the Hired Gun

A Novel

KATHLEEN Y'BARBO

WATERBROOK
PRESS

ANNA FINCH AND THE HIRED GUN
PUBLISHED BY WATERBROOK PRESS
12265 Oracle Boulevard, Suite 200
Colorado Springs, Colorado 80921

All Scripture quotations are taken from the King James Version.

This is a work of fiction. Apart from well-known actual people, events, and locales that figure into the narrative, all names, characters, places, and incidents are the products of the author's imagination or are used fictitiously. Any resemblance to current events or locales, or to living persons, is entirely coincidental.

ISBN 978-0-307-44481-3

ISBN 978-0-307-45912-1 (electronic)

Published in the United States by WaterBrook Multnomah, an imprint of the Crown Publishing Group, a division of Random House Inc., New York.

WATERBROOK and its deer colophon are registered trademarks of Random House Inc.

Library of Congress Cataloging-in-Publication Data
Y'Barbo, Kathleen.
    Anna Finch and the hired gun : a novel / Kathleen Y'Barbo. — 1st ed.
        p. cm.
        ISBN 978-0-307-44481-3 — ISBN 978-0-307-45912-1 (electronic)
    1. Single women—Fiction. 2. Women journalists—Fiction. 3. Holliday, John Henry, 1851-1887—Fiction. 4. Pinkerton's National Detective Agency—Fiction. I. Title.
        PS3625.B37A56 2010
        813'.6—dc22
                                                    2010000756

Printed in the United States of America
2010—First Edition

10 9 8 7 6 5 4 3 2 1

To Jess
Which rhymes with "bless"
For rescuing my mess!

And to my village.

He was a dentist whom necessity had made a gambler; a gambler whom disease had made a vagabond; a philosopher whom life had made a caustic wit; a long, lean, blond fellow nearly dead with consumption and at the same time the most skillful gambler and the nerviest, speediest, deadliest man with a six-gun that I ever knew.

—*Wyatt Earp, regarding Doc Holliday*

We had a little misunderstanding, but it didn't
amount to much.

— *Doc Holliday*

April 30, 1885, Denver, Colorado

Daybreak found Anna Finch astride her horse, Maisie, heading for
the foothills west of Denver. Her father had given her the mare before
he decided riding horses across the high plains was not for well-bred
women of marriageable age.

As the youngest of five daughters, Anna had always been able to
tug on her father's heartstrings and get whatever she wanted from
him, and what she'd wanted was a proper saddle. Not one of those
sidesaddle contraptions where a lady had to balance herself and her
bustles to avoid falling and injuring more than just her pride. Despite
her mother's vocal protests, Anna soon had exactly what she wished
for. That old saddle still served her well, though Papa long ago
believed she'd retired it, along with her habit of watching the sun rise
out on the prairie, astride a trusty horse.

As an observer of people, Anna had learned by watching her sisters, who'd been forced to give up all but the most docile pursuits,
that there would come a day when this would be asked of her too.

And once that day came, she'd no longer have the freedom to ride like the wind. Instead, she'd be left knitting in some parlor, praying for a breeze.

Shrugging off the thought, Anna urged her horse to a trot and let the mare find her own pace across the plain. Wild streaks of orange and gold teased a sky painted deepest purple as she loosened her hairpins and tossed them behind her.

If the maids wondered why they had to fetch so many hairpins from the mercantile, they never said. Nor did anyone question why Anna's skirts were often coated in trail dust or why the occasional set of youth-sized trousers found their way into the carpetbag she carried on her rides. Those who resided under the Finch roof, be they servant or family, preferred a sort of self-induced blindness that relegated all but the most obvious to the edges of their vision. And sometimes even the obvious was missed.

Anna, on the other hand, prided herself in seeing details. As a girl, she'd begun the custom of writing in a journal. Once the risk of Mama or Papa coming across a written record of her life became a concern, Anna had turned to poetry and, on occasion, fiction. Writing poems and stories couldn't be counted against her, she reasoned, so she'd created characters and events that gave her staid life in Denver a sparkle it might not otherwise have.

Her dream, however, was to use her love of writing to make a difference. Wouldn't Mama and Papa be shocked to know their youngest daughter's fondest wish was to become a journalist? She smiled at the idea of someday seeing her byline beneath a headline on the front page of the *Rocky Mountain News* or the *Denver Times*.

Maisie sidestepped a rift in the ground, jolting Anna back to a more careful observation of the trail ahead.

It did not escape her that tomorrow was May Day. How odd to think that the girls at Wellesley College would don their best gowns tomorrow morning and make merry at the May Day celebration, just as Anna had each year while there. Odder still that she'd gone from that to this, from a woman longing to be a wife to a woman bent on escaping the title by writing about it.

But that was another story, one she'd told time and again through the now-retired character Mae Winslow—named for the May Day celebration that spawned the first story.

Even her best friend Eugenia Cooper Beck, ironically one of Mae's biggest fans, had no idea the real author of those embarrassing dime novels was Anna Finch herself.

Or had been, Anna corrected as another hairpin went flying. She'd negotiated for a dozen of those silly books, falling into the career backwards when a story she wrote as a joke for her literature class at Wellesley was mailed to an editor at Beadle & Adams on a dare.

Still, Mae's stories had given Anna a venue for expressing how she felt about the confining institution of marriage as embodied by the arranged alliances her sisters had made. The fact that the only way she could get out of her contract was to marry the character off still galled Anna. At least she had escaped with a nice sum, now gathering interest at the National Bank of Boston.

An amount she would have gladly traded for the opportunity to garner a different type of interest from Daniel Beck, the only man who'd made her reconsider her feelings about donning the shackles of a wedding gown. However, her handsome neighbor, now Gennie's husband, had never seen her as anything more than the girl next door.

Another hairpin fell, and a strand of hair blocked her vision. She swiped at it and shook her hair free to blow in the fresh breeze. The last day of April looked to dawn kind and gentle rather than with the harsh chill of last week. It was still cold enough, however, for Anna to wish she'd chosen clothes for greater warmth rather than greater anonymity.

The mare slowed, which meant she'd caught the scent of water. To the south lay a creek that had proved not only reliable but also safe from prying eyes. After a quick check of the sky, Anna decided to allow Maisie her favorite treat, a cold drink of spring water and the carrot Anna had in her pocket.

Beyond the scrub that lined the stream, the bank tilted at an angle just steep enough to allow a horse to traverse it without sliding in. At the water's edge, the shadows were still long, showing little of the daylight that crept across the plain. The weather was glorious. The last of the April snow remained only in sparkling patches. Soon the upstream melting would begin and, if combined with a decent thundershower, turn this peaceful stream into a raging river.

Anna guided Maisie to her favorite spot and slipped off the horse. Stretching the kinks left in her back from a night of too much reading and not enough sleep, she debated whether to reach for the Smith & Wesson pistol in her saddlebag and see if she could still match her record of five straight hits on the old log on the other side of the stream. It had been some time since she'd made the attempt.

To keep her hair from hindering her vision, Anna fashioned a hasty braid and retrieved the hat from her saddlebag. She lifted the Smith & Wesson from the bag as well and made short work of filling its chambers with six bullets. After all these years of performing the same rote action, loading the weapon still gave her the tiniest of thrills. Probably because shooting was another in a long line of pastimes she'd been required to give up. At least as far as her father knew.

But then, there was so much he didn't know.

Anna set the pistol on a rock, then hobbled the horse in case the sound frightened her. Maisie was a high-strung mare under the best of conditions, though she always returned when she bolted. Still, this might be the time she did not, leaving Anna to find her way back to Denver on foot.

Anna raised the pistol and took aim on the log. The fallen tree was slightly larger than a man and of sufficient age to have been used for target practice for two winters. In summer the faded green of the grass made for easy shooting, but in winter the long shadows, occasional covering of snow, and brown earth upped the ante. Here in the golden glow of early morning, the sun danced across the log's imperfections, invitingly highlighting several places at which to aim. Anna chose a knothole and closed one eye, bringing the makeshift target squarely in her sights.

A squeeze of the trigger, and she saw the first bullet zing off the end of the log. A good shot, but barely, and certainly not close enough to the knothole. Easing her aim a bit to the right, she fired two more rounds directly into the center of the log.

Then she heard the bear. At least she thought it was a bear from the volume of its howl.

Maisie heard it too and began to spook. Wherever the bear was, he'd either been hit by one of her bullets or awakened before his winter nap ended.

In either case, Anna didn't want to meet him.

She tucked the gun into her waistband and ran for her horse. The faster she tried to remove Maisie's hobbles, the longer it took. Finally she kicked the last one free, pulled out the gun, put one foot in the stirrup, and swung her leg over the saddle.

Only somehow, Maisie slipped from beneath her.

Anna was vaguely aware of the horse's hindquarters as they trotted over the rise to disappear into the prairie grass. Most of her attention focused on whatever yanked her from the saddle and now held her by the middle in a grip so tight her breath came in short gasps.

Her flailing boots struck something solid, and her attacker dropped her. Anna skittered backwards out of the bear's reach. The sun blinded her, but she could see the grizzly's proportions. When her boots refused to find solid ground, she rolled to her belly and began to crawl.

Only then did she realize she still held the Smith & Wesson in her hand.

Panicked math told her three bullets remained in the chamber. Three chances to save her skin. Three shots between her and meeting Jesus well before she expected to.

Taking aim wasn't possible, so she turned and fired off two quick shots. The second one felled the bear, and he went down with a mighty roar and a string of blistering words.

Words?

Anna sat bolt upright.

The bear had transformed into a crumpled mass of buckskin and boots, but appeared to be human. And from the sound of his growl, decidedly male. Leaning out of the sun's glare, Anna eyed her writhing attacker, definitely man and not grizzly, though shaggy and trail-worn.

A few yards ahead, Maisie appeared over the rise, her desire for spring water obviously overruling any fear or good horse sense she might have. Even with an aching backside, Anna thought she could reach the horse faster than this stranger could find his feet and give chase.

But with a howl, he surprised her as she scrambled to her feet by lurching forward and hauling her up by the back of her pants.

"I ought to tan your backside, boy," he shouted, "but I'll let your pa do that. Where is he? I doubt he'll appreciate his son shooting at an innocent man. And the law's not going to like that you probably chased Doc Holliday himself away. You're not with Holliday, are you?"

"Don't be ridiculous." Her arms swinging wildly, Anna tried to free herself. "Release me this instant, you brute, or I'll see that my father has you shot. Again."

It was a stupid comment made in panic, but the bluster did its trick. The man let her go. Anna scrambled for Maisie.

"You won't get anywhere running off like that," the stranger shouted. "I'm bigger and faster, and my aim's a whole lot better than yours. Now *stop*, or you won't have to wonder if I'm telling the truth."

The boy froze. Or rather, the *girl* froze. This was definitely a girl.

Jeb Sanders had become painfully aware of the fact as soon as she spoke. If he were a man given to embarrassment, this would have been the point where he'd have felt it.

Instead, he felt the sting of the shot that winged past him, the one that woke him from the first good night of sleep he'd had in a month of Sundays. It was the second shot, however, that wounded his pride, because he'd stood right there and let her do it.

At least the first time around she'd snuck up on him.

Come to think of it, that was nothing to brag about either.

In an effort to ignore his wounds, Jeb focused on his attacker. That he'd assumed the shooter to be anything but female proved he'd been sound asleep when he made the determination. Though the oversized shirt and trousers she wore looked stolen right off a miner's clothesline, what lay beneath was pure female and hard to hide. Her expression begged him to believe she'd shoot him again, but her wide eyes told him she'd likely swoon before she could pull the trigger.

That alone disqualified her as an associate of Holliday. Anyone who traveled with him had seen blood and plenty of it.

Jeb followed her gaze to his torso, the apparent cause of her discomfort. Lifting the hem of his shirt, he showed her the slash just above his hip bone where the bullet had grazed him. Cold air hit his bare skin and stung the wound, which was only a few inches long and just deep enough to bleed.

She swayed but caught herself. "That's a lot of blood," she said, all her bluster gone.

"It's only a scratch."

Wide eyes looked up at him through a tangled curtain of dark hair. He couldn't see much of her face, but what he did see, an upturned nose and a dimple in her right cheek, he liked.

She still stared at his midsection, so he looked down to see what she found so interesting. He was bleeding like a stuck pig, but it was nothing a few hours and a bandage wouldn't cure. The woman, however, looked as if she might keel over at any minute. The last thing he needed was a frantic female on his hands.

"This is nothing." He let go of his shirt and gestured to the place above his heart where a scar served as a souvenir of his run-in with a would-be train robber back in '82. "You should see this one. It was right after they got Johnny Ringo. Took a bullet that nearly did me in. A man has no idea how much blood he's got until he's shot in the chest. Train didn't get robbed that day after all." Jeb chuckled then noticed the woman hadn't caught the humor in it. "Oh, now, come on," he said, taking a step toward her.

She flinched and backed away. "You mean you were…"

She didn't seem able to finish the question, so he did it for her. "Shot?" He nodded. "It happens in my line of work, but most bullets that come my way I manage to dodge. Guess that makes you among the few who actually hit what you were aiming for."

"But I don't shoot people." Her lower lip trembled. "N-not in real life."

"Well, darlin'," he said slowly, "you did today."

When she swayed again, he reached out to grab her elbow. She allowed it, but only for a second. Feisty, this one, though she appeared to be losing her spunk faster than he was losing blood.

"I didn't kill you," she whispered so softly he wasn't sure he'd heard it.

"Well, not yet," he said with humor he shouldn't have felt. His gaze fell to the gun still in her hand. "You don't plan to, do you?"

She stared at the revolver in horror. "Oh," she gasped. "Oh no, oh no, oh…"

"You all right?" he asked.

She staggered backward and made a run for the horse.

"Hey," he called. "Come back. You just winged me."

Why he wanted her to return, he couldn't exactly figure. She'd shot him fair and square and likely hadn't known she'd done it until afterward. After all, who expected a man to be taking a nap behind a log in the middle of nowhere? Certainly not a city girl dressed in country clothes.

Though the way she slid into the saddle and spurred her horse into a full gallop was too impressive to believe she'd spent all her days in town.

Jeb might have whistled for his horse and tried to catch her, but that seemed foolish. After all, if she was carrying a six-shooter, she still had one shot left.

2

My father taught me when young to attend to my
own business and let other people do the same.
—*Doc Holliday*

Anna raced all the way back to Denver, fear chasing her faster than
Maisie could gallop. While Mae Winslow wouldn't have given a second thought to firing a round into some fictional bad guy, Anna had
actually done it.

Had actually shot a man.

She swiped at her cheek and took a deep, shuddering breath.
"Lord, forgive me," she whispered through the sobs. "I didn't mean
to shoot that man."

As she rode toward Denver, the trail blurred by her tears, Anna
wondered if she, like the man back at the creek, might now be considered an outlaw. Ludicrous as that seemed, she had shot a man,
then fled the scene.

Perhaps she'd done the noble thing by preventing him from com-
mitting whatever crime he had planned for that day. Though he
seemed to be a nice man and not in need of shooting in any way, he
had admitted to some discourse with train robbers. She tried to rein
Maisie in so she could better logic this out.

If a potential crime was not committed due to her panicked mistake, then shooting him wasn't the awful act it felt like. And it did feel awful to actually put a bullet in someone. Or rather "wing him," as the stranger had said.

Her conscience stinging, Anna knew she should go straight to the police and give them a description of the criminal. He was tall, a full head above her in height, and broad of shoulder. Much more so than Papa or any of the men her sisters had wed.

What else? Her writer's eye sought out the details.

Dark hair. Longish and a bit mussed, though likely from his nap behind the log. His skin was burnished brown by the sun. He had a scar just to the left of the dimple in his chin.

Despite good breeding and better sense, she thought of what he'd revealed with a lift of his shirt. His skin was darker than hers even in places that should have rarely seen the sun. And a scar lay just to the right of…

She blinked to remove the image, then felt like a fool. What modern woman was shocked by the dark and muscled midsection of a healthy specimen of the opposite sex? Hadn't artists made great sculptures and paintings from the same subject matter? Between her time at Wellesley and her many trips to the Continent, she'd seen her share. And the man had worn trousers. It wasn't as if she were staring at Michelangelo's *David*. Though what little she saw of his torso bested the Italian statue by a Colorado mile.

Anna blushed at her own brazen thought.

Bypassing the secluded spot where she usually slipped out of her trousers and into her more feminine riding attire, Anna took a deep breath and let it out slowly as she lowered her head, allowing Maisie to find her way home. While she never completely lost the fear of being recognized, Anna had learned that a slight youth astride a mare attracted little attention on any street in Denver. Even hers. Today she had neither the strength nor the steadiness of hand to negotiate the ordeal of buttons and ribbons involved in her other set of clothing. Better she slip home unnoticed and race to her chambers.

Anna kept her hat low and her head down as she rode the last quarter mile past familiar gates and beautiful lawns. As was her custom, she jumped off the horse behind the Finch stables and allowed the groom to take the reins. Only then did the reality of what happened—of what could have happened—hit her with full force.

She could have killed a man.

Or, given that he was obviously sleeping in a log because he didn't want to be found, he could have killed her.

A welling up of emotion stalled her and rendered her legs useless. The familiar world blurred, leaving only smudges of color. Green, blue, and gold swirled around her.

Her legs began to shake, and her feet inched forward. The stable boy asked a question and she managed a nod, though she had no idea what he'd said. Another inch forward, another victory for knees that knocked and hands that shook as they felt for the rough boards of the stable.

She could have killed a man.

This was not fiction. Not some Mae Winslow adventure with guns blazing and outlaws fleeing to Boot Hill in a bloodless battle that killed them nonetheless. This was real.

He was real. A real, live, breathing man, with eyes the color of a gray winter day and hair that matched the cherry wood of Mama's grand piano. A man who would forever be scarred by the bullet that, had it hit him a hair's breadth to the left, could have ripped through his gut and caused a slow and painful death.

While Maisie was led away, Anna slipped into the thick shrubs that lined the border between her home and the Beck property and fell to her knees. A wave of nausea hit, and she lost the remains of her hurried, predawn breakfast.

How long she remained kneeling, Anna couldn't say. At some point she turned to prayer, though her pleadings felt as dry and dusty as the banks of the spring where she'd spent her morning.

When she could manage it, Anna rose and dusted off her trousers, then swiped at her mouth with the back of her sleeve. Another wave of nausea chased her as she darted across the gap between the stables and the kitchen. By the time she reached the door, however, the feeling had subsided.

Hurriedly stabbing hairpins into her hopelessly ruined coiffure, she slipped into the kitchen and bolted for the back staircase.

"Anna Finch."

Papa. She froze, unable even to respond. Her father called her name again, and Anna slowly turned to see him standing in the kitchen entrance. His glower made her feel half her age.

"Come with me," he said shortly, turning and marching down the corridor. Anna followed helplessly.

Her father entered the library, leaving the door open. Anna stalled in the doorway, knowing that as soon as this conversation began, her freedom ended. She squared her shoulders and breathed a quick reminder to herself that she was a modern woman with no desire to have her father treat her like a child. Then she stepped into the room.

And instantly the woman gave way to the girl, and Anna Finch lost all interest in her personal declaration of independence. Tucking what she could of her hair back into place, she ran sweaty palms over the garments she now wished she'd never donned.

As if her thoughts paraded before her, irritation tightened her father's usually kind face. "Shut the door," he commanded.

She managed it on the second try. The bindings holding her chest flat began to slip, and Anna pressed her arm to her side to avert disaster. At least this disaster.

"Sit down."

Anna considered taking the seat nearest the door should the need to escape overwhelm her. She made a poor attempt at removing any sign of unease from her expression. *I am a grown woman. A woman who shot a man.*

"Sit," her father repeated as his gaze slid the length of her with obvious disdain.

"Yes, Papa." Anna sank to the edge of the chair nearest Papa's desk and tried to still her shaking knees as she noticed her borrowed boots had tracked a mixture of mud and leaves across the carpet. At least she hadn't brought any of the man's blood with her.

Another wave of nausea bubbled up inside her, but Anna bit back on it until it passed. In its place came the urge to unburden herself to Papa. To tell him the horrible events of the morning and ask— no, *beg*—him to make them go away. To right the wrong of shooting a man, whether innocent or not.

But she couldn't do it. He already thought so poorly of her. Given his demeanor, he likely expected she'd done much worse.

When finally his stare met hers, Papa seemed ready to speak, but then he looked away and studied something on the opposite wall. Anna swiveled to follow his gaze and saw the portrait on which his attention rested.

Five young ladies in their best Sunday dresses smiled back at her. Finding herself in the portrait was easy. She was the smallest of the group and the only one who refused to smile. Not that the casual onlooker would notice, for the artist, who'd earned a hefty commission for commemorating the gathering of the Finch girls, had taken the liberty of painting a smile on her anyway.

Slowly Anna became aware of her father's silence, a silence that stretched far and deep into the chasm between them. Though she longed to find the easy banter that had rarely failed her where Papa was concerned, no words would come.

Anna watched the light glint off the heavy gold chain that attached her father's pocket watch to his vest button and wondered if the ticking was as quick as her heartbeat. Her bindings slipped another notch, and she crossed her arms over her chest.

Her father walked around the desk to stand before her. "If you were a child, I'd know how to remedy this. Unfortunately, tanning your backside for this ridiculous indiscretion of yours would solve nothing. Am I wrong?"

There was no good answer to his question, so Anna said nothing. She did, however, realize that her father was the second man to make that threat today, and it was not yet noon.

"When a female of marrying age is no longer amenable to

remaining under the guidance of her father, it is my opinion she should be handed off to a husband who can perhaps do a better job of it." His eyes, the color of her own, narrowed. "And you, Anna Finch, have proven by your audacious behavior today and, I daresay, on many as-yet undiscovered occasions in the past, that you are well beyond any control I might have over your person and behavior."

Anna took a deep breath and let it out slowly, fighting to hold her tongue. After all, this was Papa, and she was his favored child, his baby girl. Surely calmer heads would prevail once he had a chance to think on things.

"I'm terribly sorry," she said. "I never meant to bring any—"

"Tarnish to your reputation or the reputation of your family?" He paused. "I fear it's far too late for such concerns."

This statement wounded her far deeper than she expected. "But, Papa, I've not done anything that would cause such tarnish. I swear it." *Other than shot a man.*

His gaze slid over her once more as he walked back to his chair, and she cringed. "Did you purchase that outlandish garb or steal it off the servants' clothesline?" Before she could answer, he held up a hand. "No, don't tell me. I truly don't care which you've done. What I do care about is how this whole debacle can be quietly made to go away."

She stiffened with panic. "Papa," she said, the words pouring out of her, "I promise you I had no idea that outlaw was there. Who sleeps inside a log meant for target practice?"

Her father's expression turned from serious to shocked, and Anna realized her mistake. Of course Papa had no idea she'd discharged her Smith & Wesson into a man. How could he?

His face reddened, and a vein on the side of his neck began to throb. She'd seen him this mad only once, and the horse that had thrown him was sold before sundown. Likely she would suffer the same fate.

She probably deserved it.

"You shot a man? Today?" he demanded.

"By the river, but I promise I hadn't any idea he was behind the log. I only thought to practice with the Smith & Wes—"

"Quiet."

She ducked her head. "Yes, Papa."

He made a note on the page spread before him. From her vantage point, Anna could see the words *Pinkerton* and *Thompson,* and a sum in excess of one thousand dollars. When he spied her looking, Papa turned the paper over. "Did anyone see this transgression?"

"He's fine. He said so himself. And quite strong. Despite his blood loss, he managed to haul me up against him and…" Anna bit her lip to stop babbling.

"Who was he?"

She shook her head. "I truly don't know."

"No one whom you've seen before? Not a son of friends or well-placed clients? Not anyone we might come across on the streets of Denver? Or at church?"

"No." She'd never seen him before, but should she ever meet the stranger again, Anna would know him. She doubted a girl ever forgot the first man she shot.

"We're done speaking of this. You will never repeat this foolishness. Now, to the more important matter." He paused, rose from his seat, and seemed to think a moment. "Indeed it is a conundrum as to which gentleman I shall honor with the duty of taming you."

Anna felt her brows rise as she absorbed the statement. "Apparently you've not read that awful Mr. Mitchell's gossip column. I'm a hopeless candidate for a bride."

The first sign of amusement showed on her father's otherwise stoic face as he closed the space between them. "Anna, darling, when you've the resources of the Finch family, one can never be considered hopeless, and there are *always* choices."

She rose carefully and inched toward the door. "Then perhaps I choose to go up to my chambers and—"

Papa caught her wrist and held her in place. All signs of good humor disappeared from his face. "You've tested me since you first learned to say the word 'no,' Anna." His grip tightened just enough to get her attention. "Know with no uncertainty that you've tested me for the last time with today's escapade. Now—go and change before someone other than the help sees you."

"Yes, Papa." She managed to remain upright despite her once again churning stomach.

"And rest assured you will marry, Anna Finch. And soon." Her father released his grip but held his position. "If I choose a man who will keep you in the parlor rather than the paddock, so much the better. In fact, I think I'll make that a requirement to gain your hand. What do you think?"

Anna squared her shoulders and turned toward the door, feeling the eyes of her married sisters staring back from the awful portrait. As she reached the hall, Papa called after her.

"Anna, you've ignored my question."

She froze. "I assumed it was rhetorical." She eased around to face him. "But if you're truly asking my opinion, I don't think much of your requirement. As you've said, a Finch always has choices." Her temper flared and her voice betrayed her. "And I choose not to marry a man for whom I have no feelings. So there's your answer, Papa. No."

Papa's chuckle held little humor. "In this you do *not* have a choice, even if you *are* a Finch."

3

We never sleep.

—*Pinkerton Detective Agency motto*

May 1, 1885, Denver, Colorado

The noon hour on the following day found Anna languishing at a table at the Windsor Hotel while Gennie, her lunch date, was nowhere to be found. Used to Gennie's penchant for adventure and late arrivals, Anna had brought ample reading material to keep her occupied.

While a perfectly nice table near the window sat unoccupied, the awful waiter—barely old enough to shave—had seated her in the middle of the dining room filled with people who might listen to her conversations and report back to her father. To make things worse, the heating system and overcrowded nature of the room had raised the temperature far above comfortable levels. Anna dabbed at her brow with her handkerchief.

As she picked up that day's copy of the *Rocky Mountain News,* she noticed a tall man enter the dining room with a lovely dark-haired woman in a fashionable hat. Something in the older man's face seemed familiar. But from where? Perhaps he reminded her of a character in one of her novels. That happened sometimes. Anna would

swear she knew a person only to realize afterward she'd instead written about someone similar.

The couple's progress across the packed room brought them past
Anna's table, where she heard the woman say, "Really, dear, perhaps
this isn't such a good idea. Look at the crowd."

"The crowd's exactly why it's a good idea. We won't stick out like
sore thumbs," the deep-voiced man replied. The clatter and chatter
of the room rose to drown out any further comment.

From the corner of her eye, Anna watched the waiter gesture to
the table she had begged for, the one set squarely before the windows
of the hotel's main facade. While the lady seemed pleased, her companion shook his head and argued with the waiter.

Interesting.

Anna let the paper slide from her fingers, stood, and moved
toward the trio with a smile. "Perhaps you'd like my table."

The gentleman smiled. "Thank you, miss, but we couldn't possibly intrude on—"

"Oh, it's no intrusion at all. I can easily move my things to this
table." She noted the waiter's aggravated stare with a measure of glee.
"In fact, I'm sure it can be arranged, can it not?"

"Yes," the waiter said with effort. "Of course."

"Thank you," the woman said. "You've done us a great favor. You
see, we're meeting someone and—"

"What my wife means is lawmen are not people given to sitting by
windows." The man shook Anna's hand, and she recalled where she'd
seen him: the newspapers. She'd read about him somewhere and even
cut out a photograph as a model for a character in one of her novels.
He'd been a lawman in that story too. His name escaped her, however.

"Old habits die hard," he said with a shrug. "I do appreciate the favor. And you will allow us to buy your lunch."

"Oh, no," Anna said as she gathered up her things and vacated the table. "It's my pleasure. Really."

He tipped his Stetson and grinned. "That wasn't a question, miss, so do enjoy yourself." The gentleman spoke with the authority of someone who generally got his way. He glanced around. "You're not alone, are you?"

"Alone? Oh, no, I… That is, no. My friend, she's, well…" Anna swallowed hard, suddenly flustered under his steady, all-male gaze. "Gennie's been known to…"

"Arrive slightly past the appointed time?" the lady offered.

"Yes." Anna slid a thankful look her way.

"Well, then. That's settled." The man tipped his hat again, and the couple turned to take possession of their table.

"She's very pretty, Wyatt," the woman said as Anna stepped away.

Wyatt? Anna glanced back to watch the older man fold his long legs under the table, his back squarely to the wall and his eyes on the only exit.

"Wyatt Earp," she whispered. "Oh my."

While dime novels painted the man as a hero, Anna's impression of the legendary lawman Wyatt Earp, garnered from newspaper reports, was less than favorable. Looking into the man's eyes and watching how he treated his companion made her wonder if he truly was the cold-blooded killer the papers said he was, bent on revenging his brother's murder through the so-called Vendetta Ride.

Stories of one death after another, all connected in some way to the Tombstone killing of Morgan Earp, had filled the papers for years. Names like *Clanton* and *Ringo,* along with hints of things not reported by the law, were usually mentioned. Alongside the requisite photograph of the bullet-ridden corpse generally came a photograph of the one deemed responsible: Wyatt Earp and, on occasion, his old friend Doc Holliday.

The same Doc Holliday the man at the river had mentioned. Coincidence? Perhaps.

But perhaps not.

And now Wyatt Earp sat just a stone's throw from her, in the very chair she herself had occupied. Looking around, she noted that no one else in the Windsor seemed to realize a man of dubious reputation and some renown was in their midst. Anna tugged at the lace on her collar and contemplated the situation.

Until this moment, her journalistic aspirations had been limited to reading the paper instead of writing for it. But the opportunity of a lifetime had just offered to buy her lunch.

ᏯᏨ

"Welcome back to Denver."

Jeb looked up to see Hank Thompson moving across the expensive carpet toward him like a tomcat circling a mouse. "I always figured you for the straight-arrow type, Hank, but this has all the marks of a decently aggravating practical joke."

"I assure you I'm quite serious. You look awful, by the way. You couldn't have bathed before you came by? You're more trail dust than skin."

Jeb shook his head, ignoring Hank's jab at his appearance. "You know I'm not a man given to complaints, but I'm standing my ground on this one. You'll just have to find another fool to put on…" He snatched the paper out of his pocket. "The 'costume befitting a Roman gladiator.' Didn't they wear dresses back then?"

"Togas, Jeb, and all the staff will be wearing them. Helmets too, so your anonymity will be easier to maintain. Surely you don't expect to be an effective shadow if you stick out like a sore thumb?"

"It's a dress," Jeb said as he fought his temper. "Besides I'm going as a guest, remember? I'll fit right in."

His old friend made the mistake of grinning. Only the fact that he owed Hank more than just his life kept Jeb from slugging him. That, and he still ached something fierce from being shot by a girl the previous morning.

"All right," Hank said, "I can see your point." He seemed to think hard on something. "If you don't want this job, I've got something else I can offer."

"I'll take it." Jeb paused. "What's the catch?"

Hank shrugged. "It's a promotion. More pay, next step up the ladder." A grin spread across his face. "I can assure you it'll keep you busy."

It only took Jeb a moment to realize what Hank was offering. "Oh no." He gestured to Hank's desk. "I don't want your job. I've never been a man who could keep his boots under a desk for long without itching to get some trail dust on them, and you know that."

"Fair enough."

Jeb gave Hank's blank expression a suspicious look. "That's it? You're making this too easy. Just give me another assignment, and I'll get out of here and let you get back to work. I've got something I can see to for a few weeks, anyway."

Hank narrowed his eyes. "Carrying the Pinkerton badge gives you access to resources you wouldn't otherwise have. I reckon that's come in handy on occasion."

"It has."

"Like when you're off hunting Doc Holliday."

"That's not fair, Hank." Jeb snatched his hat off the desk, where he'd set it when he came in, and jammed it back on his head.

Jeb bit off the rest of what he wanted to say, though he would've given his best saddle to be able to have a real conversation with Hank about Doc Holliday. The other Pinkerton's instincts were sharp and his network of informants nearly as good as Jeb's. He'd like to know whether Hank had heard anything about the half dozen trail hands over in Kansas who'd been dispatched to fresh graves just last week by the Georgia dentist. The informant who'd promised to meet Jeb yesterday at dawn had either been scared away by the shooting or never intended to show, so anything Hank could provide would have helped.

"I haven't balked at an assignment since you convinced Mr. Pinkerton to give me my job back, but I won't wear a dress, and I won't be shackled to a desk." He paused. "And as for Holliday, you know I work that investigation on my own time."

"Doc Holliday's an innocent man, and until there's solid evidence to the contrary, there's nothing you can do about that. As for what you'll be wearing tonight, I'll take your complaint about needing a place to carry your gun under advisement." Hank's exasperation showed as he pointed at Jeb's midsection. "Speaking of guns, it looks like you've got yourself a new bullet hole."

A glance down at his shirt told Jeb his wound had soaked through the bandage again, despite a day's worth of healing. "It's just a scratch."

Hank's snort of disbelief provided a welcome moment of levity. "Don't suppose I'll be getting a report on it."

"Don't suppose so." Jeb changed the subject before thoughts of big brown eyes and chestnut curls derailed his conversation entirely. "Beck's getting a good man." Jeb would never admit to Hank that he'd recommended Hank to Daniel Beck after turning down the job himself. The last thing his friend needed to know was that he was Daniel's second choice for chief of security at Beck Enterprises.

"So you know. I guess I shouldn't be surprised." Hank cleared his throat. "About this assignment, I suppose I could refer the client to J. F. Farley down the street at Thiel's, though I would have to let Mr. Pinkerton know our agent was unable to take on the job."

If the taunt was supposed to sting, it missed the mark. "And I could go down the street to Thiel's and tell Farley I'd like to do some real detective work instead of baby-sitting rich people," Jeb replied. "Especially when that involves following them to ridiculous costume parties."

"You think I don't know about the special assignments you did for Beck?" The anger in Hank's voice matched the look on his face. "Let's start with that honeymoon stunt. What kind of detective work did it take to arrange that little horse ride with Mr. Beck and his bride down Fifth Avenue? That ring shaped like a hairpin you convinced

Mr. Tiffany to make? You think I don't know you had a hand in that? And the arrangements for Mr. Beck to reunite with his father? Those didn't just happen."

Jeb refused to react. Those had been favors to a friend, not assignments, but he wouldn't admit that to Hank. There was no need.

Hank slammed his palms on the desk and stared. "You're not just the best we got at hiding in plain sight, Jeb. You're also pretty darn good at working for rich people. All you have to do is keep Anna Finch out of trouble. The job's shadowing her until her pa finds some fellow to marry her off to. If that means wearing a toga, then you wear a toga. Simple as that."

"Simple as that?" Jeb felt a grin come over him as the puzzle pieces began to fit. Hank wasn't usually this touchy. Something must have set him off. Jeb pushed his hat off his forehead, sure he'd discovered the source of the case of unrequited love Hank had been nursing for months. "I think I've got a solution that'll work for both of us. *You* marry her, her father won't need me, and I won't need to get fitted for a dress. Problem solved."

"Out," Hank snapped. "Before I change my mind and put you in for a promotion." He pointed at Jeb's middle. "Wait. Did Doc Holliday do that?" he asked with more than the appropriate level of sarcasm.

Jeb looked at the fresh stain on his shirt. The wound definitely needed a new bandage. He made a note to stop in at the apothecary in the Windsor lobby before seeing to that bath and shave.

"The truth?" Jeb asked. *Why not?* "I had a meet-up planned with a fellow who had some information I needed. Figured I'd get there early, so I went out the night before and made myself a fine little campsite."

"So your informant put a bullet in you?"

"Nope. I got shot by the prettiest gal I've seen in a long time," Jeb said. "Tiny thing with big brown eyes and a horse with a streak of pure evil in it. The kind of girl that leaves a mark, in more ways than one."

"Some hired gun you are."

"You know I'm the best there is."

"Yeah, I do." Hank stared at him as if waiting for the punch line. "Go," he finally said. "Before I change my mind and have you fitted for a decent suit and a desk chair."

"I'm going, and I'll baby-sit Barnaby Finch's daughter." Jeb adjusted his hat and gave Hank one last glare. "But you're going to let me do it my way. Otherwise I'm heading up the trail to home and you can find yourself another Pinkerton to wear my badge."

"Deal," Hank said without hesitation.

"In that case, I'll see you tonight." Jeb reached for the door, then glanced over his shoulder. "And I *won't* be wearing a dress."

He would, he decided, be wearing a few stitches to bind up the mark that feisty gal had left on him. Jeb left the building that housed the Pinkerton office, then turned left at the corner and hauled himself into the doctor's office.

He took a seat in the waiting room with his pride dented and a fresh resolve to sleep with one eye open. At least the woman he was assigned to watch over wouldn't be as dangerous as the one who'd put a bullet in him.

She couldn't possibly be.

4

I tell you all this talk about Holliday is wrong. I
know him well. He is a dentist and a good one.

—*Bat Masterson*

"Anna, you're still here!" Gennie Cooper Beck swept into the dining
room, causing more than a few heads to turn. No matter where she
went, Gennie always arrived looking like she'd just stepped off the
page of a fashion magazine.

If Anna didn't love her so much, she might have been jealous of
her stylish friend, for today Gennie wore a lovely shade of green, her
coat and matching hat trimmed with fur. The feather in her hat
matched the brooch pinned to her neckline. Both coordinated with
her belt, shoes, and handbag. The beaded bag caught the light and
sent a shower of sparkles across the room each time she took a step.

Anna too had a wardrobe full of beautiful gowns and accessories,
but none of them looked like this on her. Gennie could stop traffic
in a burlap sack.

As she made her way toward the table, Gennie greeted those she
knew and smiled at others. An elderly couple called her name, and
she paused to make conversation, catching Anna's eye. A wave and a
shrug, and Gennie returned her attention to the couple for a moment
longer before making her exit.

By the time Gennie reached the table, the fair-haired beauty appeared out of breath and in need of a glass of water. She paused to nod at the mayor's wife, then returned her attention to Anna. "I'm terribly sorry I'm so late," she said as she reached into her purse to retrieve what looked like a letter to fan herself with. "Why is it so warm in here?"

Anna pushed her water glass toward her friend. A waiter approached, then retreated when Gennie waved him away.

"I can't stay but just long enough to let you know what's happening," she said.

"You can't?" Disappointment tempered the question, and Anna made no attempt to hide it. "But I had something important to discuss with you." She glanced around the dining room then back at Gennie. "Really important."

Indecision colored Gennie's expression, but only for a moment. "So do I," she said. "It's dire."

"Dire? Is something wrong with the baby?"

"No," Gennie said quickly. "Danny's fine. A beautifully perfect little boy. He got a new tooth last week. Did I tell you about that?"

She had, but Anna didn't stop her from telling it again.

"It makes six. Or is it seven? Goodness, I'll have to count when I get home. I lose track. He's growing up too fast. But that's not why I came."

"But it's dire," Anna echoed. "Well, mine's not dire. At least not in the strictest sense of the definition." She leaned forward. "So I'm listening."

Gennie drew a deep breath, then let it out slowly. "You know

Daniel has a younger brother. Edwin?" When Anna nodded, she continued. "Well, you're not going to believe this, but he arrived this morning without any warning at all." She shrugged and took a drink of Anna's water. "Just knocked on the door and expected to be welcomed like, well, family."

"Honey," Anna said gently, "he is family."

Her friend looked as if she might cry. "I know, but this is Edwin. He runs the family business in England, and then there's the thing with—well, there are other things." She paused. "There's so much about him you don't know. About Daniel. And about Charlotte."

Anna looked questioningly at Gennie. "I'm getting lost. Perhaps you should start at the beginning."

She shook her head. "Even if Daniel gave me permission to tell the whole story, I don't have time right now. The driver's waiting outside. I have to get home so I can pack."

"Pack?" Anna asked. "Are you going somewhere?"

"New York." Gennie looked nervously out the window. "It's been ages since Mama and Papa have seen Danny. And I'm taking Charlotte. She does love the city."

"What young lady wouldn't? Especially one who is almost grown and has started entertaining the thought of fancy dress balls and beaus."

Gennie's first genuine smile emerged. "Don't let her father catch you talking about his little girl like that. Why, just try reminding him Charlotte will be sixteen soon and see what happens. He's positively in denial, I tell you, though he did consent to allow her to attend the reception tonight."

Anna returned the grin. "It's a father's job to be in denial," she said with an enthusiasm she did not quite feel. "He forever sees his baby girl as just that, a *baby.*"

"Oh, I agree." Gennie sighed. "Miss Charlotte, now, she has other ideas. As you can imagine, it's interesting to watch the two of them, but not so much fun playing referee when he's trying to keep her a child and she's trying to be a grown woman before she's ready."

"Sorry to hear that." Anna reached for her napkin and began to twist it. The words she longed to say burned the tip of her tongue, but to interject them into the conversation at this point would be beyond rude.

"I'm perpetually warning him to treat Charlotte like she's older and Danny as if he's still a baby," Gennie continued. "He frightens me terribly when he puts my little boy in front of him on the saddle and goes galloping about."

"I'm sure." Anna's mind strayed to her own galloping about the previous morning. "So, you're leaving for New York when?"

"Edwin has provided the use of his rail car," Gennie said, "so it's simply a matter of collecting what we need. The reception will go on as planned, and then we'll be off tomorrow morning."

"What's the rush?" Anna asked. "I mean, it seems odd that Daniel's brother arrives from England this morning and you and the children leave on some surprise trip the next day."

Gennie seemed a bit indecisive, almost pensive. As if, perhaps, she wanted to say more. Then, in an instant, the moment passed and she became her usual cheerful self again. Still, something in her happy expression didn't quite reach her eyes.

"It's a fortunate accident," Gennie said. "I'll write just as soon as I can and as often as the children and my parents will allow. And depending on the circumstances, perhaps the children and I will be home sooner than expected."

"When exactly is 'expected'?"

"Well," Gennie said slowly, "I'm not sure. It depends on...well. Daniel said we should enjoy our visit, perhaps go and see the Boston cousins, and generally have a wonderful summer."

"Summer?" Anna shook her head. "You'll be gone all summer? It's only the first day of May." She took a deep breath and let it out slowly. "That's forever, Gennie."

"It is, isn't it?" Gennie rose from her chair. "I'm terribly sorry, dear friend, but I must rush. Daniel wouldn't be pleased to know I've slipped off to meet you, but I couldn't leave without telling you first. Especially after your invitation to lunch today. That was quite unexpected, by the way, though under other circumstances, it would have been most welcome."

Gennie leaned down to pick up the water glass, and Anna grasped her wrist. "You can't leave before I tell you what I called you here for."

Their gazes met. "All right," Gennie said slowly.

Several possible statements came to mind, but Anna decided to use the most direct of them all. "I shot a man yesterday, and until five years ago I wrote Mae Winslow's dime novels for Beadle & Adams."

Anna let go of Gennie and leaned back in her chair, waiting for the expression of horror she knew would come to her best friend's face. Though Anna's heart pounded furiously, there was something freeing in having said the words out loud for the first time. She glanced around to see diners going about their business, not realizing something of momentous importance had just been revealed in their midst.

Gennie, her expression blank, slowly shook her head as her fingers worried with the string of her purse. "Would you repeat that, please? I don't think I heard correctly."

"I said," Anna repeated, "I shot a man yesterday, and I used to write dime novels. Mae Winslow's stories, actually." When Gennie didn't respond, Anna continued. "The man lived. It was just a flesh wound. As for Mae, once I met you and realized how many women I'd been deceiving with those storylines, I had to stop. Though I'm very thankful that through Mae I met you." She paused. "If it were up to me, Mae would have ridden off into the sunset and left Henry at the altar to cook his own meals and darn his own socks. Unfortunately, the publisher refused to see things my way."

While Anna watched, Gennie sank slowly back onto her chair. She dropped her handbag on the table and turned to look out the window. Between the fur hat and fur collar, her face was mostly obscured. Only a sweep of golden hair and the tip of her nose could be seen as Gennie peered down at something on the street below. Anna followed Gennie's gaze and saw a trolley clang past, filled to the doors with people. Close behind was a delivery wagon pulled by two mules. Passing on either sidewalk were fashionable folks mixed with common people. As much as Anna had loved Boston, it could never replace Denver for interest.

A tall, thin fellow sauntered by the hotel, pausing to look up at the awning over his pale head. He held in his hand a bundle of letters wrapped with string. When the man stepped into slanted sunlight, a diamond on his lapel caught the light. He noticed Anna staring and looked away.

Anna looked at her friend, who hadn't moved. "Gennie?"

Her friend's shoulders began to shake, and Anna heard the beginnings of a giggle. By the time Gennie turned to face her again, she had her hand over her mouth and looked about to burst.

"What?" Anna said.

"One more time," her friend managed between stifled chuckles. "Please."

"I hardly think this is funny."

And yet Gennie obviously did. "Again," she squeaked, her voice as high-pitched as the laughter that followed. "And don't forget the part where you wrote the—the…" She dissolved into a fit of laughter that caused the diners around them to turn and stare.

"Honestly," Anna said, her temper rising. "I try to admit something that's burdened me for years, and this is how you respond?"

Gennie sobered enough to purse her lips. "Oh, Anna, you are the best friend a girl could ever have. The very, very best."

While Gennie dabbed at the corners of her eyes with her handkerchief, Anna sat back in her chair to collect her thoughts. "Really, Gennie," she finally said, "I hardly expected this kind of reaction."

Gennie reached across the table to pat Anna's hand. "Well, of course you did, and that's what makes you my very best friend." Gennie folded the handkerchief and returned it to her handbag, then retrieved a letter and resumed fanning herself with it. "Thank you so much for lifting my mood. You always know just what to say." She giggled. "This time you really took me by surprise."

"That's what the man with the flesh wound said," Anna muttered as she grabbed the glass of water and drained it.

Gennie gathered her purse strings, pushed away an errant strand of hair, and rose. "I wish I could stay, but I truly must go. You'll be at the reception tonight, yes?"

"Of course." Anna followed suit, dropping her napkin onto the table. There would be other opportunities to unburden herself. Surely Gennie would believe her next time. "What if I walk you downstairs?"

"That's not necessary. You've not eaten a bite."

"I'm going anyway," Anna said. "I'm not really hungry, and I need to send McMinn into the post office for stamps if I'm going to write to you."

Perhaps she could say in a letter what she hadn't managed to say in person. It might be fun to send Gennie one of her manuscripts as well, just to prove her point. After all, she had a trunk full of them in the attic.

"Oh goodness," Gennie said, "I almost forgot. Might I trouble you to post this for me? I know Daniel will have someone send a telegram to Mother and Father, but I think posting a letter's probably best. Send it by the fastest means, would you?"

"Of course." Anna took the letter that had been used moments earlier as a fan and followed in Gennie's wake as the one and only Mrs. Beck crossed the room and walked out onto the upstairs landing. Anna was surprised to see they were one of the last lunch parties to leave the dining room. She hadn't realized so much time had passed. They parted ways at the top of the stairs. With a wave, Gennie hurried ahead and disappeared into the pharmacy.

Anna was about to descend the stairs when she spied walking toward her the thin but well-dressed man she'd seen through the window. He reached the top of the stairs and stopped to lean against the banister. The stickpin in his lapel caught the light and glittered, a bright contrast to his pale skin and paler hair. Anna moved closer. The man had a general look of poor health, though his blue eyes followed her with great interest.

Curious but unwilling to pry, Anna pressed past the man, but as her heart overruled logic, she paused. "Sir? Are you ill?"

The man straightened and regarded Anna with something akin to surprise. He seemed, however, at a loss for words. Before he could find his voice, Wyatt Earp came bolting toward them.

In all the excitement with Gennie, Anna had forgotten the lawman was still there. She stepped back to watch the pair, who were obviously well acquainted.

"It's you," Mr. Earp said as he embraced the frail fellow with the gusto of a man gone a long time between visits. "It's really you. I didn't think you'd…"

Wyatt's voice trailed off as he held the man at arm's length, then embraced him once more. Finally, the lawman stepped back and shook his head. "What am I thinking?" he said. "Why don't we go sit down? You look like you'd blow over in a stiff wind. 'Sides, there's not a man alive who couldn't use a square meal and a cup of coffee at the end of the trail."

When Wyatt released him, the other man wobbled backward before righting himself. "I might at that, though I think I'll just have the coffee." He glanced at Anna. "Is this the lucky woman? I don't believe we've met."

Two sets of eyes turned Anna's direction. "Who, me? No, I'm his Anna…that is, we are not acquainted."

The legendary lawman stepped in to place his palm on his friend's shoulder. "Come in and meet my wife," he said gently. "I'm sure this young lady has other things to do besides watch two old-timers reminisce."

"I ought to go mail these," the thin man said abruptly. "Coming to Denver at all was a bad idea."

Wyatt Earp shook his head. "This little lady was kind enough to give up her table for us," he said with a tone that seemed strangely casual considering his companion's nervous demeanor. "I'm sure she's not going to mention to anyone she's seen you."

"Seen who?" Anna said before she could stop herself. "I don't believe we've met, and it appears that's exactly as it should be."

The lawman broke into a grin. "You don't recognize this man, little lady? This fellow here, he's famous."

"He is?" Anna gave him a closer inspection. "Really?"

"Yes, of course," Mr. Earp said. "This here's the outlaw William Bonney. You won't tell the law he's here, will you?"

The pair seemed close to laughter.

"Never mind," Anna said, shaking her head. "I'm sure you're a nice fellow. You certainly don't look like an outlaw."

In fact, he looked like a nice old man, unless one studied his face. Only then could a person see that rather than being of advanced years, he was middle-aged at most. His skin may have been pale and his cheeks gaunt, but there were no wrinkles around eyes as blue as the Colorado sky.

If he'd been younger, she might have pegged him for the famous outlaw Doc Holliday. But while this man was indeed on the unhealthy side, as newspaper reports claimed of Holliday, the fellow standing before her bore little resemblance to the young, dark-haired man in the newspaper photographs.

The lawman reached out to shake her hand. "Pleased to meet you," she said. "And you're Wyatt Earp."

"I am. A pleasure to make your acquaintance, ma'am." He cut his companion a look. "If you'll excuse us, Mr. Bonney and I have plenty to catch up on."

"Of course." Anna's gaze dropped to the packet in Bonney's hand. "Would you like me to post your letters?" She held up Gennie's letter. "I'm already taking this for a friend, and I don't mind dropping them off at the front desk on my way out."

"No," Bonney said quickly, pressing the letters against his chest. "I'm sure this is a fine establishment, but I prefer to send my correspondence through the postal office." He winked. "Cut out the middleman and avoid the diversion of the curious, as it were."

"I see. Well, I'm stopping at the post office for stamps on my way home." She paused to give him time to consider her offer. "Though if you're particular with your mail, perhaps you'd prefer to deliver them yourself."

His smile was dazzling despite the paleness of his skin and the weakness of his demeanor. "You do understand, then."

"Yes, of course." And with what she hoped was a graceful exit, Anna turned and swept down the stairs to the main lobby. "What an odd man," she said to herself as she took a few tentative steps toward the door and the sidewalk beyond. "I wonder who he really was."

The chill air hit her square in the face, and Anna's breath caught. The dining room had been so warm that she'd completely forgotten the remainder of last month's snow on the ground. Anna shrugged deeper into her coat and pressed on.

Only when she'd crossed Eighteenth Street did she realize she'd just missed the perfect opportunity to investigate the aging lawman. She looked at the Windsor. Then turned away and left her aspiring career in journalism in a heap on the curb.

"Home, miss?" her driver, McMinn, asked as he handed her into the buggy.

Anna shook her head and handed him Gennie's letter. "We need to post this for Mrs. Beck, and I need some stamps."

"Yes, miss."

"There you are," a deep and distinctly Southern voice called. "Am I too late to avail myself of your kindness?"

Anna swiveled to see Mr. Earp's mysterious, fair-haired friend walking toward her, the packet of letters in his hand.

"Not at all," she said.

When he reached the buggy, he leaned heavily against it as if exhausted. Despite the chill in the air, perspiration glistened on his high forehead. He reached into his pocket for a handkerchief to mop his brow, then handed her the letters. "Thank you."

As she took the packet, he slipped a folded bill into her hand. She could feel his fingers trembling.

"This should cover the cost," he said.

"Oh no, I couldn't possibly…" Anna's attention moved from the folded bills to the face of the man who held them. The harsh afternoon sun revealed the sickly pallor of the man's skin, and his gaunt look clearly stemmed from more than his thin build. "Are you unwell?"

Rather than respond, the man merely shrugged. "This cold air is lovely, don't you think? Gets a man's blood racing. Again, thank you. I am in your deepest debt."

Anna tried to return the funds to him. "No, please. It's just a few letters."

"To you, perhaps," he said, "but to me it is much more. A pity I must resort to such lengths just to keep my letters from being accidentally mislaid before they reach their intended recipient."

Anna felt his fingers tremble and realized she still held his hand. "I don't understand."

"No," he said slowly, "I suppose you don't."

He took a step backward, and the money slid from her gloved fingers, landing at her feet on the floor of the buggy. When she reached down to grasp the bills, the man Wyatt Earp referred to as Mr. Bonney turned his back on her and slipped into the crowd. Anna had no trouble following his progress among those strolling up and down the thoroughfare. Between his almost-white hair and his superior height, one would be hard pressed to miss the man who shuffled along with the slow gait of a fellow much more advanced in years.

The packet of letters lay in her lap, and Anna noticed the top one addressed to a convent in Georgia. She looked down at her feet, where the man's money had fallen. An idea formed in her head.

McMinn cleared his throat. "Post office?" he asked, gathering the reins.

"First the post office and then back here to the Windsor," Anna said quickly before she lost her courage. If she truly wanted to be a journalist, what better time to begin than when she knew the exact location of the infamous Wyatt Earp?

5

He is the last man anybody would ever take for a
killer...
—*Kansas City Star, May 15, 1883, regarding Doc Holliday*

Two steps outside the doctor's office, Jeb nearly keeled over. There
in broad daylight, on the sidewalk in front of the Windsor Hotel,
stood a man who strongly resembled the murdering coward Doc
Holliday.

Jeb edged closer, keeping his hat low over his eyes and a pair of
well-padded matrons between him and the suspect. Holliday had lost
weight since their run-in back in Leadville. His suit hung on shoulders that seemed less broad than Jeb remembered, but the silver
revolver was deadly familiar. He wore a look of ill health that
explained the fit of his clothes, and more than once he paused to
cough. Abruptly Holliday turned, and Jeb backed into the shadows
to watch from under the brim of his Stetson.

Doc zigzagged across Eighteenth Street, then leaned into a nicely
appointed buggy to talk to its occupant. The society gal shook her
head, causing the blue feathers on her hat to obscure Jeb's view of her
face. He could see chestnut curls and hands that moved as if she
couldn't manage to speak without them.

It didn't take a Pinkerton to figure out what was going on between Doc Holliday and the woman in the buggy. Jeb's temper flared. Was money changing hands? It appeared so.

It never ceased to amaze him how easily a woman got caught up in turning a bad man good. Jeb gave the stylish society belle a second look. Though he couldn't see her face, she was shapely enough that in his previous existence, before he'd learned the Lord had a better way of doing things, he might have practiced his skills on the poor girl. Instead, he'd have to be satisfied with watching Doc Holliday make the attempt.

That the man walked free on the streets of Denver galled Jeb to no end. Except for the longstanding, almost antique warrant in Arizona, which probably wouldn't be honored anyway, John Henry Holliday had nothing to keep him from enjoying what few years he had left in any way he chose.

Unlike all those he put in the grave.

Returning his attention to the buggy, Jeb assessed the situation. From his angle, he could make out nothing of the woman's features under the silly hat, but from the style of buggy and fine horse, she was clearly a woman of some worth.

Stilling his urge to race over and confront Holliday, Jeb rested his palm on his pistol. A part of him hoped Doc might commit some crime right in front of him so he could use the Colt on the gunfighter.

Not likely, and Jeb knew it. If there was one thing besides gunplay Doc Holliday excelled at, it was staying one step ahead of the law.

The pair seemed oblivious to his intrusion on their private

moment, such was the intimacy of their conversation. There seemed to be some point of debate, for the woman continued to thrust the money back at Doc only to have him return it to her. Finally the former dentist stepped away from the buggy and headed back across Eighteenth toward Jeb.

The possibility Doc might recognize him did not keep Jeb from getting a direct look at the criminal, who'd aged beyond his years. He seemed to wear his troubles in his expression as well as his posture.

Not that Jeb cared. Even though he'd read of Doc's supposed battle with illness, to see that Ella's killer suffered gave him some measure of satisfaction. That the consumption was a slow, cruel death was slightly comforting, as well.

The Bible said he should let go of any concern over what the Lord did with Holliday. This was an ongoing project at which Jeb failed more than succeeded.

Jeb slowed his pace to allow a harried mother to herd half a dozen children into the Crutcher Mercantile, all the while watching Doc's back. The Georgia dentist plying a society matron with money intrigued Jeb as much as it put him on alert. Doc was up to something.

Jeb glanced behind him to see if Doc's friend still waited, but the buggy had already disappeared. He turned his attention back to Doc, who made slow but steady progress through the bustling crowd until he disappeared inside the apothecary that was located inside the Windsor Hotel. *Figures.* A man in his health probably spent a considerable amount of time and money buying potions and powders to keep himself upright and moving.

All the better, for that was a stop Jeb too needed to make.

Jeb took a deep breath of clear, bracing air and paused to survey the scene around him. Though Holliday mostly traveled alone, only allowing his supposed wife Kate any access to him, there was nonetheless a possibility some of his less law-abiding friends might be lurking about. Jeb saw no one he recognized, but he knew there could still be new hangers-on whose names he might only learn the hard way. By way of habit, he rested his palm on his Colt and gave one last hard look to anyone who might be glancing in his direction.

Jeb spent the next several minutes staring at the apothecary door, trying to decide just how bad an idea it was to go inside. His stupid side won out. He took two steps forward, then stopped as the woman's buggy came around the corner and rolled to a stop in front of the Windsor Hotel.

So they were meeting after all.

Jeb crossed the street and caught up to the woman as her driver helped her down. She paid Jeb no attention, though from his spot behind her Jeb could see she gave particular interest to the upper floors of the hotel.

"I'll be in the dining room," she said.

The voice sounded vaguely familiar. Before Jeb could figure out from where, the driver spied him staring and moved toward him.

"You need something, pal?" the undersized Irishman asked.

Jeb pulled his hat lower over his eyes and shook his head. He turned and moved a few yards away, then retraced his steps in time to see the pretty lady entering the Windsor's front doors.

A glance at the driver, who had already climbed into the seat and slouched his hat over his eyes, and Jeb followed the mysterious female inside.

The lobby stretched half a block in either direction, and a double staircase led to one of the dining rooms. For a city girl who probably got little in the way of exercise, she took the steps at a decent pace. When a group of men in business suits obscured his view, Jeb watched her hat, a concoction of feathers and ribbon, bob and bounce as she climbed above the crowded lobby. Careful to blend in as best he could despite the fact he still wore a full beard, Jeb crossed the lobby and waited at the bottom of the stairs until the woman disappeared into the main dining room.

A fellow in a hotel uniform caught sight of him and frowned. Jeb tipped his hat and pretended to leave, then circled around behind the man to wait for his chance to get upstairs undetected. It came a few minutes later in the form of a screeching child who threw herself onto the floor in the middle of the lobby. While the hapless parents attempted to console their little one, the uniformed employee watched intently, giving Jeb a moment to race up the staircase without being noticed.

Jeb reached the second-floor landing and stumbled to a stop. In the center of the nearly empty dining room sat Wyatt Earp and his wife. And with them was Doc Holliday. This Jeb certainly hadn't expected, for the once inseparable duo had not been seen in public in years. From what he'd heard, Wyatt had settled into quiet obscurity as a family man bent on living to a ripe old age. The woman approached the outlaws' table as boldly as if she'd known them all her life.

The lack of a crowd in the dining room gave Jeb only one place to hide that still offered a view of the table in question, and he slipped behind the forest of palm trees in the corner without hesitation. Secure in his hiding place, Jeb returned his attention to the drama playing out at the only table in the room occupied by diners. At least it appeared to be a drama, though the woman's flustered body language was almost humorous. Few things were funny, however, with Doc Holliday sitting across the table from his old friend Wyatt Earp.

Quite a meeting, especially considering the old friends had chosen to come out into the open.

Jeb squatted down to get comfortable. Whatever was about to transpire, he didn't intend to miss any of it.

Then the woman turned and glanced in his direction, and the breath went out of him. It was her.

The woman who'd shot him.

6

Throw up your hands, Doc Holliday.
I have you now!
—*as reported by Perry Mallon, Denver Tribune, May 1887*

Anna hid her shaking hands behind her as she opened her mouth to begin the speech she'd practiced in the buggy. Three sets of eyes looked up at her, and yet not a word would come.

An odd situation for one who had more trouble stopping her speech than starting it.

Whereas she'd planned to be forthright and professional in her journalistic endeavor, now Anna had to settle for looking foolish.

In the hope that some brilliance would materialize as an opening line to the wanted men, Anna opened her mouth and said, "Gentlemen." She paused to smile at Mrs. Earp. "And you, of course," she added. "I suppose you wonder why I came back." She presented the folded bills to Mr. Earp's friend, who merely stared at her outstretched hand. "You've overpaid, Mr. Bonney."

A fair brow, barely visible against his pale skin, rose in response. "While I thank you for returning the excess," he said, "I must protest. As my angel of mercy, I wonder if you realize the value of the favor you've done for me."

Anna gave the Earps a sideways glance before shaking her head. "I'll not hear of it, sir." She paused long enough to take a breath. "You see, I—"

"'Scuse me, miss."

A plate piled with more food than a girl could eat in a week landed on the table in front of her. The waiter grinned, then placed similar dishes in front of the other three diners. "Enjoy," he said before tucking the tray under his arm and turning on his heels to head back toward the kitchen.

"But wait, I—"

"Please join us," Mrs. Earp said.

"Truly, that was not my intention."

Mr. Earp shook his head. "Never argue with the help," he said in his slow drawl. "Or, for that matter, with the spouse." His serious expression only lasted a second. "I suppose that just works if you're not the wife." He nudged his friend. "Ain't that right, Mr. Bonney?"

The fair-haired man revealed the beginning of a smile. "I don't suppose I've spent enough time with mine to know for sure."

Mrs. Earp looked perplexed. "Where is Kate these days?" she asked.

Anna noticed the former lawman's almost imperceptible shake of the head along with the way he narrowed his eyes when his wife attempted to speak further. Their companion seemed inclined to go along with the silence, continuing to regard Anna with an even stare. His message was clear.

Any questions she'd had about the identity of the man were answered. She was indeed in the presence of the gunfighter Doc Holliday. Anna took a deep breath and let it out slowly as the realization sunk in. Her fingers only shook for a second, though it took more than that to manage another look at the fellow.

From the faces of the trio, she had already overstayed her welcome. Despite the potential for her first scoop as a reporter, Anna wasn't going to find any help here. The only story appeared to be a public meeting between friends who had not seen each other in years. As ill as Doc Holliday looked, the meeting might be their last. Further reason to make her exit as quickly as possible.

Anna stepped back from the table. "I'm terribly sorry to have intruded on your meal. You see, I had this harebrained idea of writing something for the newspaper that would vindicate you, Mr. Earp. I've followed your career since your time in Kansas, and I happen to be among those who believe there has not been a complete accounting of things where that matter with the cowboys is concerned. However, I've realized this is neither the time nor the place for such an endeavor. So if you will excuse me, I'll just be going."

Anna moved toward the exit, taking her pride and nonexistent journalism career with her.

"Wait, miss!" Anna turned to see the waiter giving chase. "That man there," he said, "he asked that you come back. Says he's going to take you up on your offer."

"My offer?" She looked past him toward the table. Mr. Earp caught her gaze and nodded. His wife gestured for her to return, and Anna could only grin. "Might I trouble you to fetch writing paper and ink?" She slid a few coins into the waiter's hand. "There's more if you hurry."

"How many sheets of paper?" he asked.

"Enough to tell a compelling story." His expression went blank. Anna sighed. "Buy up all they've got," she said and sent him running for the mercantile.

When the waiter had scurried off, Anna returned to the Earps' table to find the men engaged in a good-natured disagreement over what year some unnamed incident took place.

"I'm telling you it was '77," Earp said.

Holliday leaned back and crossed his arms over his chest. "It wasn't either," he insisted. "It was '78, and if your brother was here he'd say so."

"Thank you for your offer." Mrs. Earp touched Anna's sleeve. "It wasn't right, all those lies that were told. The things those awful men did to our family and to Doc and the others. People need to know that."

Earp cleared his throat and looked away while Holliday's face remained expressionless.

Emboldened, Anna leaned forward. "I'll do what I can. What is it you'd like my readers to know?"

The aging lawman's piercing blue eyes narrowed and a muscle in his jaw clenched. For a moment, there was nothing but silence in the empty dining room. How anyone who'd dined in this man's presence missed noticing him was beyond Anna's understanding.

"Little lady," he said slowly, "I suppose there's been a grain of truth in just about every story printed about me and the boys." A pause. "And Mr. Bonney over there."

The other man's chuckle became a cough that he quickly covered with his handkerchief.

Earp eyed his friend with concern before returning his steely gaze to Anna. "If you publish the truth, the whole truth as I give it to you, without adding or taking away any of it, then you'll be the first."

Considering she'd made up every word of every book she'd ever written, Anna was more than ready to take on her first publication of truth. Especially if it was a truth that needed telling.

The waiter returned with the writing materials, including more paper than she could use in a month, and Anna sorted out what she needed. "Shall we get started?" she said, her pencil poised over a sheet of paper.

"All right." Mr. Earp leaned back and regarded her with an even stare. "What do you want to know?"

"Maybe you'd like to tell me what really happened with Mr. Ringo."

"Johnny Ringo's a tale best told by Mr. Bonney here," Earp said.

The man in question swiped at the sheen of perspiration on his brow and offered Anna a smile. "Then I regret it's a tale that must wait for another day. It's Mr. Earp's story you're writing, not mine."

"Fair enough," Earp said. "I reckon I've got stories enough to fill up more pages than you've got there, little lady."

Anna grinned. "Lack of paper will not be an issue, I assure you."

Her.

Jeb's fingers brushed the Colt and he felt the pull of his stitches. Was *she* the informant he'd been waiting for? She wasn't what he'd expected, but then he'd figured the source to be male. With her aim, had she come to inform him or dispatch him to his reward? Hard to tell. He could read a man like a book, but knowing what went on in a woman's mind had never been his strong suit.

He watched her, studied her, noted the dimple in her cheek and the way she leaned her head back when she laughed. Whoever this woman was, she had decent aim and was well connected enough to dine with Wyatt Earp and Doc Holliday. With her Smith & Wesson nowhere in sight, she appeared every inch the lady, although she did seem to be taking notes as Earp talked.

If he hadn't been determined to see Holliday tried and hanged, he might have forgotten about everything else and concentrated on figuring out just who this fancy gal was. While Earp droned on about who knew what, his wife and Holliday sat in silence. The woman continued to scribble on the stack of pages in front of her like she was some kind of reporter?

He skittered out of sight just as chairs scraped across the floor and the woman and Holliday rose. The odds of Holliday identifying him as the Pinkerton from that long-ago Leadville card game were little to none, but Jeb wasn't willing to take the chance.

"Thank you," Earp's wife said. "I'm sure we'll meet again."

"What about you, Mr. Bonney?" the woman with the deadly aim asked. "Perhaps you'll change your mind."

Ironic that the murderer was using the alias of the dead outlaw Billy the Kid. Jeb shifted slightly and found a better view of Doc Holliday and the dark-haired society gal. She'd cleaned up quite nicely. He tried not to remember how she felt against him. He had a job to do.

As Holliday leaned toward the feisty female, his diamond stickpin caught the light, as did the nickel-plated pistol in his shoulder holster. In an instant, Jeb's mind tumbled back to Leadville and a card game where he'd won it all but lost the only thing that mattered.

There, within reach, was the man whose life he'd sworn to end.

His hand went once again to his pistol. Only when his fingers touched the cold steel did his thoughts shatter. Jerking his fingers away, Jeb let out a long, silent breath. The man who'd made a vow to kill Doc Holliday had not yet met up with his Savior or been baptized in Cold Creek. Since then he'd learned a lot about forgiveness, about giving the other man the benefit of the doubt. And about letting God take His own revenge in His own time.

Why, then, did the need to put a bullet through the Georgia dentist's heart still bear so heavy on him?

"Perhaps another time," the woman said, "once I've gained your confidence."

"Confidence, my dear, is a relative thing," Holliday replied. "Unlike my friend Wyatt, I've a motto I live by: if you're not a relative, there's no confidence." He chuckled. "And trust me, there are even relatives in whom I have no confidence."

Jeb held still, barely breathing. From his vantage point, he saw Holliday sway, then right himself. The woman muttered some words of concern to which Holliday merely laughed.

"What about Mr. Earp?" she asked. "Is he some distant cousin of yours?"

Holliday's chuckle dissolved into a fit of coughing that continued until the pair moved out of Jeb's sight. "As, might it be argued, are you. After all," the gunfighter finally said, "I did allow you to post important correspondence."

They must have stopped just outside the dining room, for their voices remained strong and loud though the pair could no longer be seen.

"Oh, you allowed me, did you? And to think I was under the mistaken impression I did you a favor. Instead I received a privilege." She laughed again, and Jeb realized she was flirting. "Next time I'll know the difference."

"You're confident there will be a next time," Holliday said, "which makes me wonder just how…"

And then they were gone, leaving the last of the conversation trailing in their wake. Jeb waited a full minute, then rose and made his way to the door. He stopped short when he saw Holliday turn back toward the dining room. Jeb let his hand drop to the Colt but didn't touch it.

Holliday continued walking toward him as the feathered hat bounced down the stairs atop the head of the retreating woman. Holliday stopped to wipe his chin, then studied the handkerchief for a second before stuffing it into his pocket. He shuffled back toward the dining room with his attention focused on the rug. Then the outlaw looked up.

Their eyes met.

Jeb's heart lurched, but then he noticed Holliday's expression. Nothing. No recognition.

As far as Doc Holliday was concerned, Jeb had never crossed his path. That much was obvious by the way the pale man walked past him without so much as a tip of his hat.

Cold anger sparked within him and flamed bright as Jeb curled his fists. A man of less honor would have taken his best shot right then. Would have called Holliday out right there in the Windsor's fancy dining room and watched while the bullet did to the dying gunslinger what it had done to Ella.

Jeb cleared his throat and said, "You there."

Holliday froze, then turned slowly as Jeb moved toward him. Wyatt Earp and his woman looked up from their coffee cups. "Were you speaking to me?" Holliday asked.

"I was." Jeb rested his palm on his Colt. The room was warm, his gun cold. Holliday was fast, but Jeb knew he was faster. In a fraction of a second he could easily dispatch this man to meet his Maker. Earp might send him there right on Holliday's heels, but Jeb didn't care. Not at that moment. Not with Doc Holliday in his crosshairs.

A half-hearted grin crossed Holliday's face before disappearing. "Might I be of some assistance?"

Jeb stared into the face of evil and realized this man bore only a passing resemblance to the Holliday he remembered. The features were there, to be sure. Consumption could be the only explanation for the change in him.

"Yes," Jeb said as evenly as he could. "You got the time?"

The gunfighter reached into his vest pocket, and Jeb half expected him to pull a pistol just for sport.

Instead, he consulted a gold watch, then returned his attention to Jeb. "A quarter past one," he said as he replaced the watch in his pocket.

Time hung between them a second longer than it should have as Jeb memorized the killer's features and corrected the image in his memory. As he decided whether or not to end it all right there.

His trigger finger found its place. A quick tug, one shot, and Ella's death would be avenged.

A murder for a murder.

If he pulled the trigger, Jeb would be no better than the man standing in front of him.

With a curt nod, Jeb turned his back on Doc Holliday and walked out of the dining room before his need for revenge trumped his sense of morality.

Once he crossed the dining room threshold, Jeb forced his hand off the weapon and into his jacket pocket. With each step, he made another promise to Ella. The investigation would continue. Proof would be found. And then he would put Doc Holliday in the grave he'd earned long ago.

A flash of blue caught his attention, and he knew he'd found the next fugitive on his list: the woman who'd put a bullet in him. Jeb headed her direction.

What he'd do with her when he caught up to her was another question entirely. As he recalled, she still had one more bullet in that gun of hers.

7

He would no sooner be out of one scrape before
he was in another...

—*Bat Masterson, regarding Doc Holliday,
from Gunfighters of the Western Frontier, 1907*

Anna walked out of the Windsor Hotel's dining room with a story
and no idea what to do with it.

My readers. Had she actually said that? She'd had no readers since
the last time Mae saddled up, but she aspired to reaching a whole
new audience.

She tucked the pages under her arm and descended the stairs. It
was a heady assignment, this righting of the wrong against the Earp
name. Even Mae's story paled in comparison to the reality of the life
of Wyatt Earp.

There had to be a way to gain the attention of the press. But
how?

Papa had friends at both the *Denver Times* and the *Rocky Mountain News,* but neither would likely publish a story written by a nobody like her. Besides, Papa would never stand for any female bearing
his good name giving the appearance of being employed. Especially
in the mood he'd been in of late.

His good name. Anna stopped in the middle of the staircase. That was it. She just needed a new name.

Anything but Finch.

She'd not had to make this decision when writing the Mae Winslow books. All of them had Anonymous listed as the author, which was fine by her, but a factual piece would never be printed without some kind of credit.

Anna began to run through names in her mind.

"My favorite little birdie!" called the familiar and despised voice of Winston Mitchell as Anna reached the lobby. "I've been waiting for you, Miss Finch. I wondered if you might tell me what's going on at your neighbor's house, though I'm willing to listen to anything you might want to tell me about your lunch as well."

From the top of his bowler hat to the tips of his freshly shined shoes, Winston Mitchell was a study in fashion. His jacket matched his cravat, which coordinated with his vest and likely his undershirt and socks. Were he not as well known for his ability at fisticuffs, the middle-aged journalist might have been considered too unmanly to survive in a town such as Denver. Despite his popular gossip column "Perish the Thought" at the *Denver Times,* Mitchell's British accent was the object of much speculation. Some said he only affected the accent to hide his true background, while others said he was a lost or wandering nobleman who came to Denver to keep from being found.

Anna didn't really care where he'd come from. She just wished he'd go back there. Over the last few years, he'd made her his favorite subject, documenting in embarrassing detail her failed attempts at securing a husband. It was hard enough dodging all the men her father threw at her without having Winston Mitchell mock her every move.

Little bird. That's what he called her in print as a thinly veiled attempt at keeping her identity secret while making sure she and most others who counted knew exactly to whom he referred. Just this week, he'd mentioned her in a column she'd been unable to forget.

What little bird refuses to leave her finely feathered nest despite her longsuffering parents' best efforts? This reporter knows all too well the travail associated with the lengthy process of sending the fifth and final hatchling forth, as he has reported on many of the events created for this very purpose. Perhaps, as Papa Bird was overheard suggesting, the little one's wings have grown weak from flapping. Oh, perish the thought!

Biting her lip against the words she longed to speak, Anna put on a smile. She'd learned the hard way that angering Mitchell was never a good idea. The entire city read his column.

"Is that so?" she said. "Then you'll be waiting a long time, for I've nothing to say."

"Of course you do." He smiled. "So, about the Becks. A house-guest arrived via private rail car. What can you tell me?"

"I've no idea what you're asking," she said. "Perhaps you should go to Mr. Beck with your concerns."

"I have, but he refuses to comment."

She shrugged. "As do I. Now if you'll excuse me—"

Anna darted around the column at the base of the stairs, but unfortunately so did Mr. Mitchell. With a shake of his head, he fell in step beside her.

"Mrs. Beck spent a brief amount of time in the dining room with you. And she handed off a letter."

"Aren't you informed?" Anna picked up her pace. "I suppose you know I also had business at the post office. I intend to write letters, and unless the rules have changed, the postal service requires stamps." She gave him an exasperated look. "Am I wrong? After all, you seem to know everything that goes on in Denver. If there's anything you miss, well, perish the thought."

There. She felt slightly better, except Mr. Mitchell still kept up with her.

He frowned. "There's a story here, and I'm going to find it. If you helped me, I might consider it a personal favor." He paused. "And you a personal friend and valued source. Have I mentioned I have a rule regarding personal friends and valued sources, little bird?"

Little bird. Looking straight ahead seemed the best and safest response. It also allowed Anna to see that the exit was not as far as it seemed.

"Personal friends and valued sources rarely appear in my column, Miss Finch. I find that a conflict of interest." The vile man chuckled. "Thus you might wish to attain that status. So, about this mysterious visitor. I'm told his trunks bore a royal crest, though not a single one of my sources could say what it looked like with any certainty."

Anna giggled. "Then perhaps you need a better quality of valued sources. Oh, and personal friends too."

"You're quite funny, Miss Finch," he said in a voice that held no humor. "I'm certain you must amuse yourself to no end on those long, lonely nights at home with your mother and father. And with that view of the Beck home out the window."

She ignored the jab with an effort worthy of Mae Winslow.

"I fail to see why you protect him, considering in all the years you've been in love with him, he never looked twice at you."

"Of all the nerve." Anna stopped short, blood pounding at her temples. "How dare you? I have overlooked all the awful things you've said about me in your wretched column. Until now." She took a breath and let it out slowly, hoping it might give her time to re-think her feelings. It didn't. "So, *Mr. Mitchell*, I will have an apology from you immediately or I will have to seek further recourse. I assure you, you will hear from my attorney before the end of the day."

She had no attorney, but likely Papa did. As angry as she felt, Anna would walk the length of Eighteenth Street until she found one.

When Mitchell merely stared at her, she swallowed hard. That they stood in the very public Windsor Hotel lobby was not lost on Anna. But the fact that she had finally stood up to the horrible fellow who wounded her for sport felt exhilarating.

Thus, she couldn't help saying one last thing. "I see you're not of a mind to make the apology I demand. Very well. I have a question of my own."

He looked amused. "And what might that be, Miss Finch?"

"What part of England are you from again? I've traveled extensively on the Continent as well as in Great Britain, and I can't quite seem to place your accent."

The color drained from his face, as did a good portion of his bravado. "Yes, well, we moved around quite a bit, my family and I."

"You're not misrepresenting yourself to your readers, are you, Mr. Mitchell? Your name *is* Mitchell, isn't it?" She paused to enjoy his obvious discomfort. "For a journalist to bend the truth—well, perish the thought."

"All right, then." He sighed heavily, then made a great show of bowing before her. When he straightened, the amusement had returned to his face. "Miss Finch, I intended neither to offend nor to upset your delicate sensibilities in any way." He paused and glanced around the lobby before his gaze met hers. "I am asking your forgiveness, though I do not deserve it, wretch that I am. Would you do me the great and glorious honor of accepting my apology?"

When she merely crossed her arms in response, unwilling to let him get away with mocking her yet again, the awful man fell to his knees. All around her, people stopped to stare. Some whispered comments to companions while others merely indicated displeasure with a raised brow or a frown. Still others seemed amused.

"Get up this instant," she demanded. "You're making a scene."

"Forgive me, Miss Finch!" Mitchell cried loudly. "I beg you!"

Wishing she'd just ignored him from the moment he appeared, Anna turned to flee and slammed into a wall of buckskin and brawn. The man, obviously fresh off the trail and far out of his element in this place, grasped her by the shoulders to keep her upright.

"So sorry," she said as her gaze collided with eyes the same smoky gray as a Colorado winter sky.

A jolt of recognition hit her. She had looked into those eyes before. How could that be?

The mountain man said nothing, but his grip remained firm, his stance unwavering. When he released her, Anna stumbled backward. Once again the stranger saved her from landing anywhere but on her feet, this time by wrapping his arm around her back and hauling her against him.

Anna looked up. The vantage point was familiar, as was the feel of muscle beneath rough cotton. The stranger, his face covered with a month's growth of whiskers, looked down. He had saved her from hitting the floor, but he couldn't save her from her shaking knees.

Or from losing her brand-new hat in the scuffle. She looked down at the creation, its feathers hopelessly ruined by the oversized boot that had stomped it nearly flat.

The mountain man gently released her, though his palm remained at her waist as he reached down to sweep up the remains of her hat and offer it to her. "My apologies, ma'am."

That voice. She knew it, had heard it yesterday morning at the river when it bristled the air with words of surprise then made quick amends by soothing her fear that she'd done him in with her panicked shooting.

Anna stared at the man's midsection.

Him. It had to be.

Anna braved another glance at his face and found the scar on his chin. The lobby began to spin. "You."

She blinked hard, remembering what lay under the layers of clothing, the damage her Smith & Wesson had done.

Looking for a way—for words—to right the wrong she had inflicted on him, she pressed her hand against the spot where she'd drawn blood. His quick intake of breath told her she'd either shocked the poor man or hurt him once again. Even through her glove she could feel the bandage.

His hand covered hers, and she froze. Her gaze trailed up the length of him, darting across a shirt that deserved to be thrown in the rubbish bin rather than washed one more time, up the tanned skin of his neck. Finally she met his gaze. The mountain man lifted her hand and held it, then released her.

The man she'd shot.

The room tilted and faded away.

When Anna snapped back to herself a few seconds later, she realized the mountain man had once again saved her from falling. Somehow, he'd also managed to remove her from the middle of the Windsor Hotel. From the humiliation of being seen foolishly fainting over some strange man.

He'd tucked her into a curtained alcove off the main lobby, where a hallway likely meant for employees lay hidden. Anna found the wall and leaned against it, closing her eyes until the swirling stopped. She opened her eyes expecting to find the mountain man gone.

He was not.

He leaned over her, his palms flat against the wall on either side of her head. Whether out of concern or some other reason, he studied her intently. If anyone happened upon them, they might suppose she and this unkempt fellow sought privacy for more pleasant reasons.

Anna ducked out of his almost-embrace and positioned herself between the mountain man and the curtain. "Truly, I owe you an—"

"You naughty girl!" Mr. Mitchell called. "I see where you're hiding, and I'll have your attention or know the reason why." He threw open the curtain.

Anna fought the urge to scream as she whirled to face the menace with a pen.

"Go away."

Of course, he did not. "I only sought to return this lovely chapeau." His gaze slid down to her toes then back to her face. "Did I see yet another attempt to pair up the poor girl with someone?"

"You are truly insufferable."

"You've had quite a string of gentlemen today. The first one looked a bit old for you," he continued, "and the other seemed to be suffering from some sort of ailment, though I completely understand that in your position you might have to compromise in certain areas. The good health and extended life span of the groom, for instance. As for your latest attempt…"

The columnist looked past her and his face fell. Anna glanced behind her and found the mountain man was gone. He must have slipped out through the other end of the corridor.

Unless he'd been a figment of her overactive imagination. But the glee of Winston Mitchell told her otherwise.

"What a slippery fellow! Oh well."

Anna pushed past Mr. Mitchell and the curtain, searching the expanse of the lobby for the man with the smoky eyes and telltale scar.

"So which is the lucky man, little bird? The older man? The invalid? Or is your intended the fellow who looked as if he'd not seen a woman since the dawn of time? Nor a barber, for that matter."

He chuckled. "Quite an interesting exchange between the two of you before he swept you off behind the curtains."

Though her temper once again threatened to spark, Anna only contemplated her response for a moment. "As another apology from you would likely not be sincere either," she said slowly, "I suggest you cease speaking at once and do not take up the habit again until you are well away from me. Far, far away." Anna punctuated the statement with a direct stare at the columnist. "Unless you're more intelligent than I think and you're willing to just leave me alone."

"You wound me, Miss Finch."

"If only that were possible, Mr. Mitchell." She turned on her heel and stormed toward the door.

"So?" Mitchell pressed. "Who's the lucky man?"

"You're the reporter, Mr. Mitchell," she said when he'd caught up to her. "Figure it out."

"Here's what I'd like to figure." He moved between Anna and the sidewalk, blocking her path. "Has your father resorted to importing foreigners? Or perhaps it would be more accurate to ask if he has taken to exporting daughters."

She shook her head and stepped around the vile man, waving to McMinn. When the traffic on Eighteenth came to a lull, Anna hurried across.

"Want me to make him disappear, Miss Finch?" McMinn asked, nodding toward Mitchell. Strong words from a man whose job was to drive the family, not protect them. Anna wasn't completely opposed to someone pummeling the journalist on her behalf; after all, what woman didn't relish a little jousting in her honor, even if it did come from a paid employee?

She allowed Mr. McMinn to help her into the buggy. "Thank you, but it truly wouldn't be worth the effort."

Nor did she intend to allow the thought of extracting revenge on the columnist to slow her trip home. As the buggy picked up speed and slipped onto Eighteenth behind an overly crowded trolley, Anna had already begun to review her notes from that afternoon's chance meeting.

"Divine appointment," she whispered. Surely only the Lord could have arranged such a fortuitous meeting. How the tale that dispelled the lies told about Wyatt Earp would find its way to the page of a newspaper was another miracle only He could manage.

As for the other unplanned meeting of the day, the one with the man whose blood Anna had accidentally drawn, perhaps she might be allowed an opportunity to right that wrong as well.

8

This is funny.
—*Doc Holliday's reported last words*

From the looks of the activity outside the Beck home, preparations for tonight's event for Governor and Mrs. Grant proceeded on schedule. In a few hours the stately house would be full of guests. Jeb had seen the list and approved the plan for keeping Denver's elite safe and secure, including changing the hired help's garb from Roman togas to a more dignified suit that allowed the three dozen men on duty to hide their guns and still appear part of the staff.

Hank probably wouldn't take well to Jeb sticking his nose into the business Hank would soon be paid to handle, but for now Jeb was still the man to whom Daniel turned when he needed something impossible done well and fast. Money never changed hands between them, as it would with Hank, so Jeb called the things he did for Daniel favors rather than Pinkerton work.

"Uncle Jeb!"

He looked up toward the familiar voice and found Charlotte Beck waving from the window above the parlor.

"You'd better not let your pa or Gennie catch you behaving like a heathen, Charlie," he called. "What are you now, twelve? Thirteen?"

Daniel's daughter affected an indignant expression. "Don't pretend you don't know I'll be sixteen soon," she said. "Very soon."

"Can't be." He shook his head. "I told you a long time ago I'd not settle for you growing up."

"Too bad." She tossed her curls. "Guess what? Tonight I'm to join the adults at the reception. Isn't that a daisy?"

"It is indeed. Now get on back inside. I'll see you when you're ready for your big debut."

Charlotte blew him a kiss and slipped away from the window, leaving lace curtains swaying in her wake.

"That one's a handful," he said under his breath as he slipped through the kitchen door of the Beck home.

Tova, Daniel's housekeeper, had already poured him a cup of hot coffee and set it in his usual spot at the table.

"Can't tarry tonight." He kissed her cheek and reached for the mug. "I'm on the clock."

"Hey, now." Elias, Daniel's houseman and longtime friend, looked up from his newspaper and shook his head. "If my woman needs kissin', I'm the one's gonna do it. You got enough to worry about with Pinkerton business anyway, especially given who showed up 'round here this mornin'. So just leave her t'me."

"Yes sir." Jeb saluted with his free hand. "And about that, what's your—"

"Your woman, is it?" The Norwegian woman's *harrumph* let both men know exactly what she thought of that. "He calls me such a thing and yet when it comes to marrying me..." Her words faded to muttering, which didn't seem to surprise Elias at all. Rather, he seemed to delight in it. Tova's scrubbing became a symphony of pots, pans, and spoons clanging together.

Jeb set aside the questions he'd intended to ask Elias about Edwin Beck and turned his attention to stirring up the pot of trouble already brewing between these two. "When're the two of you getting hitched, Elias?" Jeb asked over the noise. "This engagement's gone on for how long, Tova? Two years?"

"Three, come Christmas," Elias said, "but who's counting?"

"I am," Tova said. "But until that man gives up those awful cigars, he'll not be marrying me."

Elias placed his copy of the *Denver Times* between himself and Tova. "I've had them cigars a whole lot longer than—"

"I get the idea." Jeb took his place across the table from the old codger. "But sometimes what you give up's worth what you get." He gestured over his shoulder at the housekeeper, who no longer banged pots and pans in the sink. "And Tova here's quite the prize. Why, if I weren't already sworn to permanent bachelorhood, I'd have to give serious consideration to the fact that you've been dragging your feet to make her your missus."

Elias's bushy gray brows rose nearly to the brim of his Confederate cap. "Now see here."

"Come and look," Tova said.

Jeb swiveled in his chair to see the housekeeper staring out the window, a dishtowel covering the lower half of her face. He jumped up and joined her at the sink. "What is it?"

Tova began to giggle. The reason stepped into the clearing between the stables and the kitchen. Tova's son, Isak, had forsaken his usual stable hand garb and made his way toward the house in an odd combination of trousers, boots, and a bed sheet wrapped around him to form a makeshift toga. Atop it all he'd placed a helmet-looking hat that under other circumstances might have given him the appearance of a gladiator.

"Looks like that boy done gone off the deep end," Elias commented as the back door opened and Isak tromped in.

"I know the boss wants us all to dress like century mans but—"

"Centurions," his mother corrected.

Isak shrugged. "That's what I said. But I can't do it. I won't." He shrugged out of the bed sheet and handed it to Jeb. "You tell me how a man can see to the horses without losing his dignity in that thing."

"Too late for that, son." Elias pointed to the hat. "Even I wouldn't wear that."

The young Norwegian tugged the helmet off and thrust it toward Jeb. "You're the one who's good at disguises. See how you feel wearing this. As for me, I'm going back to the barn to put on some decent clothes." When his mother opened her mouth, he held up his hand to silence her. "Don't say it, Ma. I've made up my mind."

He marched out of the kitchen, the door slamming behind him. Jeb didn't have the heart to inform Isak all that rebellion was for naught.

Tova's face turned scarlet, and she snatched the bed sheet from Jeb. "I tell him he must dress as the others. This occasion is important to Mr. Beck. What sort of boy won't listen to his mama?"

Elias moved between them and grasped Tova's wrist. They stood eye to eye, the tall Norwegian and the Confederate veteran, and neither seemed inclined to so much as blink.

"Leave him be, Tova," Elias said, his voice low, his tone brooking no argument.

Jeb stepped back, set the helmet on the table, then picked up his coffee cup. This was a conversation he didn't intend to miss. Likely this would be the best entertainment of the whole evening, the Denver Orchestra and whatever else Daniel had planned for the governor's reception included.

Tova blinked first. "Leave him be? I'm his mother."

"And he's a grown man."

The bed sheet fell to the kitchen floor, but neither seemed to notice.

"A grown man," Tova repeated with disdain. "What kind of man—"

"The kind who finally figured out where to draw the line, Tova."

"But—," she sputtered, though Jeb noticed she made no attempt to move away.

"The kind who decides one day that enough is enough." Elias inched closer. "The kind who won't be told to change his ways when there ain't no good reason for it 'cept to delay what ought not be delayed, you understand?"

"Elias?" Tova's normally restrained voice cracked. "We're not talking about Isak anymore, are we?"

"No, we're not, woman," he said. "Now, I'm determined to marry you come Tuesday afternoon right here in this kitchen, and soon as I kiss you proper, I'm going to fetch the reverend and tell him to expect us. You get me, and you get the occasional cigar, though I promise not to smoke indoors or on Sundays. What say you to this?"

Jeb took another sip and watched Tova's pale features color bright crimson. It was all he could do not to chuckle.

"What say I?" Her spunk returned full force, and Jeb half expected her to turn back to the sink and resume her cooking utensil symphony. "What say I?"

"Tova, darlin', you're repeatin' yourself," Elias said.

"Here's what I say." She kissed Elias soundly, then abruptly pushed him away. "I say what sort of man wants to wait until Tuesday? Am I not worthy of marrying today?"

Elias seemed flustered, though Jeb couldn't say whether it was from the kiss or the question. "You wouldn't happen t'be a preacher, would ya, Jeb?"

"Me? No," Jeb said quickly. "I'm afraid not."

"Here you are." Daniel Beck stepped into the kitchen and closed the door behind him. "I wondered if you planned to arrive with the crowds through the front door or slip in the back." He looked past Jeb to his housekeeper and Elias. "What's going on here?"

Jeb gestured to the back door. "How about we talk outside? Wouldn't want to interrupt true love."

Daniel gave the pair a confused look, then followed Jeb. "I didn't expect to see you so soon," he said when they stopped a safe distance from the house. "Aren't you here as a guest tonight?"

A chill wind blew across the lawn, and Jeb huddled in his coat. "I am. Thought I might borrow a spare room to change clothes so I'm not spotted until I want to be."

"Of course," Daniel said. "You know you're always welcome here, my friend."

"I appreciate that." Jeb kicked a rock out from under his boot as he decided how to tackle the subject of Edwin Beck, Daniel's younger brother and the man who both fathered Charlotte Beck and removed Daniel from the family business back in England.

His old friend had never offered details, and Jeb never asked. He saw all he needed to know: a man who'd come to Denver to make a new life and succeeded.

There was only one reason Edwin Beck would come looking for Daniel. He wanted what Daniel had, be that wealth or family. As long as Jeb drew a breath, he would have neither.

Daniel gave him a sideways glance. "Securing a room at the Beck Inn is not why you've got me standing out here, is it?"

"No," Jeb said slowly. "I hear Edwin's paid you a visit."

He looked up sharply. "Yes."

Jeb chose his words carefully. "Do you want him out of Denver?"

"No." Daniel let out a long breath. "Much as I would like not to, I'm going to try to settle things with my brother."

"That's admirable," Jeb said.

"It's for Charlotte." He paused. "And our father. The earl's not getting any younger, and I know his fondest wish is that Edwin and I settle our differences."

"Does he know what those differences are, Daniel?" Jeb shook his head. "Forget I asked that. None of my business."

"You've been a friend to me and my family too long to claim that," Daniel said. "The truth is, I'm unsure what my father knows." He looked up at the house, then returned his attention to Jeb. "I hoped you were here early to talk me out of hiring Thompson. You know you've always been my first choice."

"I appreciate that," Jeb said, "but you're getting a good man with Hank, and I'll still be around if you're of a mind to lose at cards."

Daniel's hearty laugh was answer enough. Then he sobered. "This assignment of yours. Should I be concerned?"

Jeb laughed. "I'm almost ashamed to tell you. I'm playing hired gun to your neighbor."

"Someone after Barnaby Finch?"

Jeb spied activity at the stables, but it was only Isak speaking to a pair of stable hands. "I'm shadowing his daughter."

"Anna?" Daniel shook his head. "Why? Surely she's in no danger."

"According to her father, her only danger is from herself. Apparently he's having some trouble marrying her off."

"I repeat: Anna?" Daniel paused. "I've known Anna at least ten years, and I can't recall a single time when she's been anything other than a proper lady. What man wouldn't be delighted with someone like that? Surely you recall meeting her at some point. You must have."

Daniel described her, and Jeb shrugged. "Might be best if you just pointed her out. I'll take it from there."

"Of course, and I would ask one favor from you."

Jeb met his stare. "Anything."

The look on Daniel's face told Jeb this was no simple favor. "Should Barnaby Finch decide my brother is a candidate for Anna's hand, I would very much appreciate you preventing that from happening."

He didn't need to think about his answer. "Consider it done."

Daniel consulted his watch, then gestured to the door. "Gennie will be wondering where I've gone."

Jeb fell into step behind Daniel.

"One more question," Daniel said. "How did you convince my wife to change her Roman theme at the last minute?"

"Oh, that was simple." Jeb shrugged. "I told her it was your idea."

9

There was something very peculiar about Doc.
He was gentlemanly, a good dentist, a friendly
man and yet, outside of us boys, I don't think
he had a friend in the Territory.
—*Virgil Earp, The Arizona Daily Star, May 30, 1882*

Long after she'd returned home, Anna thought about the mountain man. Questions darted across her mind, but only one paused long enough to stick.

How could she make this right?

There was no good answer, of course. Money would not repair the damage her bullet had done. An apology, heartfelt and sincere, would be the beginning. And of course, she'd insist on seeing he received proper medical treatment.

But how to find him? Anna paused to consider her options. Were it not for the need to give an explanation, she might have sent Mr. McMinn back into town with a description of the man. She briefly considered speaking with Papa about making some sort of restitution but discarded the option. He was angry enough with her already.

Unable to solve the problem of the mountain man, Anna set her mind on the notes she'd taken on Wyatt Earp's story, looking up from them only when the maid knocked to ask if she wished for any help in dressing for the evening. After spending the day toiling over a factual tale that was much more exciting than any dime novel, the last thing Anna wished to do was spend yet another evening away from her desk. But it would be her final chance to see Gennie for some time, so Anna set aside her pen and paper in order to play the obedient daughter to her doting parents.

At least that was the image Anna attempted to convey as she passed through the familiar gates of the Beck home. The night was crisp, and the ring of misty clouds around the moon promised wet weather before dawn. With the twilight's dusting of stars came a chill wind that her wrap, chosen for looks rather than effectiveness, did little to dispel.

It was a night meant for snuggling under her quilts and reading—or preferably writing—until her eyes refused to remain open. If only she could flee these festivities and return to her story about Wyatt Earp.

"Evening, Mr. Finch," a familiar voice called. When she and Mama turned, Mr. Thompson, Papa's Pinkerton friend, tipped his hat. "Evening, ladies," he said.

"Good evening, Mr. Thompson." Mama slid Anna a sideways look, and Anna responded with a similar greeting.

"Meant to discuss something with you," Papa said to the Pinkerton as they fell into step together. "That situation we talked about. It's under control?"

While Mama pretended not to listen, Anna held no such pretense. In fact, she was extremely interested in whatever situation Papa felt worthy of discussion with a Pinkerton.

"The project's in better hands than mine," Mr. Thompson said. "I've put my best man on the job." He fixed his attention on Anna. "You see, tomorrow I'm turning in my badge and taking on the job of chief of security at Beck Mines."

"It'll be a shame to lose you," Papa said. "Is Daniel paying you well enough to leave the Pinks?"

"He is paying me very well, actually." Mr. Thompson again turned his attention to Anna. "And while I'm leaving the agency, I won't be leaving town. Rest assured you'll still see plenty of me."

Papa clasped Hank's shoulder. "Good to hear, isn't it, Anna?"

"Yes, of course," she answered, though Papa hardly noticed her response.

"I've got a meeting with Hiram Nettles in Leadville, which will likely keep me out of Denver for a spell." Hank slowed his pace to allow Papa to go ahead of him. "But once I return, I'll be able to keep an eye on the situation even if I'm no longer in Mr. Pinkerton's employ."

"That's comforting," Papa said, "though I'd like an introduction to the man who'll be taking over. Might that occur tonight?"

"Yes, sir. Absolutely."

They reached the door, and though Mr. Thompson continued to speak, Anna's mind had moved well past the words coming out of his mouth. Instead, she tried to imagine why a man would leave one career for another. What would cause a Pinkerton to leave the agency for a job where the best he could expect was to be at Daniel's beck and call?

Unfortunately, before she could form a theory, Mama spied the ink stains on her fingers.

"Where are your gloves?" she whispered while Papa entered the house and began greeting the other guests.

Before Anna could answer, her mother pulled a spare pair from her bag and thrust them into her hands.

"I'll not have you meeting a potential husband in such a manner."

"Potential husband?"

"Didn't your father mention it?" Mama asked with an innocence Anna recognized as pure fabrication. "Well, nevertheless, you'll be on your best behavior as the gentleman in question is certainly unused to women who conduct themselves as heathens."

Heathen? "Mother, what are you—"

"You shall be lucky to land him, Anna. That is my last word on the subject."

Anna tamped down her frustration and kept her voice low. "Mother, are you saying Papa intends me to be looked over by someone who *might* be interested in marrying me?"

"Yes, isn't it wonderful?" Her mother's smile was broad and quick, but it disappeared as she made a grab for Anna's wrist. "You've been close to the altar before, Anna, and each time something unfortunate prevented the marriage. Your father doesn't see what I do." She narrowed her eyes. "And I see a young woman repeatedly causing her own trouble."

Anna swallowed hard. "Whatever do you mean?"

Lady Montclair and her husband drew near, and her mother paused to exchange endearments, all the while keeping a tight grip on Anna. "You're not getting any younger, Anna. This may be your last chance at a man with all his teeth and decent eyesight."

"If so, then he's already better than the last three Papa sent my way." Anna shook her head, not caring who watched them. "No, four. There was that railroad man. What was his name? Ah yes. Mr. Turnbull. Mr. Turnbull, Senior. Emphasis on 'senior.' How old was he? Sixty?"

"He was a young fifty-three, and if you do not lower your voice and convince everyone staring at us that you've been making the most charming joke, I shall go immediately to your father and tell him you've embarrassed us yet again." Her mother managed all of this in a tone just above a whisper and yet with more emphasis than if she had shouted.

So, obligingly, Anna smiled. Then, as her mother nodded, she giggled.

"Now put on the gloves." With a look that promised later discussion, Mama swept off in a swish of skirts, trailing after Papa as their names were announced.

Anna briefly considered tossing the awful gloves behind the nearest potted plant, but Papa and Mr. Thompson were watching her, and she'd already disappointed her father enough for one week. Should he catch her in yet another act of defiance, she might find herself engaged before the orchestra struck the first note.

Maybe even to Mr. Thompson, especially now that he'd be in Daniel's inner circle. Perhaps the soon-to-be-former Pinkerton was the man to whom Mother referred. Anna could feel him watching her, and when she met his stare, his ears reddened.

She sighed. Where was the Pinkerton whose exploits capturing murderers, thieves, and other villains made the papers? Surely he didn't stammer when he demanded the surrender of the criminals he caught. There seemed to be two of him: Thompson the brave Pinkerton agent, and Hank, the man with the puppy dog stare and perpetually scarlet ears.

If he was the potential suitor to whom her mother referred, at least his inability to speak clearly in her presence would give her ample time to run from any proposal of marriage he might attempt.

Anna searched the ballroom for her hosts, but Daniel found her first and waved. Her old friend's easy smile had once set her heart aflutter and made her babble like a fool whenever she attempted polite conversation. In recent years, however, Daniel had become like the brother she never had, a man given to gentle teasing and warm affection.

"Daniel," she said, smiling.

"Beck. Always a pleasure." Papa moved between Anna and Daniel. Her host opened his mouth to speak, but Papa clasped his hand on Daniel's shoulder and gave him a friendly shake. "Where's that brother of yours?" he asked. "I—"

"Darling Anna!" Gennie called as she moved toward her. "You're here."

"Is this Anna?" A man who looked vaguely familiar removed himself from Mama's embrace and focused his attention on her. "Enchanted."

Anna stared at him. Green eyes. A smile at once warm and wicked. A soft yet firm handshake that lasted just a moment longer than proper.

"Anna Finch," he continued, and her name rolled like soft thunder toward her. "It is a pleasure. I've traveled far to make your acquaintance."

"Mine?" she managed to squeak.

He turned to Gennie. "Do introduce us." Anna noticed his tone was not nearly as sweet when he spoke to Gennie as it had been with her.

"Yes, of course," Gennie said with a sideways glance at Daniel. "Anna, do meet—"

"Edwin." The stranger released his grip on Anna's hand and captured her wrist. "Edwin Beck."

"Edwin Beck," she echoed.

Of course. She should have known. And yet everything she'd heard about this brother of Daniel's had led her to believe he must look as unpleasant on the outside as he had to be on the inside.

She was wrong. Very, very wrong.

Though he bore a striking resemblance to his older brother, Edwin Beck had taken the features that were pleasant on Daniel and wore them with a rakish air that made *handsome* an inadequate description.

"I must apologize for the unkempt manner in which I've been forced to greet you," Edwin said, "but I fear I'm still suffering from the journey. Perhaps once I've rested I will be worthy of making your acquaintance."

"Unkempt?" She studied him from head to toe then back up again. "I fail to see how any part of you could be improved whether by rest or any other such contrivance. Why, given the distance you've traveled, you're certainly fit to be—"

Papa cleared his throat. "Forgive Anna. She does go on."

"Yes, well," Edwin said, "I confess I'm entranced by her. I could listen at length. Do continue."

He punctuated the statement, spoken with the British accent his brother had all but lost, with a wink. She should have protested, but now that she'd stopped talking, she didn't seem able to start again.

She looked at Gennie, who watched Edwin with an odd expression on her face. Daniel joined his wife, and a look passed between them that Anna couldn't help but notice.

"Miss Finch?" Edwin said.

Anna braved another glance at his face. "Yes?"

"You're not a stranger to my name, are you?"

An accusation for sure, though he seemed amused rather than angry. "Of course not," she said, intending to be succinct and demure, but his expression appeared to ask for more and she found herself obliging. "Why, I practically called this place my second home until Gennie arrived, so you can imagine Daniel mentioned his family on occasion. Though I admit he did not prepare me for the fact you might be, well…" She clamped her mouth shut to stop the gush of words.

She looked around the room. Around them the party guests mingled while up in the ballroom the orchestra struck the first chords of a waltz. Anna studied her mother's gloves and willed her heart to stop racing.

"Might be what?" Edwin prompted.

"I'm sorry," she managed. "I've completely forgotten where I left off." The truth, but only barely. Though the actual statement escaped her, the embarrassment still lingered.

"Then I shall help you." Edwin leaned forward as if relating a secret. "You were about to tell me how your expectations of me were not only met but exceeded."

"I was?" Had she said that? It was certainly possible. "Yes, well, I hope you're not offended by the admiration, because I truly thought you'd be—well, that is, I didn't expect you to be a man of such…"

Thankfully, her breath ran out just as Gennie tapped on her shoulder. "Anna, darling, might I borrow you a moment?"

Edwin chuckled. Was he laughing at her?

Gennie linked her arm with Anna's and repeated her question. "Anna, could I see you, please?"

The Englishman's amusement grew, and others turned to stare. Daniel made his way toward them.

"Edwin, the governor is asking to meet you," Daniel said.

Suddenly overwhelmed with the realization of everything she'd just said to Daniel's rogue brother, Anna slipped from Gennie's grasp.

"Perhaps later?" she whispered. Then she took her humiliation and fled.

10

You're a daisy if you have.

— *Doc Holliday*

It had been a long time since Jeb had played the dandy. He resisted the urge to tug at his collar and focused on the plan for tonight. First order of business would be locating the subject, and then he would maintain visual while keeping watch on the surroundings.

No different than any other assignment. That the person in question was a pampered princess rather than a hardened criminal held no interest to him. It was a job.

Just a job.

And when he completed his mission, Jeb could set aside his Pinkerton badge and go home long enough to let the hole in his side and the weariness in his soul heal up.

One last check to secure the wrappings covering his bandage, and Jeb was ready to make his entrance. He decided against his usual routine of taking on an alias in favor of being himself. After all, if he didn't remember Anna Finch, it was highly unlikely Miss Finch remembered him.

Squaring his shoulders, Jeb stepped out of the guestroom and into the hall leading to the second floor ballroom. Daniel spied him, as did Governor Grant, and he soon found himself embroiled in a debate regarding the ongoing construction of the state capitol.

Halfway through his statement regarding his belief that the wrong people were in charge, Daniel tapped him on the shoulder and gestured to his left. "She's coming our way."

Jeb nodded. "Governor," he said as he attempted to discern which of the well-dressed ladies was his quarry, "if you'll excuse me, duty calls."

"Ever the Pinkerton, I see," Governor Grant said.

"I'm afraid so." He leaned toward Daniel. "Which one?"

"There." Daniel made a small gesture toward the crowd. "Green lace with flounces."

Jeb scanned the crowd, unfortunately populated with a multitude of females. "Flounces? What are those?"

Daniel pointed him toward a dark-haired woman moving quickly through the throng. Her chestnut curls sparkled with diamond combs, and her emerald dress was cinched tight and fitted to perfection. Surely he couldn't be so lucky as to be paid to follow her.

"Stop joking around, Daniel. Just tell me which one's Anna Finch."

"Her," Daniel insisted. "The one your fellow Pinkerton's trailing after like a puppy."

Sure enough, he saw Hank Thompson tagging two steps behind the gal in green. No wonder, Jeb decided. If he wasn't supposed to remain discreet, he'd be following her too.

"There you go, buddy," he said under his breath as Hank caught up with her and made contact. She whirled around and offered the former Pinkerton a smile, and Jeb saw her face.

"No," he said as the breath went out of him. "It can't be."

He moved in for a closer look, ducking his head when she glanced his direction. With a sideways glance, he saw Thompson had her occupied.

He also saw he was right.

Anna Finch was the same woman who'd shot him yesterday, then nearly caused him to kiss her today. What she'd have him doing by midnight was anyone's guess.

Pasting on a smile came naturally to one whose occupation for most of the last decade had been attending mindless social gatherings. Anna offered greetings to those she knew and those she didn't as she worked her way toward the back door.

The amount of traffic at the front entrance made escape that way impossible, so she'd turned toward the broad expanse of doors flanking the back of the home. Behind the curtains—which were of substantial weight to hide a grown woman in a ball gown should she be required to disappear—was access to the back lawn. From there, it was a decent hike to the Finch home, across grounds that would likely ruin the gown her mother had shipped in from Paris.

She had a third option: the kitchen. She might have to endure the cross-examination of Tova and possibly Elias, but neither of them would fault her for fleeing.

Her plan resolved, Anna turned around and nearly slammed into Hank Thompson. The Pinkerton's ears reddened as he tipped his hat.

"Forgive me," he said.

Anna shook her head and looked past him. The kitchen was beyond the stairs, a decent distance from where she stood but an expanse she could cross in a short amount of time if not otherwise hindered.

"I am sorry," Mr. Thompson said again.

"Mr. Thompson, you must stop apologizing. It is neither required nor requested." When he began to laugh, Anna felt her temper rising. "Am I so funny that men cannot help but be struck with uncontrollable mirth in my presence?"

"Oh, Miss Finch, I do love to listen to you speak, especially the way you put words together. A man like me, I'm—well, I'm just impressed, is all."

"That I might be educated?" she demanded then wished she hadn't. She sighed. "I'm afraid it is my turn to beg an apology. You see, the evening has begun on a rather sour note and…" No, she'd not share her humiliation. "That is, I am in need of good humor. Perhaps you could cheer me up. Tell me about yourself, Mr. Thompson. Have you always been involved in the world of law enforcement?"

That would work. She often tossed the conversational ball back into the gentleman's court, with great success. On this subject, Mother was right: all men love to talk about themselves.

Hank Thompson was no exception. He launched into a story about train robbers, and Anna stared determinedly at the clock on the wall behind his head so she wouldn't look for Edwin Beck. She didn't want to encourage him to resume their previous conversation. Not that she was averse to a second attempt at making a good impression on Daniel's brother. He was, after all, practically family.

And practically perfect, at least from a visual standpoint.

Anna glanced across the room and found him. When he caught

her watching and smiled, she hurriedly returned her attention to the clock.

"You've not said a word, Miss Finch," Mr. Thompson said.

Anna shook her head, but before she could say anything, her mother appeared next to Mr. Thompson.

"Mr. Thompson, might I borrow Anna?" her mother said.

Anna just caught a glimpse of Mr. Thompson's befuddled face as Mother whirled her around and marched her back toward the party.

"He's a nice man but not our sort. At least not yet," Mother amended. "Now that Mr. Beck, Daniel's brother? He's quite the catch, isn't he?"

"Is he?"

"Well, of course he is." Mother waved at the man in question, who obliged by starting in their direction.

Thankfully Anna spied Charlotte standing alone at the top of the stairs. "Please excuse me, Mother," she said, "but I promised Charlotte I would introduce her around, and she's just now made her appearance." She slipped free of her mother's grasp, ignoring her protests, and moved toward the staircase.

Charlotte was truly on her way to becoming a woman, whether Daniel would admit it or not. Her curls had been tamed and properly styled so that few would recognize her as the impudent child she once was. In profile, Charlotte was very much a Beck, though her late mother—Daniel's first wife—must have played some part in her slender build and the tilt to her chin. The tapping toes, however, were purely the influence of Gennie Cooper Beck, as was the lilac ball gown that fit her so well, a last-minute substitute for the more child-ish dress Daniel originally deemed appropriate for this event.

Anna met Charlotte halfway up the broad carpeted steps on a landing that provided views of both the ballroom and the reception area. The orchestra played an up-tempo tune that had Charlotte almost bouncing in place by the time Anna reached her.

When they embraced, Daniel's daughter whispered, "What do you think of Uncle Edwin?"

Anna broke off the hug to hold Charlotte at arm's length. "Not you too." At the almost sixteen-year-old's perplexed look, Anna hurried to explain. "I'm sorry, sweetheart, but it appears I'm to be married off soon, and my mother thinks your uncle should be on the ever-growing list of potential grooms."

The girl sighed. "It all sounds very exciting."

"Not really."

Charlotte's green eyes widened. "Oh, Anna, I so look forward to the time when I can discuss suitors with Papa." Her gaze swept the room below, then lifted to take in the ballroom above. "He's so difficult."

"Your father?" Anna found Daniel in the crowd. While he carried on a discussion with Governor Grant and the mayor, part of his attention was obviously focused on his two ladies, Gennie and Charlotte. "He only wants the best for you."

"As does yours," Charlotte said as she grasped Anna by the elbow. "Now, let's listen to the orchestra."

"Listen?" Anna tried to keep Charlotte to a sedate pace as they ascended the stairs. "I saw you tapping your toes. I wager dancing's what you want to do."

Charlotte skidded to a halt at the edge of the ballroom. "Not tonight," she said as she craned her neck to peer around the room. "I promised Papa I wouldn't. It's the only way he would allow me to attend. Oh look, the Millers are here. I wonder if my friend Augusta was allowed to accompany them." Her curls bounced as she slipped in front of Anna for a better view of the room. "Yes, there she is. Oh, I'm so glad her father changed his mind. Isn't that a daisy?"

"A daisy? Yes, of course."

The ballroom was populated with the usual collection of party-goers, chatting in groups or twirling around the dance floor. As Anna surveyed the crowd for someone she knew, she spied one man lingering in the shadows. He was tall but not overly so, with the look of an observer rather than a participant. The cut of his suit coat was stylish, the expression on his face one of watchful boredom. He seemed, however, to be looking right at her.

"Forgive me for abandoning you?"

Anna looked down at Charlotte, who gave her a pleading look.

"Go," Anna said smiling, "and enjoy your evening."

Charlotte giggled. "And you enjoy Uncle Edwin."

As the girl skipped off, Anna looked for the man in the shadows only to find he'd disappeared.

"Did I hear my name?"

Anna jumped. Edwin Beck stood beside her.

He offered a courtly bow. "Might I have this dance, Miss Finch?"

"Dance?" She looked up into his green eyes, and her feet refused to move.

"A waltz, to be precise. Surely you've heard of it." Daniel's brother placed his hand against her back and moved Anna toward the dance floor. "If not, I'll be happy to offer instruction."

As Edwin led her to the center of the dance floor, Anna spotted the strange man again. He still watched, still moved on the edge of the room. A woman paused to speak to him, and he leaned toward her. She smiled, and he nodded.

"After you," Edwin Beck said. With his persistent push, Anna found herself in the midst of the crowd and no longer able to see the stranger. "We'll have to begin dancing now, Miss Finch, or the others will run us over."

"What? Oh yes, of course." She stepped into the waltz and found Edwin to be a delightful dance partner. After a few moments, she was even able to relax and enjoy the music and the elegant flow of the dance.

Until Edwin whirled her around, and she came face to face with the stranger. And saw the familiar scar.

11

It seems that this quiet state of affairs was but the calm that precedes the storm...

—*Tombstone Epitaph, October 27, 1881*
(*the day after the gunfight at the OK Corral*)

Jeb moved away from the dance floor and into the shadows at the edge of the room before he got too close to Anna Finch again. Until he decided his plan, there would be no contact with the subject. At least she hadn't recognized him, though he had certainly recognized her.

He stole another glance at her. There was no doubt the woman gliding around the dance floor wearing the latest in Paris fashion began the previous day wearing oversized trousers and a working man's shirt. Working *boy,* Jeb amended as he assessed her size, remembering he'd already held her against him twice.

And not at a safe distance, as Beck's brother did now.

"Not a bad assignment compared to some, eh?" a voice at his side said.

Jeb barely took his eyes off the woman he was being paid to shadow long enough to acknowledge Daniel's presence. "Think so?"

"Sure beats passing as a miner or taking fire from train robbers." Daniel nudged him. "I see you've noticed she's pleasing to the eye."

Jeb might have nodded. He wasn't completely sure. "But dangerous when armed."

"I'm sorry?"

He spared Daniel a moment's attention. "Don't be. As you said, I've handled worse."

"You say you're following Anna until an announcement of her marriage is given?" When Jeb grunted, Daniel continued. "Perhaps the assignment will be brief, then. I think my new chief of security is besotted."

Jeb thought of how Hank had trailed the Finch woman through the party. If he hadn't known Hank Thompson to be among the best men that Mr. Pinkerton ever handed a badge, he would have sworn his fellow agent was nothing but a lovesick schoolboy.

Rubbing his palm against his freshly shaven chin, Jeb contemplated how to proceed. Hiding in plain sight would only work if the woman and Doc had no idea he was a Pinkerton. He'd stared into Doc's eyes and not been recognized, but any time that passed might change this.

It wasn't too late to find a disguise, though the idea of spending the next few weeks—or more—pretending to be someone else sounded like a lot of trouble.

Another look at Anna Finch told him he was in for trouble either way.

"Worried about something?" Daniel asked.

Jeb shrugged. "Just figuring."

"Figuring?" Daniel laughed. "Is that what they call it now? Looked to me like you were figuring how to get Hank and Edwin out of the picture so you could move in."

"I'm going to ignore that." The crowd swirled thick around them. No place to converse without being heard. "How do you think that gal will take to knowing her pa's plan?"

"Anna?" Daniel paused to acknowledge a guest, then returned his attention to Jeb. "I don't know. Why?"

"Just figuring."

"So you said." Daniel turned and looked him square in the eye. "Anna's practically family, Jeb. Anything I need to know?"

If she was family, maybe Daniel knew more than he was saying. "Can I speak with you privately?" Jeb asked, eying the surrounding crowd.

"Now?"

"Now."

The entrance to Daniel's library was well hidden behind the palms and columns brought in to turn the ballroom into a Roman ruin. With the door shut, the sounds of people and chamber music disappeared.

The room smelled of cigars and leather, and the spot Jeb chose in the cowhide chair by the narrow window was as familiar to him as the kitchen table. Daniel joined him and reached for the humidor. Jeb waved away the offer.

"All right, Jeb," Daniel said. "What's wrong? And don't give me the cleaned-up version. You know I'm trustworthy."

"Yeah, I reckon you are." He spent a moment deciding what to say. "Doc Holliday's back in town. Saw him at the Windsor." He paused. "With Wyatt Earp."

"That's interesting but hardly news," Daniel said. "Not anymore, anyway."

Jeb considered how much to tell him, then decided to keep it
simple. "They were with Anna Finch. And there was money
exchanged."

"I see."

"That's it?" Jeb stood. "No reaction to the fact that this woman
you supposedly know so well is cavorting with two known outlaws?"

"Did it appear she was having a social visit?"

He had to think a minute. "She did a lot of writing, which was
odd. And talking. Earp, he talked more than Holliday. His wife didn't
say much."

"Interesting." Daniel leaned back in his chair. "So it's possible
Anna was taking notes. Possibly doing research. Both of those gentlemen have inspired more than one book."

"What does that have to do with anything?"

Daniel slowly stood so that he matched Jeb in height. "I'm going
to tell you something I probably shouldn't." He shrugged. "Maybe
you already know."

"I only know what Hank's told me, and that's precious little. Her
pa wants her married off. Thinks she's a danger to herself. Well," Jeb
said as he let out a long breath, "I say Barnaby Finch is right. I just
want to know if he realizes who she's been spending time with."

"She's a good girl, Jeb, but there's a lot Barnaby doesn't know. At
least, I assume he's not informed on her literary career."

"Literary career?"

Daniel shrugged. "Our Anna has a history of penning dime
novels."

"C'mon, Daniel. I've no patience for jokes."

"It's no joke, I assure you. I found out accidentally when I arranged a meeting with the publisher with the intention of luring Mae Winslow's creator back for one last book as a gift to my wife."

"Yes, I recall that series was a favorite of hers."

Daniel smiled. "The publisher was astonished that I didn't just walk over and knock on the author's door." The clock chimed the half hour, and Daniel moved to the desk. He reached for his pen and dipped it into the ink. "Sorry, but I can't linger. Just let me tell you two things about Anna Finch. First, there is absolutely no reason for her to need anyone's money. None. What she hasn't earned herself from her novels, Barnaby has provided. She's very well set." The expression on the Englishman's face left no doubt at his sincerity.

"All right."

"And second, Anna Finch was like a mother to Charlotte during those years when there was no one else to love my daughter except me. If I'd allowed it, she might have become my wife. And until Gennie came along, I was near to considering it for Charlotte's sake."

As much as Jeb knew of the friendship between Finch and Beck, he hadn't anticipated that. Evidently his surprise showed, for Daniel began to laugh.

"Were you to repeat that, I'd deny it."

"Understood."

"What I'm saying is a man doesn't let anyone around his child unless he's done his due diligence in finding out exactly who that person is. Agreed?" When Jeb expressed his agreement, Daniel continued. "Whatever you saw is not what you saw."

"Then what was it?"

Daniel set the pen aside and rose. "You're the Pinkerton. Figure it out."

"Oh, I plan to."

Daniel moved toward the door. "Enjoy yourself tonight, Jeb. And do keep me informed."

The door opened, and Daniel slipped out as the noise from the party tumbled in. Jeb started to follow, but his legs felt tired and heavy. What he wouldn't give to be on horseback heading for home right now.

But not until he'd finished the job and healed a bit. The jostling that came from a spirited horse on a mountain trail wouldn't do any good for his bandaged side. And leaving town with the murderer Doc Holliday so close to being captured wouldn't set well. Not after all these years.

Jeb paused at the door to give his reflection a glance. Considering what he'd looked like only a couple of hours ago, no one would recognize him as the man who made a fool of himself in the Windsor lobby. Only his mama would know him covered in trail dust and beard hair, and then only if she wore her spectacles.

Jeb grinned. He just had to see to his duties tonight unnoticed, and tomorrow he'd figure out how to proceed.

"Easily done," he said as he passed through the door. "As Miss Charlotte says, 'It's a daisy.'"

⚭

Anna stumbled slightly as Edwin spun her back into his arms. "I fear I lost you for a moment, Miss Finch."

She looked quickly over her shoulder, trying to find the man with the scar, but he'd slipped away into the crowd. She focused on her dance partner. "I'm terribly sorry."

They resumed their dance, but the damage was done. Her hands shook, and everywhere she looked, she saw someone who might be him.

Anna allowed Edwin to sweep her into the center of the dance floor, where they moved easily among the others.

She spied the man again and stiffened.

"Miss Finch?"

He stood near the stairs, his face partly obscured, but from Anna's vantage point, he looked very much like the mountain man. She had to know for certain.

"Forgive me." Anna stepped away, breaking his hold on her waist. Without looking back at him, she hurried to follow the stranger.

This time Anna refused to allow the man out of her sight. Whether he knew she gave chase or not, he seemed intent on not being caught. She lost him in the reception area, then spied him slipping into the hall near the kitchen.

"Miss Finch," Hank Thompson called. "Miss Finch."

She sighed and pretended not to hear him as she kept her attention focused on the man. From her knowledge of the Beck home, the only exit from that hallway was through the kitchen. Thus, if the stranger were fleeing, he was already gone. If he'd merely become lost, he would quickly return.

Anna contemplated whether to wait or pursue. Then Hank stepped into her path, and she had to stop short to keep from slamming into him.

"Please, if you would," he said. "I'd appreciate a moment of your time."

"Really, I'm…" She looked anxiously down the hall. "Excuse me, Mr. Thompson, but I'm on my way to powder my nose."

Mr. Thompson blushed, mumbled an apology, and stepped out of her way. Anna hurried down the hallway and prayed Mr. Thompson would not follow.

The kitchen door opened just as she reached it, and a waiter nearly ran her over. On his heels was the stranger.

"You there," Anna said, regaining her balance, as the dark-haired stranger avoided her stare. "Stop. I know you."

"So sorry, miss. May I help you?" The apologetic waiter halted, blocking Anna's path and allowing the stranger to escape.

Obviously he did not want to be found, which made Anna even more curious.

By the time she trailed the man back up the stairs and into the ballroom, she'd nearly decided he wasn't the mountain man from the river at all. Then he slipped into Daniel's library.

Anna paused only a moment before reaching for the doorknob. As the door swung open, a slice of light traced a path across the carpet and a pair of decidedly male boots, which quickly moved into the shadows.

In a move she would either regret or celebrate tomorrow, Anna stepped inside and allowed the door to close behind her, plunging the room into darkness. The sounds of the celebration outside were muffled, her intake of breath oddly loud.

"I know you're in here," she said. "And I know where the lamp is."

But when she reached for it, she found it gone. Any fool would have turned and walked out, but Anna stayed.

"Look, I just want to speak to you. I don't think you're supposed to be in here, and I'm a bit troubled that you seem to be following me."

She heard a shuffle to her left and moved toward the sound, arms outstretched.

Jeb felt like an idiot. A grown man—and a Pinkerton at that—and he'd been reduced to hiding like a common criminal. Instinct had failed him, and not for the first time, when it came to Anna Finch.

Outside the door someone laughed and the orchestra struck up another tune. Jeb backed into Daniel's desk and froze. Miss Finch hadn't spoken for several seconds. Perhaps she'd give up and leave soon.

He caught the scent of flowers. Roses, he decided. Definitely roses.

Then her hand grazed his arm, and he felt her fingers wrap around his bicep.

"I'm not afraid of you," she said softly. "I only meant to offer an apology. You see, I'm not in the habit of aiming my gun at innocent strangers. I feel terrible about the whole thing."

No good response came to him, so Jeb kept his mouth shut. Her hand found his belly and his breath froze.

"Forgive me," she said, "but I need to see if this is really…"

Her hand traveled east just a notch and Jeb caught it before her fingers could stray to the bandage. Her free hand made the attempt, and he caught it too. Holding both her hands in his, with the desk behind him and Anna Finch in front of him, there was nowhere to go.

She wrangled one hand free. When she reached to touch his face, he once again snagged her wrist.

Then the door flew open, and Jeb found himself staring past the shocked brunette to the surprised face of Winston Mitchell, social columnist for the *Denver Times*.

"Am I interrupting anything, Miss Finch?" Mitchell's eyes followed the path of light toward them. "Now isn't this cozy?"

Jeb braved a look at Anna Finch, whose face was thankfully in shadows. He released her hands. "It's not what you think, Mitchell."

"Of course it's exactly what I think." The columnist bent to pick up the lamp. "Looks like this is what you were both groping for."

Miss Finch took a step backward, and Jeb reached for her. "Let me handle this," he whispered against her ear. "Nod if you understand."

She did, and he moved her out of the light.

"Mr. Mitchell," he said slowly, "might I have a word with you?" He paused. "Man to man?"

"Of course," Mitchell replied, though his enthusiasm was tempered with a healthy amount of caution.

When he was sure Miss Finch wouldn't bolt, Jeb wrapped his arm around Mitchell's shoulder. "Walk with me," he said, guiding the man out the study door. Keeping up the pretense of friendship was difficult, but Jeb managed it until he'd walked the columnist out of the house and onto the lawn.

The air was cold, the breeze stiff. Jeb walked until he reached a spot where he felt sure none of the party-goers could see them, then released Mitchell, using a little more force than was probably necessary.

"You and I," Jeb said, "are going to have a private conversation that's going to stay private. Nod if you understand." Mitchell did, and Jeb continued. "You know who I am?"

"The next prospective groom?" Mitchell asked with a bravado he seemed to immediately regret.

Jeb leaned forward and the smaller man cringed. "I'm a Pinkerton, Mr. Mitchell, and regardless of what you might think you saw, I am here on assignment."

Now the columnist looked interested. "Assignment? What sort?"

"Nothing I can tell you at the moment." Jeb paused. "But perhaps with cooperation on your part, I might offer up more details at a later date."

Mitchell studied him for a minute. "What assurance do I have, sir?"

"None," Jeb said, "but I've got an assurance for you."

"What is that?"

Jeb leaned closer, careful to offer nothing in the way of humor in his expression. "If I read one word of this in your paper, be it in your column or anywhere else, I'll want an explanation for why you saw fit to interfere in an official Pinkerton investigation." He paused. "Now, Mr. Mitchell, is there anything in what I've just said that you do not understand?"

"No," Mitchell said softly.

"All right, then why don't you go on home? I'm sure you've got work to do." Jeb took a step backward. "Just nothing that has anything to do with me or Miss Finch."

"Wait a minute." Mitchell shook his head. "You can't tell me not to write about Anna Finch. That's not legal."

Jeb merely stared at him.

"Understood," Winston Mitchell said, deflated, before he slipped away into the night.

12

My lawyers will have a petition drawn up. Everybody in Tombstone knows that we did nothing but our duty.

—*Wyatt Earp*

Any other woman would have been happy that her reputation had such a gallant protector. The fact that the protection came from a man Anna might have shot was more than a bit confusing. And interesting.

A fatal combination for a woman bent on a career in journalism. She had to find him.

Anna opened the library door just wide enough to peer out. To her left she spied Charlotte and the youngest Miller girl with their heads together and their attention fully focused on the dance floor. Scanning the crowd, she found neither Mitchell nor the stranger. She slipped out of the library. It was time to leave.

Seeking out Daniel took some doing, but she finally caught up to him. "Thank you for the lovely evening," she said, "but I fear I must plead exhaustion."

Daniel searched her face a moment. Did he guess her true reason for fleeing the festivities? "Are you unwell?"

"No, truly, I'm fine." She forced a smile. "Just tired."

"I see." He nodded at Abe Miller and his wife, then returned his attention to Anna. "Can we chat before you go? I'll be brief, I promise."

He did know. Anna swallowed. "Of course."

He nodded and a waiter rushed to his side. "Have Miss Finch's wrap ready for her departure, please." Daniel turned to Anna. "Join me in my library?"

"No," she said hastily. She didn't think she could reenter the room where she'd just been humiliated. "I don't think that would be wise."

Daniel frowned. "I wish to discuss my brother but do not intend to be overheard."

She sighed. "I see the dilemma. Perhaps we could use a code?"

Daniel laughed. "Anna, you truly are unique." He snapped his fingers. "Of course. I'll refer to him as the prize mule."

"Daniel!" Anna gave the Englishman an impertinent jab, and her burst of laughter drew more than one interested stare. "You're incorrigible."

"My wife would agree." Her host gently eased her away from listening ears. "The truth about that mule is he kicks."

Anna stopped short. "Excuse me?"

"Some mules can be domesticated so that they hardly resemble those in the wild. The mule in question, however, will never accept the yoke."

"Daniel, I fail to see why I need this information. I'm neither in the market for a mule nor interested in any I've seen thus far." When Daniel looked unconvinced, Anna continued. "Papa's plans and mine differ. He's upset and feels that I need a, well, a mule. He's probably mentioned it to you."

"I've heard him speak of it, yes."

"I hope to disabuse him of the concern," she said.

"Impossible, I'm afraid." Daniel touched her sleeve. "Though I'll try to persuade Barnaby to look in other pastures."

Anna smiled. "Why, Daniel, that's quite clever."

"I can't promise I can keep it up for any length of time."

Anna's gaze swept the ballroom, searching for the mystery man. "You know, Daniel, I'm wondering about a gentleman I met tonight. I thought you might tell me who he is."

"Well, now, another mule for the pasture?" At her warning look, Daniel nodded. "Which one is he?"

Again she searched the crowd. "I don't see him, but he was tall, broad at the shoulders. A bit rough around the edges. Perhaps a cattleman."

"Cattleman?" Daniel rubbed his chin. "That could be half a dozen men. Any particular reason you're looking for him?"

"Reason?" Anna stumbled over the rest of her excuse, finally giving up. This was Daniel, after all, the man who knew her well enough to remain her friend despite her many faults. "We may end up in Mr. Mitchell's column tomorrow," she said. "I wanted to learn his name before I read it in the *Times*."

Daniel looked amused. "Anything you'd like to confess, Anna?"

"I'm innocent, I promise." But as she protested, Anna knew that wasn't completely true. She'd trapped the poor man in the library and practically accosted him without his permission.

And all of it in the dark.

"I hate it when you wear that expression." Daniel paused. "You're blaming yourself again, likely for something you didn't do."

"No." Anna met his stare. "This time I truly did it."

"Will I be reading about it?"

Anna shrugged. "Perhaps."

"Then I'll wait for the morning edition to get all the details. You do look exhausted. Radiant," he quickly amended, "but exhausted." Daniel gestured to the reception area. "Go find my wife and bid her good-bye before you leave. She'll be lost without you."

"And I without her," Anna said. "Can I ask that you see to her speedy return?"

He nodded. "Soon as the pasture's empty."

"Of course." She knew just enough about Daniel's troubled relationship with his brother not to ask when that might be.

Anna found Gennie easily enough and slipped into her conversation with Senator Hill and his wife. "Darling," Gennie exclaimed, "you cannot leave. You just cannot."

"And yet I must."

Gennie made her excuses to the Hills and linked arms with Anna to walk toward the door. "I can't bear it that I'm going to New York without you."

Anna noticed Papa watching her, and smiled, but he looked away. "I know it will be terribly lonely for both of us, but—"

Her friend yanked on Anna's arm and halted their progress. "Oh, Anna, I've the most brilliant idea. Why don't you come with us?" She warmed to the topic. "You don't have to pack a thing. We'll buy whatever's needed when we arrive. Or, better yet, I'll loan you a wardrobe. Return the favor you extended to me when I first arrived in Denver."

"The idea is lovely, but truly I cannot go. I shall miss you terribly." Anna embraced Gennie and sent her back to her guests after promising three times to write.

She turned to find her wrap in the hands of one of the servants. While the man helped her don the garment, she took one last glance around the room for the mysterious stranger. Wherever he'd gone, at least he appeared to have taken Mr. Mitchell with him. Anna could only pray that was good news.

Or, better yet, that the evening's incident would become no news at all.

But when she stepped beyond the Becks' gate and found the mystery man waiting, Anna knew the story had only just begun.

Everything in her wanted to stop and interview him as she had Mr. Earp, but she didn't. Not with their proximity to the Beck home and Winston Mitchell still out there somewhere, possibly taking notes for tomorrow's edition. As much as she wished to speak to the man, she knew she needed to do so beyond the view of those gathered behind the gates.

"My, you're brazen," she said as she walked past him and prayed he would follow. "Have we not had enough trouble with each other tonight?"

As she hoped, he fell into step beside her. "Miss Finch—"

She stopped short. "How do you know my name?"

The shadows hid his face, but the clench of his jaw and the tilt of his head was impossible to miss.

"Simple," he said. "I'm the Pinkerton your father hired to keep you out of trouble."

"No. I don't believe you," Miss Finch said flatly, though her face told him otherwise. Slowly, she began to shake her head. "So that's what Papa wanted to discuss with Mr. Thompson."

"Might be."

Her expression turned indignant. "How dare he treat me like a child in need of...of..."

"Protection?" Jeb offered.

"Minding!" She whirled and stomped three paces toward her home, then stopped again. When Jeb caught up to her, she burst into laughter.

"What?" he asked, thoroughly confused.

Anna Finch's laugh was no soft ladylike giggle. Instead, the society gal didn't seem to care that anyone passing on the street could hear her sudden amusement.

"If you're supposed to keep me out of trouble, then it appears you've already failed," she said once she had her breath back.

The truth, but he wouldn't let the comment go uncontested. "That remains to be seen. The proof will be in tomorrow's edition of the *Times*. Mr. Mitchell and I had a conversation about appropriate subjects for his column."

As she offered him a sideways glance, the moonlight washed over features he'd not yet had the luxury of studying. He'd seen her several times, but tonight, with no witnesses and no bullets flying, Jeb finally managed to really look at her.

Anna Finch had the kind of beauty that grew on a man. The

kind that might make him forget any time he spent with her was in the line of duty.

Miss Finch set off walking again. "So what have you done to Mr. Mitchell, Pinkerton man?" she asked when he caught up. Before he could respond, she once again stopped in his path. She reached out to touch his side before he could step out of the way. "I've not yet properly apologized, though I'm uncertain what one says to one's shooting victim, as I've never shot anyone before."

Was she teasing? Jeb couldn't tell. He was still trying to catch up with her abrupt change in subject. "You've got me there, Miss Finch. I've shot my share of men, but conversation afterward was never something I concerned myself with." He caught her wrist and moved her hand away from his side. "I am glad to hear you don't make a habit of this."

She dipped her head in response, and he lifted her chin with his free hand. Lovely, indeed.

Jeb cleared his throat. "I'd be remiss in my duties if I allowed you to stand out here at this hour of the night unattended." He released his grip. "So if you'll just cooperate, I think tonight's mission can be accomplished easily enough."

"And what mission is that?"

He grasped her shoulders and turned her to face her home, then pressed his palm against her back. "Tonight's assignment was twofold. The part I can tell you about is getting you home without incident." He shrugged. "Other than that situation in the library."

"Which, if I understood you correctly, will not be written about?" she asked.

"If it does, my next encounter with Mr. Mitchell won't be as civil as the first." Her back was warm against his palm, and Jeb knew he shouldn't walk so close. *The better to protect her,* he told himself. And yet it was he who needed the protection, he decided when she glanced up with wide eyes and flashed that dimple at him.

"And the second part of the assignment?" she asked.

His smile came without warning. "That's not for you to know." She would find out soon enough that his job only lasted until her father found some poor fool to marry her.

"I see." Miss Finch studied him a moment longer, then gestured ahead. "That's my gate. I assure you I'm safe now."

Jeb watched her until the grand front doors opened and she slipped inside. "I'm not so sure I am," he whispered.

13

John Henry Holliday, dentist, very respectfully
offers his professional services to the citizens of
Dodge City and surrounding county during the
summer. Office at Room No. 24, Dodge House.
Where satisfaction is not given, money will be
refunded.

—*Dodge City newspaper, 1878*

Anna went to bed with her thoughts a jumbled mess, the memory of
the stranger's palm against her spine still fresh. When she realized
sleep would not come, she went to her writing table and tamed her
tangled thoughts by writing them down.

The next morning, Anna opened the *Times* and braced herself
for whatever the horrible man had written about her. To her surprise,
there was no mention of her adventure in Daniel's library. Nor did
anything appear the following day, making Anna think that perhaps
her hired gun had achieved what she'd decided was impossible: breaking the poison pen of Winston Mitchell.

And then Papa left for an extended stay in Leadville, and her
mother announced a visit to San Francisco. While Anna usually cher-
ished a trip to see her aunt and cousins, she opted to remain home.
Once Mama was safely deposited on the train, Anna returned home

to request a plate of fried chicken and a fresh bottle of ink from the stationer's downtown. Thus supplied, she set to work on her story about Wyatt Earp.

When the article was done, Anna leaned back to savor the moment. All that remained was folding the pages and sealing them so that McMinn could deliver the letter for her.

"Not exactly all," she whispered as she reached for the pen and dipped it into the inkwell. "First a note of thanks to Mr. Earp for this opportunity." She paused before touching pen to paper. How ironic that Winston Mitchell had provided her with the perfect pseudonym. "Signed by A. Bird, journalist."

That done, Anna sealed the pages and summoned Mr. McMinn to dispatch the article to the paper. "Now what?" she said as she rose to stretch.

Unlike with her novels, Anna knew she couldn't wait for the publication of one article before she began writing another. The only question was whom to write about next.

Anna pulled a fresh sheet of paper from the stack and dipped her pen in the inkwell. Recalling as much of the conversation as she could, she began to list everything she knew about the man she believed to be Doc Holliday.

She noted his lack of good health, his superior height, and the pale silver white color of his hair. His pistol was nickel plated and unusual in its design and size. More research would be needed to identify it, but she knew it was not a common Smith & Wesson or Colt. This told her he either possessed the weapon through luck or skill, or he had come from money. The cut of his greatcoat and a tailored suit made from fine fabric made her believe the latter.

Remembering his blue eyes, she wrote that down, along with his distinctly southern accent. Then there was the mention of a woman named Kate and the Georgia address on the letters she mailed.

Finished, Anna set aside the notes on Doc Holliday and began another list, this one populated by people she wanted to interview. Poring over newspapers, she stopped to write down every person of interest she came across. Soon she had several pages of potential names.

Now she just had to locate them and secure interviews. Perhaps she should start with those men and women who lived in the Denver area. She noted those, then moved on to the people she could find through addresses provided in the papers, creating a list of people to whom she would write letters of inquiry.

Perhaps once her piece ran, Mr. Earp might give her a reference. Or better yet, he might recommend his friends speak to her. But until that happened, Anna was on her own.

Then, out of the blue, she recalled something. Anna scrambled for the stack of newspapers. Hadn't she seen Doc Holliday's picture recently? Something to do with a murder or robbery.

She tore through editions of the *Rocky Mountain News,* the *Denver Times,* and the other newspapers she'd collected until she found what she was looking for.

On the front page of the Tombstone, Arizona, newspaper was a story about Doc Holliday.

On the first day of May, the former Georgia dentist dispatched two of our less stellar citizens to uncertain glory during a night of drunken debauchery at the Bird Cage Saloon. His person is now being sought as a man wanted for murder.

Anna set the paper down. "But that's impossible. He was in Denver." The man in the photograph accompanying the story was not the same man who sat across the table from Wyatt Earp. "How can that be?"

She retrieved her notes. Placing them next to the newspaper, she went over each detail several times. Then she rang for the maid. "Would you have someone bring the rest of these downstairs to Papa's study?" she asked, gesturing to the overflowing bin of periodicals.

After carting downstairs all the papers she could carry, Anna settled behind her father's desk and spread them out, organizing them by date. Then she began to search for the name of the famous gunfighter. After setting those with mentions of Doc Holliday aside, she reached for more and continued the process.

By the time the lamps were lit, Anna had a mountain of discarded papers on the floor and a neat stack of several dozen on the desk. Resting her elbows on the desk's polished surface, she stared at the newspapers.

All had run stories of crimes committed by Doc Holliday, and if these journalists, who often quoted eyewitnesses, were to be believed, Holliday was a busy man. So busy that he could shoot a sheriff's deputy in Salt Lake City the same day he robbed a man of his gold watch and his life in Tucson.

Anna could draw only one conclusion. Someone—perhaps more than one individual—was impersonating John Henry "Doc" Holliday. And that meant a story needed to be told. The man Wyatt Earp had so enthusiastically embraced was in no health to commit some, if any, of the crimes the reporters and supposed eyewitnesses claimed.

Anna spent the week working on the story, scanning each day's periodicals for further mention of the outlaw. She also looked for her new pen name, hoping to find it under a letter to the editor or, in her wildest dreams, under a byline as a real article.

When she'd all but given up on a journalism career, Anna spied a letter in the *Denver Times* not written *by* her but *to* her.

The editor of this paper wishes to contact Mr. A. Bird directly regarding further endeavors of the journalistic variety.

Anna looked around the dining room, where she'd elected to take her breakfast, then back at the paper to read it again. The editor of the *Denver Times* wanted to talk to her. Her story had obviously been read and appreciated.

"Further endeavors of the journalistic variety," she echoed in an excited whisper.

Even with her father still away on whatever business kept him in Leadville and Mother happily extending her visit to her sister in San Francisco, Anna couldn't quite bring herself to say aloud what she'd held inside for so long.

She was a bona fide journalist. A writer of something with lasting importance.

Her breakfast forgotten, she quickly wrote a letter to the editor of the *Times*. In a moment of bravery, she signed her own name. Then, before she could change her mind, Anna sealed it up and sent for Mr. McMinn to deliver it directly to the recipient.

"Should I wait for a response?" he asked as he eyed the envelope.

"Yes, please." Anna handed over what could very well be the ticket to an arrangement that would change her life.

Which meant the job of delivering it belonged to no one but her.

"Wait," she said. "I'll take it myself."

Mr. McMinn gave her a nod. "I'll ready the buggy."

An hour later, after changing her outfit three times and her hairstyle twice, Anna stood at the door to the *Denver Times* office and prayed she appeared as serious as the work she intended to do. The office was situated on the corner of Sixteenth and Larimer in an area of Denver called the Tabor Block, and she could see the Windsor from where she stood.

She took a deep breath and let it out slowly then looked around for the Pinkerton who was nowhere in sight. *Good.* The Lord had granted her the ability to write, and if this was the outlet He chose for her skills, then He would already be in the editor's office, waiting to pave the way for her employment.

Anna easily located the paper's offices and walked into the newsroom, a place of much noise and activity. A sweeping glance of the room assured Anna that she knew none of these people and that the awful Mr. Mitchell wasn't in residence. Until that moment, she hadn't considered the possibility of seeing him. So far, it seemed God was on her side.

She snagged the sleeve of a young man as he brushed past her. "Might you point me toward your editor's office?"

He gestured toward the back of the room. "Behind the door on the left. Watch your step."

"Thank you," she said, but the boy had already moved on.

Anna carefully made her way through the maze of people, tables, and equipment to the door and stepped inside a tiny office.

An elderly man sat hunched over a desk littered with papers, leather-bound volumes, and a large dusty globe. A plaque on his desk proclaimed him to be O. A. Smith, Editor in Chief.

He looked up, and his spectacles fell from his brow to his nose. A push with his forefinger set them in place. "May I help you, young lady?"

She closed the door and swallowed hard. "Are you the editor?"

"I am." He set aside what he'd been reading to peer at Anna. "Who are you?"

Anna clasped her hands in front of her to keep them from shaking. "I'm your letter writer. My name is Anna Finch, but I am also A. Bird."

"You're a bird?" He glanced behind her, then returned his attention to her face. "How did you get in here, miss?"

"No," she said with an authority she didn't feel. "I am A. Bird. The author."

Mr. Smith sat up a little straighter. "I'm sorry, but you're a woman. And Barnaby Finch's daughter unless I'm mistaken."

"I am." She gestured to the chair across from him. "May I?"

"Yes, please," he said. "Now tell me the truth. Who is the writer? A friend, perhaps?" The editor rested his elbows on his desk. "You can tell me. The story is brilliant, by the way. I'm not sure it's the truth, but it's brilliant. Managing to speak to the one and only Wyatt Earp—well, I'm impressed. And a quote from his wife? That just doesn't happen."

"Oh, it's the truth. I have a witness who will attest to the whole thing." She folded her hands in her lap and waited for the older man to speak again.

"You understand I have some difficulty believing a woman wrote that letter." Mr. Smith's stare was not kind. "It was, well, quite eloquent."

Rather than wasting time with anger or clouding her reputation by mentioning the lengthy list of dime novels she had to her credit, Anna began to recite what she'd written. Three paragraphs in, the editor lifted his hand to stop her.

"Who's your witness?" he asked.

Anna told him about the waiter at the Windsor, and the editor nodded. She almost mentioned that Doc Holliday had also been in attendance but decided to keep that fact to herself.

Mr. Smith looked down at the letter then back up at Anna, concern etching his features. "There's one thing I've got to ask before we go any further in this conversation."

"Of course."

"We're a fair paper, Miss Finch. Fair and honest, despite what some of the others would have you believe." He paused to run his thumb across the top of the page. "I make it a practice not to tell my writers how to conduct their business. I give the assignment and they bring me the story. If it's true, I print it."

"Understood," she said, though she really didn't. Not completely.

He pushed back from the desk and met her stare. "You can't draw a breath in Denver without knowing who Winston Mitchell is, so I won't insult you by asking. Nor will I insult Mr. Mitchell by requesting any special favors or insisting that anyone in this town, me included, be excluded from his reporting."

"I understand."

He shrugged, his gaze unwavering. "How do you feel about writing for a paper in which you might also read about yourself? And not always in the best light?"

Anna took a deep breath while she thought. "I think that while Anna Finch may often disagree with Mr. Mitchell's facts and reporting skills, A. Bird will never have an opinion."

He held her stare for several more seconds, then finally looked away. "Fine, then. We'll run this Tuesday, but not as a letter to the editor. I need it polished up and ready for page one by five o'clock today. Can you do that?"

Anna looked at the clock on Mr. Smith's desk. It read half past eleven. "Five o'clock," she echoed, wondering how she might accomplish the feat. "Yes, absolutely."

With a nod, he began to give her instructions on the changes needed to turn her letter into an actual piece of reporting. When he was done, he surprised her by asking, "So, what's your next story?"

"Next story?" Anna shook her head. "I'm not certain."

The editor rose to come around the desk. "Miss Finch, if you're going to have a career in this business, you'll need to have fresh articles every week or two. Sooner, if you can manage it."

"I see." She mentally reviewed the stack of notes she had at home on potential stories. "While I do have some ideas, I don't have any strong leads right now. Do you have any suggestions?"

He shrugged. "How'd you get this story?"

Anna thought about it a moment. "I suppose you could say it found me."

Mr. Smith crossed his arms and stared down at her. "Well, then, figure out how to get other stories to find you, and I'll print them."

She shook hands with him and walked out. All the way back to the buggy, Anna tried to determine how she might possibly get another scoop. Then it hit her. A simple paragraph added to the end of the story she'd written for Mr. Earp, and her problem was solved. Reaching into her bag, Anna pulled out her notebook and pencil to work up the addition to her article.

When her piece ran Tuesday on the front page of the *Denver Times* under the byline A. Bird, it ended with this:

> As Mr. Earp has trusted this author with the truth of his story,
> so can others whose tales are not yet told. Contact A. Bird
> through the editor of this paper to right any other wrong.

By Friday, Anna had her first packet of letters to choose from, all addressed to A. Bird, and all delivered in a single brown envelope addressed to Miss Anna Finch, Denver, Colorado.

She'd mailed her own letter to Wyatt Earp, alerting him to the fact that his story had been featured on the front page of the *Denver Times*. Once she'd signed it, Anna added a postscript.

"And I am enclosing a copy to give to Mr. Bonney," she scribbled before her courage failed. "Perhaps he would now be amenable to allowing me to tell his tale, especially since I've done some research that refutes a certain murder charge recently made against him. This is just one of the things I've discovered."

Fast is fine but accuracy is everything.
—*Wyatt Earp*

Jeb stood on the ridge and stared down at the valley. Daniel was late.

Returning to his saddle, Jeb yanked out his pocket watch, a useful affectation of the rich man he was pretending to be, and took note of the time. If Daniel hadn't arrived in five minutes, he'd start looking.

In the distance he saw the narrow-gauge train threading its way across the expanse of prairie, heading out of Denver. At the crunch of buggy wheels on rock, Jeb whirled. By the time he spied the rig coming over the rise, he already had the driver in his sights.

Assured it was Daniel, Jeb lowered his pistol and went to meet his friend. "Wondered if you'd decided to stay in Leadville after all."

Daniel pulled back on the reins and brought the buggy to a halt. "No need. Hiram and Thompson are earning their pay."

"By keeping your brother busy, I assume."

Daniel laughed. "My hope is they're boring him to death so he'll flee the state sooner rather than later. Appeared to be working when I last checked in on them. Edwin never did have much patience for inactivity."

"Nor do I," Jeb said. "Speaking of which, I'm beginning to wonder if your Miss Finch is slipping out to enjoy herself at my expense."

"Anna? Doubtful."

Jeb shrugged.

"You don't believe me?" Daniel leaned back in the seat. "What possible reason would she have for hiding her activities from you?"

Jeb thought of that walk home the night of the reception. His palm on her back. Green lace and chestnut curls in the moonlight. The dimple...

"Jeb?"

Jeb shook his brain back to sensible thoughts. "Might be because I told her that her pa hired me to follow her."

His friend's face registered shock. "Why would you do that?"

"Seemed like a good idea at the time," he said slowly.

His mare shifted uneasily, and Jeb scratched her behind the ear. High strung, this horse. Much like the society gal he'd signed on to protect.

"I don't suppose you told her that you and I've been friends for some years," Daniel asked.

"If she doesn't know it already, I'd like to keep things that way. At least for now." Jeb rested his palm on the saddle horn. "That's why I figured to meet you out here instead of back in Denver."

"So if you're here, where is Anna?" Daniel asked.

"Called in a favor." Jeb took another look at the pocket watch. "Cost me plenty, but your Tova's entertaining her with tea and cookies until three. After three, I'm out of luck." He paused to adjust his hat. "Ain't that a daisy?"

Daniel laughed so loud his horse spooked. "What, dare I ask, is my impudent housekeeper demanding in payment for this?"

Jeb grimaced. "She won't be happy I told you."

"Then she won't know."

"All right." Jeb gave Daniel a sideways look. "I promised I'd teach her to dance."

"Dance?" Daniel shook his head. "Tova?"

"Maybe she wants to surprise her new husband. She did mention he's quite light on his feet."

"I suppose." Daniel paused. "Why didn't she ask me to teach her?"

It was Jeb's turn to laugh. "You're her employer, Daniel."

They fell into companionable silence. "About Miss Finch," Jeb finally said. "You know her better than I do. Why would a society gal suddenly decide to spend her evenings at home? It's been ten days and other than a trip to the Tabor Block, she's only left the house twice, and that was to make trips to the post office." He paused. "Can't figure out why she likes that place so much."

"Perhaps she's writing to my wife. They're close friends, you know."

Jeb lifted his hat to mop his forehead. Though the morning had begun with a chill, the afternoon had warmed well past comfortable. Overhead a hawk circled, then dove, its cry piercing the quiet. Behind him he heard the Leadville-bound train whistle. A lonely sound when a man stood on a mountain rather than sat in a rail car.

"He's not coming, is he?" Jeb asked.

Daniel shifted positions to glance behind him. "He'll be here. He said he would." He gave Jeb a direct stare. "You're not the only one who has a few favors he can call in." They shared a chuckle, but then

Daniel's expression turned serious. "I've stuck my neck out on this, Jeb. Need I remind you the man's safety has to be guaranteed?"

"I gave you my word." Jeb looked past his friend to the lone rider approaching from the southeast. "That looks like him."

Daniel swiveled. "I'll wait with you until he arrives. I take it you'll want privacy for your discussion."

"I'd appreciate that," Jeb said.

As the rider topped the rise and lifted his hat in greeting, Daniel turned the buggy around and set off to meet him. The pair exchanged a few words, and then Daniel glanced back to wave before heading toward Denver.

Jeb stood his ground and waited for the rider to reach him. "Afternoon," he said as he tipped his hat. "One lawman to another, I appreciate you coming all the way out here, sir."

"Retired lawman," Wyatt Earp said. "Now what can I help you with?"

Jeb reached for his saddlebag and watched Earp go for his gun. He pulled out Tuesday's copy of the *Denver Times*. "You seen this?"

Earp took the paper and unfolded it.

"Front page," Jeb said. "Just below the story about the capitol building."

He watched the older man's eyes scan the page and knew the moment the article in question had been spotted. The lawman did not appear to be impressed. "You bring me all the way out here to read a paper, son?"

"It's yours to keep," Jeb said.

"'Preciate that, but I've already got a copy."

"I see." Jeb considered his words carefully as he took the paper back. "Mr. Earp, everything this A. Bird wrote about you—is it true?"

The older man made Jeb wait a shade longer than comfortable. Finally, with a dip of his head, Wyatt Earp said, "Yep."

"All of it?"

His eyes narrowed. "You hard of hearing, boy?"

"No sir," Jeb said.

Earp leaned forward. "That all you wanted to know?"

"I'd like to know who A. Bird is," Jeb said evenly, "but I don't suppose you'll tell me."

Earp had the audacity to look amused. "Don't suppose so."

"I figure it's that pretty thing you and your wife ate with over at the Windsor. When was that?" He pretended to chew on the question. "Well, you know when it was."

He watched for signs of recognition but saw none.

"All right, then," Jeb said. "Just one more thing."

"What's that?"

The sun glinted off the silver in Earp's hair, reminding Jeb that though this was no young man, he was not a man to be trifled with, for the same sun shone on the firearm strapped to his thigh. Likely at least one or two more were stashed in his saddlebags.

Knowing what he was about to say could get him shot, Jeb said it anyway. "Doc Holliday. Where is he?"

"You asking as a Pink?" The man's expression turned dangerous. "Or as a man with a score to settle?"

"Both," Jeb answered with deadly calm.

To Jeb's surprise, Wyatt Earp laughed. "Now that's refreshing."

"What?"

"An honest man." He chuckled again. "Don't meet many of those in my line of work. Or rather, my former line of work."

"I'm going to catch him, Mr. Earp. Justice will be served."

"Not with my help." Earp turned his horse and galloped away.

Jeb watched the man go. To his surprise, the lawman changed his course and returned. One hand on his Colt, Jeb watched Wyatt Earp gallop toward him, then pull back on the reins as he got within shouting distance.

"Change your mind?" Jeb called.

"Figured I'd issue a challenge." Earp paused. "One honest lawman to another, that is."

"Go on," Jeb said, his palm still resting on the Colt.

"You ask yourself if you really want to know the truth about John Henry Holliday or if you just want revenge. Which is it, son?" Before Jeb could respond, Earp shook his head. "Ain't no good ever come of revenge, Sanders. No good at all. Find this A. Bird, and you'll get the truth."

And with that he turned and headed west, away from Denver. Wherever Wyatt Earp would lay his head that night, it likely wasn't the Windsor Hotel. Jeb considered following the older man, for where Earp was, Holliday might be found, but duty called. He had a woman to keep an eye on, at least for today.

Jeb pulled out his watch, checked the time, then turned his horse. "Time to pay Miss Finch a visit," he said as he urged the mare into a trot.

All the way back to Denver, he planned his interrogation of Miss Finch and imagined the admissions she would make when he convinced her that coming clean about her involvement with Earp and Holliday was the best course of action.

How could anyone know what she knew about Wyatt Earp unless they'd spent some time on the trail with him? She'd written about the life Earp led and made the reader feel as if she sat on the horse next to him. He knew she hadn't really ridden with Earp on any of his escapades, so how had she done it? Maybe during that meal at the Windsor, though that seemed unlikely.

Anna Finch knew much more than she was telling.

And he was just the man to find out her secrets.

This bravado carried him all the way up the long drive to the Finch home. He stalked to the door, certain he would leave with everything he needed to put Doc Holliday away for life. Maybe even get a rope or a firing squad.

"Hello, Pinkerton man," he heard before the door swung fully open. "What took you so long?"

15

Holliday seemed to be absolutely unable to keep
out of trouble for any great length of time.
— *Bat Masterson*

"Pinkerton man?" the man repeated with a slow grin.

Anna forced a smile. It had taken her until this morning to figure out the combination, but the wall safe behind the portrait of the
Finch sisters had provided the man's full name and the scope of his
employment. Her feelings of betrayal at Papa's choice to hire a
Pinkerton were made worse by the fact he'd hidden it from her.

But Mr. John Edward Baker Sanders did not need to know that.
Nor did he need to know how difficult his job would prove to be.

Anna stepped back from the door. "Won't you come in?" she
asked as sweetly as she could.

The Pinkerton followed her inside and obediently settled himself
on the most uncomfortable chair in Mama's frilly and completely
female formal parlor. Exuberant use of pink, her mother's favorite
color, had caused Papa to vow never to set foot inside what he called
the Spider's Web.

It was a gentle jest between a couple long married. Today, however, Anna hoped it would be the spot where this Pinkerton man met
his match.

She'd intended the exercise as a test of the lawman's endurance, but Anna was completely unprepared for her reaction to the sight of a ruggedly male Pinkerton, even one costumed as a man of wealth, seated amongst the frill and fluff of her mother's flower-strewn tapestries and outrageously trimmed pillows.

Mr. Sanders reached behind him to remove two of the flounced offenders and tossed them onto the fur rug without apology. When he shifted positions, his suit coat opened slightly to reveal a badge that glinted silver in the light of the crystal lamp.

"I suppose you're wondering why I came calling," he said.

"You've come calling?" Anna asked innocently as she continued to study him. Objectively, of course. As an author might study a character. "Socially?" she added when he didn't seem to understand her jest. She punctuated the question with a look intended to fluster him. The attempt failed miserably.

Instead, Mr. Sanders leaned back and regarded her amusement. "Trust me, Miss Finch. I'm not on that list."

"List?"

A maid bearing tea and coffee interrupted, and Anna beckoned her in. While the refreshments were served, Anna made use of the distraction to contemplate her next move. Dare she use her rusty— if not completely untried—feminine wiles? Or perhaps battling him with intellect might succeed.

In either case, she needed this Pinkerton to either leave her alone or help her. And from the look of him and the wording on the documents Papa had signed, neither would be easily accomplished.

The parlor door closed behind the retreating maid, leaving Anna to watch while her guest spooned a heaping amount of sugar into his coffee. He lifted the cup, delicate and almost comical in his hands, to his lips.

"Sweet enough?" she asked when Mr. Sanders caught her staring.

A grin began as his gaze swept across her. She straightened her spine and pretended his impudence had no effect even as she melted inside.

"Plenty sweet," the rogue said.

Anna looked away, but his voice called her attention back again.

"Miss Finch." His sweet-as-honey tone wrapped around her name and released it slowly. "If you know I'm a Pinkerton, it's likely you know the nature of my employment." Another look slid down the length of her. "And I know something's wrong when a woman as beautiful as you sits at home for ten nights in a row."

Beautiful? She forced a neutral look onto her face. "Perhaps I'm not given to socializing."

"You haven't ridden that horse of yours either," he said evenly. "And don't try to tell me you're not given to stealing some stable hand's clothing and giving that mare of yours a run." He paused. "I'm not a man to be trifled with."

If there was a witty response to be given, it failed her. Despite her best intentions, the backhanded compliment on her appearance had reached its target. Anna rubbed her palms against her skirt and reached for the teapot. A mistake, she realized, when the liquid sloshed against the cup and spilled onto the saucer and across the tray.

"Need some help with that?" he asked, though both his demeanor and his position in the chair told her he was firmly committed to watching, not lifting a finger to assist her.

"Thank you, but no." She affected a smile and sat back without bothering to complete the task.

The rogue smirked. He knew exactly what his presence was doing to her. Ire replaced whatever errant feelings the Pinkerton's overtures had caused.

"Now, about that list," she said as firmly as she could.

His deep chuckle might have disarmed her if she hadn't been prepared. "The list? Miss Finch, are you truly ignorant to your father's intentions, or are you toying with me?"

"I gave up toys when I left the nursery, Mr. Sanders."

"But not playing games." He leaned forward, elbows on his knees. Instinctively, Anna pressed back against the settee's ample cushions. "Case in point, you know my name, and I've not yet told it to you. Wonder how that is?"

"You're a Pinkerton," she said. "You figure it out."

"I assure you I will lie awake at night pondering that great mystery," he continued. "However, what I'd really like to know is how you came to know so much about Wyatt Earp."

Anna opened her mouth, but he held up his hand to stop her.

"And before you try to deny it, as you recall, I was at the Windsor and saw you sharing a cozy meal with him and the missus. And Doc Holliday. Who seemed quite taken with you." He paused. "So maybe there's just one question I should ask."

"What is that?" she managed, grateful she'd not been required to confirm or deny her relationship to either man.

"What does the 'A' stand for?"

She took his empty coffee cup and set it on the tray. "The 'A'?"

"I understand the Bird part. That's obvious, little bird. Isn't that what Mr. Mitchell down at the *Times* calls you? Or maybe you earned that name cozying up to Earp and Holliday. I hear women of your quality aren't so keen on having their names revealed when they're keeping company with men their fathers would have shot."

Anna studied the dizzying floral pattern on the carpet.

"You don't have to answer, Miss Finch. As you said, I'm a Pinkerton. I'll figure it out."

Anna's heart jolted. "Mr. Sanders, what are you insinuating?"

"Miss Finch, I don't insinuate." He paused. "You ride better than most boys and your skill with a Colt—"

"Smith & Wesson."

"I stand corrected." Was that a gleam in his eye? "The proof of your skill with a Smith & Wesson is healing nicely."

She looked away so she could think her way out of this conversation. To her surprise, the Pinkerton stood abruptly and reached for her hand, pulling her upright. His grip was firm but gentle, his stance as steady as his gaze.

"Miss Finch, do me the favor of not underestimating me."

Despite her best efforts, Anna felt the heat rise in her cheeks. "I ask the same of you, Mr. Sanders."

"Then perhaps we should begin our association on level ground." The Pinkerton lifted her hand to his lips, his eyes never leaving her face. "Jeb Sanders, Pinkerton agent and your hired gun until such time as you manage to trick some poor man into marrying you. It's a pleasure to make your acquaintance."

Anna yanked her hand away. "You are truly insufferable, Mr. Sanders, and I wish you to leave my parlor immediately."

His chuckle was at once impudent and without humor. "Gladly, Miss Finch. All the flowers and flounces make a man dizzy." He glanced past her to the door. "Give my best to your parents when they return. I understand your mother had a lovely visit with her sister Violet in San Francisco."

"How did you know that my mother was—"

"I'm good at what I do." He adjusted his hat, stepped over the pillows, and headed toward the door. "If you need me, I'll be in the stables."

"The stables?" She started after him, then thought better of it and sat back down. "What on earth are you doing in our stables?"

"I've been sleeping there since the reception." He blinked innocently at her. "Didn't you know? I thought a reporter like you would have sniffed that out by now."

This time she did stand. "Wait just a minute, Mr. Sanders. If my father found out you were staying here with me unaccompanied, why, he'd…" Words failed her as the image of her father's wrath rose.

"He'd be thankful I was doing my job." He turned to go, then glanced back over his shoulder. "I'm bunking with the hired help, not sleeping in the house." He grinned. "Surely you don't mean to compromise my reputation."

Anna groaned and waved him away. Anything further could be handled by persons more able to tolerate the obnoxious hired gun. "Mr. Mitchell will have a grand time with this news," she muttered as she rested her head in her hands.

The Pinkerton paused in the doorway to turn and face her. "I assure you he'll not interfere in a Pinkerton investigation. He's already been made aware of the consequences of that."

"Are you sure?" she asked weakly. "Because that man's interfered in almost every aspect of my life since he took up writing for the *Times*."

"Oh, I assure you," he said with a wink. "The job of interfering is now mine. Have someone fetch me when dinner's ready. And don't forget to let your cook know I like my steaks rare and my bread well buttered."

"You know, Mr. Sanders," she said as she crossed her arms, "if marrying meant I was no longer plagued by your presence, I would accept the first proposal that came my way."

With a laugh, he turned and strode out of the room.

Anna fell back against the cushions. "Now what, Lord?" she muttered as she listened to boot heels crossing the marble floor of the entryway.

"Don't trouble yourself," the odious man called. "I'll see myself out."

Anna grabbed the nearest pillow, held it over her mouth, and screamed. When she was done, she tossed the pillow against the opposite wall and stormed into her father's library, slamming the door and turning the lock.

She had an article to write, and even that awful Pinkerton's presence wouldn't stop her.

"Excuse me," McMinn called from down the hall some time later. "Miss Finch?"

"In here," Anna called, hopping up to unlock the door.

When she opened it, McMinn handed her one of the brown envelopes from the newspaper. "This came for you."

"Thank you." Anna took the package, relocked the door, and hurried to the desk. She ripped open the envelope and began flipping through the letters it contained. When she saw the third envelope, she forgot about the rest and about the obnoxious Pinkerton apparently living in her stables.

The letter was from Mr. Bonney, and was postmarked Leadville, Colorado.

Anna sank onto the chair and cleared a spot on the cluttered desk. With care, she opened the envelope and removed a single sheet of stationery from the Clarendon Hotel on Harrison Avenue, Leadville.

Written just a few days after the article on Wyatt Earp appeared in the *Times,* the letter was brief, its message clear.

> While I remain your devoted servant, I'm as yet unwilling to tell my tale. At least not all at once, as my esteemed colleague has done.

Anna pushed back from the desk and turned her attention to the Rockies, already fading to deep purple in the afternoon shade. Her fingers found the edge of the letter and lifted it.

"As yet unwilling," Anna read again. As yet.

She smiled and reached for pen and paper. Perhaps she could convince Mr. Bonney that now was *exactly* the time.

After penning a cordial but professional greeting, Anna paused only a second before making her case as succinctly as she could.

While you are as yet unwilling, I submit that the research I've done will prove your innocence in some, if not all, of the cases charged against you. All that lacks is for you, Mr. Bonney, to fill in the details.

Anna paused. What else? She smiled.

Should you require it, I am amenable to traveling to meet you, though understandably this arrangement would have to be a private matter between us.

She signed the letter, then hastily sealed it and addressed it to Mr. Bonney at the address on the Clarendon's letterhead.

Now to get it mailed. Or better yet, sent via private messenger.

In less than five minutes she'd found Mr. McMinn mucking a stall.

"Can you spare someone to run an errand for me?" she asked.

"Of course I can." He spied the letter. "I can take that myself."

"Actually, it's not going to be posted." She paused. "I need someone trustworthy to rush this to Leadville."

"To your pa?"

"Not exactly," Anna said.

Mr. McMinn leaned against the stall and gave her a stern look. "This business?"

"Yes, absolutely. It is definitely business, which is why the errand needs to be done quickly and discreetly." Anna paused. "You have my word on that, Mr. McMinn. I would consider it a personal favor if you would do this for me."

"Yes'm," he said slowly. "I'll see someone's at the station with this first thing tomorrow morning."

"No," Anna said. "This can't wait for tomorrow. Unless the schedule's changed, there's an evening train. He needs to be on it."

"I see." He removed his hat to scratch his head. "I reckon I can spare a man. Gonna be a big rain tonight for sure, so we'll all be indoors anyway." He paused. "You got train fare and a little something for him to eat and sleep on?"

Anna reached into her pocket and handed him twice the price of a round-trip ticket from Denver to Leadville. "Whatever remains can be considered a bonus."

He nodded. "Should I have him wait for a response?"

"Of course," Anna said, "though I'm uncertain as to whether one will be offered. There is also a slight chance my friend will have already left the hotel."

"I'll be sure and mention that to whichever of the fellas ends up going." The driver paused. "Anything else, Miss Finch?"

"Yes." She took a deep breath. "I'd prefer if Mr. Sanders didn't know about this."

McMinn considered a moment. "I'll do my best, miss."

"That's all I can ask."

Determined to get rid of the Pinkerton and with an idea how to do it, Anna arrived downstairs promptly at half past eight expecting the dining table to be set and the usual evening meal waiting. Instead, she found the room empty.

And yet something smelled wonderful. She followed the scent into the kitchen.

"Cook, what's that lovely—" Anna froze at the sight of the Pinkerton standing at the stove. "You're not Cook."

He tossed a grin over his shoulder, then went back to stirring whatever was in the pot. "Gave her the night off."

It took a moment for the scene before her to register. A man whose gun and badge were still in full view would be her chef tonight?

Anna released her grip on the door and let it close behind her. "But that's impossible."

"No, Miss Finch. It's quite possible. The woman needed the evening off, and I offered to take her place. I think you'll find I'm a decent substitute." Mr. Sanders set the spoon aside and reached for a towel to mop his brow. "Gets warm in here," he said. "Now where's your bowls?"

"Bowls?" Anna glanced around, then shrugged. "I don't know where she keeps them. I could look."

"How long have you lived here, Miss Finch, and you can't find a bowl?" He turned his back to open the oven door. "No wonder you're having trouble finding a man. Any woman of mine would need to know her way around a kitchen."

"Yes, well," Anna said as she let out a long breath and tried to hang on to her temper. "I suppose it's to both our benefits that I'll never be your woman."

He looked up and grinned. "I suppose so. Counting my blessings right now with that at the top of the list."

Anna found the bowls in the third place she looked, on the topmost shelf of a cabinet in the far corner of the room. Retrieving them would be impossible without some sort of stool. She found a chair and pushed it over to climb up within reach. As she extended her hand to grab the first bowl, she was lifted off the chair.

"I'll do that." The Pinkerton's voice was as firm as his grip around her waist. Setting her on the floor, Mr. Sanders nudged away the chair and retrieved two bowls from the shelf. "Think you can find a couple of spoons?" he asked as he handed her the bowls. "And maybe a napkin or two. My trail stew's been known to need a little cleanup."

"Trail stew?" She frowned. "I've never heard of it."

"Bring the bowls over here, and then sit yourself down."

Despite the urge to protest, Anna did as she was told. From her vantage point, she watched the lawman stir in spices from Cook's collection, then reach for a spoon to taste his concoction.

"Enjoying the show?" he asked when he glanced over his shoulder and caught her staring.

"Fascinating," she said with what she hoped was evident sarcasm.

"Like a maestro conducting an orchestra," he said as he reached for the ladle and filled the bowls. "Just the right amount of each part makes for a perfect symphony." He turned to check her reaction, then began to laugh. "You are far too serious, Miss Finch."

"Perhaps it's the company I keep."

He set a bowl in front of her and settled himself across the table. Anna offered him a napkin, which he tucked into the front of his shirt.

With her spoon, Anna poked at the ingredients of the meal

before her. Something akin to beef. Definitely potatoes. A gravy of some sort.

"Where I come from, we say grace first."

Anna jerked her attention away from the food. "Yes, of course," she said. "Here too. That is, Papa always does. Would you mind?"

She tried not to peek as the Pinkerton gave thanks. Yet there was just something about a man who could shoot a gun, haul in a bad guy, and still hold a conversation with God on a first-name basis.

"Amen." He lifted his head. "Next time close your eyes, Miss Finch."

"I did," she protested, albeit weakly.

"Right." He lifted his spoon and took a taste. "Oh, this is good," he said with a groan. "I've outdone myself."

Gingerly, she touched the tip of the spoon to the brownish concoction. "What is it you call this again?"

"Trail stew." He dabbed at the corner of his mouth with the napkin. "Ingredients vary depending on what I've caught that day and what's left in the saddlebags to throw into the pot."

Anna continued to study the contents of her spoon. "Dare I ask what you caught today?"

His laughter was the only answer she got. "Dine or go hungry." He set down his spoon and gave her an "I-dare-you" look.

Under the Pinkerton's steady gaze, Anna lifted the spoon to her lips. It wasn't bad. In fact, the gravy was quite good. She met his stare. "Well?"

She braved another spoonful, this time with a smattering of the other ingredients included. "It's actually quite delicious."

"Doesn't need anything? Salt, a little cayenne, maybe?"

"No." She tried to ignore the way the lamplight slanted over features far too handsome to belong to such an irritating man. "It's perfect."

"Perfect. A man can't ask for more than that."

He went back to his meal, and the room settled into silence. Anna almost reached the bottom of the bowl before recalling she had a mission in coming downstairs tonight.

She swallowed her fear and regarded the Pinkerton with an even stare. "Mr. Sanders, I know what my father's paying you."

He paused, spoon midway between the bowl and his mouth. For a moment she thought he might ignore her. Then he placed the spoon back in the bowl and gave her a sideways look.

"And?"

"And I am prepared to double it." There, she'd said it. Anna lowered her gaze to study the trim on her sleeve.

"I see."

His chair scraped against the floor as he rose. She looked up to see him carrying both bowls to the sink. For a moment, he remained with his back to her, a dark broad-shouldered silhouette against a window, lit by the lamps on either side.

When Mr. Sanders finally turned to face her, Anna's hopes rose. His expression, while neutral, did not seem to offer any resistance to the idea.

Slowly he crossed his arms over his chest. A casual passerby might have seen a man loitering in the kitchen. Anna saw a man studying her with what she knew must be a skilled eye.

Thus, she too rose and moved to the window to stand beside him.

From her spot at the sink, Anna could see a lone lamp burning in the bunkhouse behind the stable. When the wind blew the climbing roses, the light disappeared, replaced by a zigzag of lightning that illuminated the lawn in hues of silver and gray. Soon the branches would be filled with roses, the kitchen overwhelmed with their sweet scent. Now, however, the spindly limbs were bare, the night beyond them dark and heavy with the promise of rain.

Anna pressed her thoughts back toward the carefully formed argument she'd practiced this afternoon. In profile the Pinkerton was less daunting, but only slightly.

"You've not answered, Mr. Sanders."

Outside the rose branches scratched against the window as the low rumble of thunder shook the glass. The mantel clock struck nine.

Slowly the hired gun turned to face her, one hip leaning against the edge of the sink. A muscle in his jaw twitched. "You think I put this badge on for the money? Do I look like the kind of man who can be bought?"

"Yes, well, I mean, no. I just assumed—"

"You assumed," he echoed, his jaw clenched, "wrong."

He turned and stomped toward the door, pausing just long enough to jam his hat onto his head.

"I'm sorry," Anna said. "I never meant to offend. Only to strike a deal that might be beneficial to both of us."

Mr. Sanders wrenched open the door and stepped out into the wind and rain. "The only thing beneficial to either of us right now is me leaving this room before I say something I regret."

The door slammed behind him, and he was gone.

Anna felt a headache coming on.

16

Conflict follows wrongdoing, as surely as flies
follow the herd.

—*Doc Holliday*

The sun felt glorious and warm on Anna's face, and she longed to shed her bonnet despite the impropriety involved in such an action. She fidgeted with the ribbons at her neck and gave the idea serious thought as Isak, Daniel's driver, urged the carriage away from the heart of the city.

Edwin's invitation for a morning carriage ride, arriving as it had on her breakfast tray, was a welcome distraction from her disappointment at learning the letter to Mr. Holliday had not reached its intended recipient before the man left Leadville.

Anna took a deep breath of spring air, pleased to be in decidedly non-Pinkerton company. But as the gates closed behind them and Edwin Beck slid a glance in her direction, the pleasure faded. While the Pinkerton caused her no end of aggravation, Daniel's very handsome brother reduced her to babbling schoolgirl silliness.

Neither was preferable, but she'd made her choice. Rather than open her mouth and say something foolish, Anna looked away from Edwin.

"I'm pleased your father thought to send me back to Denver early," her companion said. "He was concerned you might be suffering from lack of attention."

"I see," Anna said. That Papa felt any sort of concern over the attention she received, or didn't, was beyond absurd. Unless it had to do with finding her a husband. She closed her eyes.

"Miss Finch, have I upset you?"

She opened her eyes and found Edwin staring. "No, that would be the Pinkerton's job."

"I beg your pardon?"

"Never mind."

When Edwin Beck seemed to read her earlier thoughts and tugged on the length of green satin trailing from her bonnet, Anna gasped. His look of innocence belied the fact that he held her bonnet strings in his hand.

"Release my ribbons," Anna said, proud at the modicum of words she'd managed.

"I should," he admitted. "It would be the gentlemanly thing to do."

"Indeed it would."

The carriage veered to the right and began ascending the bridge spanning Jackrabbit Creek.

"And while our driver is no doubt a circumspect fellow," Edwin continued, "Isak would likely take offense to my familiarity with you."

Daniel's longtime employee did not respond, but Anna could feel his disapproval.

"And so, Miss Finch, while this bonnet is of glorious construction—no doubt the handiwork of some French milliner—I must submit that the curls beneath are the work of a much more talented hand."

"I don't follow," she said. "Are you toying with me or merely supposing a theory?"

It was utter nonsense, this talk, and yet when Anna braved a look at the younger Beck brother, she saw far too much of Daniel there.

"Perhaps it's time for the jest to end." She gave the ribbon a tug, but he refused to release it. "Mr. Beck, surely you can't find any good reason to continue this."

"The truth, I fear."

Her smile was quick if not steady. "Thank you for understanding. It would be quite the scandal should I be seen riding about town bareheaded."

"I do agree."

"Good."

He whipped her brand-new bonnet off her head and tossed it beneath the rolling wheels of the carriage.

"Mr. Beck!" She looked around wildly for any potential witnesses. While Anna saw no onlookers, she did watch a stiff breeze lift her bonnet and propel it over the bridge to land at the edge of the creek.

"Thank goodness it didn't land in the water. Isak, can you stop so I can retrieve it?"

Isak pulled on the reins, and the carriage slowed to a halt midway across the bridge. "I can fetch it." As he climbed down, the driver's glare was unmistakable.

"I'm so sorry," Anna said quickly. "I truly did not believe he would—"

"Do not apologize to the help," Edwin said. "Besides, it needed to be done." He gave her a penitent look, then touched the curls loosened by his prank. Wrapping a strand of her hair around his knuckle, Daniel's brother leaned toward her. "Might I plead that I was overcome?"

"Overcome?" Anna crossed her hands over her chest and chose her words carefully. "Mr. Beck, I daresay men like you are rarely overcome by women like me."

He released her curl but left his hand dangerously close to her cheek. "Miss Finch," he said as he moved closer, "how would you know the first thing about what men think of you?"

She remained still, barely breathing, and yet from the corner of her eye Anna watched what she realized was a master at work. A master manipulator of women, just as Daniel had warned her.

"Miss Finch," he whispered against her ear, "we are very much alone at this moment, for while your bonnet is being rescued, its owner has been abandoned to the man she was likely warned not to associate with."

Anna felt the heat rise in her face as she locked eyes with the Englishman. "Mr. Beck, you are incorrigible."

"I am practical," he said. "And honest, despite what my brother might have told you. Thus I will tell you without guise or deception that every moment of this morning was planned to bring us to this very place at this very time."

"Truly," Anna said, "I find your approach flattering. But to believe that you would toss my bonnet under the buggy wheels just to be alone with me for a few minutes while poor Isak mucks about under the bridge? It's a bit far-fetched, don't you think?"

"Far-fetched?" His smile was broad. "Were my intention of being alone with you the sole purpose, then I would agree." He cupped her cheek with his palm while his free hand wrapped around her waist. Before Anna could protest, he turned and lowered her head into his lap, and she found herself looking up at Edwin Beck.

And then he kissed her.

"Mr. Beck," she said when she could manage it. "Let me *go*."

His eyes searched her face, his hand still pressed against her cheek. "You are beautiful. Daniel is a fool."

"Got it," Isak called. "Isn't much worse for wear. Perhaps a good cleaning, but elsewise…"

The driver continued to talk, his voice growing nearer even as Anna ceased to hear. To feel. To think. Then, by degrees, the world righted and she found herself seated in the same spot where the journey had begun. Beside her, Edwin Beck straightened his collar and adjusted his cuff.

"Here it is, Miss Finch." Isak appeared and thrust the misshapen bonnet toward her. "I'm sure you can fix it good as new."

"Thank you," she managed as she crumpled the ribbons with shaking fingers.

A sideways glance revealed Edwin Beck smiling. "Lovely day for a carriage ride, don't you think, Miss Finch?" When she did not answer, he turned his attention to Isak. "Drive on, young man."

"No," Anna said. "Take me home, Isak." She gave the Englishman a withering stare. "Now. And hurry."

When Jeb woke that morning, McMinn had informed him that Anna Finch had gone on a carriage ride with Mr. Beck. Jeb made a mental note to thank Daniel the next time he saw him. The last thing he needed that morning was another encounter with Anna Finch. With Daniel keeping her occupied for a few hours, Jeb could relax with a cup of coffee and rebuild the professional walls Miss Finch had a habit of breaking through. He'd never had a client get to him the way she did.

When Jeb spied the Beck carriage returning to the Finch home much earlier than he'd expected, he walked to the kitchen door, intent on stepping out to meet the pair. Then he spied which Beck the Finch woman had gone off with.

Immediately he wondered just what kind of woman went gallivanting off with a man like Edwin Beck. Surely not one who might have the least bit of concern over her reputation. It didn't fit with the demure society gal image she cultivated and that he'd witnessed to this point. But then, neither did riding about at dawn in boys' clothing and dining with wanted men.

Jeb doubled back to set his coffee on the table, then made his way outside. He was about to let Anna Finch know exactly how he felt about her slipping off when he spied the expression on her face. Jeb slipped back inside and found a spot near the open window where he could listen without being seen.

"Might I speak to Mr. Beck alone?" Miss Finch said to Isak, who trotted obediently off to the stables, leaving the pair standing beside the carriage.

"Miss Finch, do me the honor of not lecturing me," Beck said. "I've no use for hearing it."

"You've no use?" Miss Finch's voice was high and strained. "After behaving as you've done, you dare tell me you've no use for hearing me?"

"I was overcome."

Jeb moved a half pace to the right for a clearer view. The Finch woman jabbed Beck in the chest with her finger. Beck laughed.

"Your spirit defies description," he said, "as I suspected it would. Now, shall we dispense with the theatrics? You and I are of an age when we shouldn't have to stand on formality. We're also of an age to strike our own bargains without the interference of family."

When Beck's hand caught her wrist, Jeb nearly went after him. Instead, he forced himself to remain in place until he had a better idea of how to remove Beck from the property without seriously injuring him.

"Mr. Beck," Miss Finch said slowly, "a Derringer is not my pistol of choice. It is, however, the pistol in my skirt pocket."

Edwin Beck released her, though the insufferable smirk didn't leave his face.

Miss Finch allowed a deadly pause before calling for Isak. When he came running, she stepped back from the Englishman.

"Mr. Beck is ready to go home." She spared him only the quickest glance. "Good day, sir," she said and stormed toward the door.

Jeb stepped aside just before the door slammed open. "Back so soon?" he called to her retreating form.

She whirled and gave him a withering look. "Mr. Sanders, what are you doing in my home? I thought you were going to remain in the barn with the livestock."

He hurried to catch up with her and fell into step beside her as she reached the stairs. "Trouble with Beck?" When she did not respond, he tried again. "Say the word, Miss Finch, and I'll handle him. I'm not just here to keep your whereabouts under surveillance. I'm also here to see to your safety. Which, by the way, might have been compromised by going off without reporting to me first."

She stopped short. "Reporting to you?"

"I am the one paid to—"

"Mr. Sanders." Miss Finch maneuvered around to stand one step higher than him, putting them eye to eye. "Had you any idea how very close I came to shooting the last man who trifled with me, you might think twice about continuing this conversation."

He laughed. "Too late to fear that, Miss Finch. You've already shot me."

When she whirled around and stormed up the stairs, Jeb went after her.

"Hey, now," he called. "I'm sorry. It was a joke."

She'd reached the top of the stairs, no doubt only a short distance from her bedchamber and the door she'd likely slam at any moment. She leaned against the newel post and stared down at him.

"It wasn't funny."

"I'm sorry," he repeated.

"Go home, Mr. Sanders." She swiped at a curl that had come loose. "Just go."

"I can't do that," he said, "but I do owe you another apology." He shrugged. "I ought not to have imposed myself on you yesterday." Miss Finch seemed interested in listening, so Jeb continued. "I had my reasons, but thinking on it now, they probably weren't enough to make up for the aggravation I caused."

Her expression softened a notch. "What reasons?" she said so quietly he almost missed it.

"I've made no secret of what I've been hired to do," he said, "but I can't do that job unless I know who I'm protecting." He paused to choose his words carefully. "I had a conversation with someone yesterday who gave me reason to wonder about some things."

Miss Finch shifted position. "Things?"

"Now's not the time to have this discussion," he said, "but we will, and soon. I thought if I visited yesterday and asked some questions, I might find out what I needed to know." Another pause. "About you."

"Me?" She shook her head. "Is that all? There's absolutely nothing to tell."

"That's where we differ," he said. "I'll go now. Not far, mind you, as I'm still on duty."

She released her grip on the post and found her bedchamber door.

"Miss Finch," he called just before she disappeared inside.

"What is it?"

"Did he harm you in any way?"

Her gaze collided with his. "Harm? No."

"Did he take any liberties?"

"He—" She seemed ready to continue, then abruptly disappeared inside and closed the bedchamber door. *At least,* he thought, *she didn't slam it.*

Jeb thought about her lack of answer with every step he took out of the Finch house and across the grounds. By the time he reached Daniel's doorstep, he knew what he needed to do.

Daniel met him at the door before Jeb could knock. "Good to see you," he said. "What can I do for you?"

"Your brother," Jeb said. "Send him outside. The stables will do."

"The stables?" Daniel shook his head. "I don't understand."

"Your brother will. If you don't mind, I'd appreciate leaving it at that."

Jeb bypassed the kitchen and went out to the stables to wait. Five minutes went by before the door opened and the younger Beck stepped inside.

"Daniel said you needed to see me about—"

One punch and the younger Beck hit the floor. "What did you do to her?"

Beck scrambled to his feet, his eyes narrowed, and raised his fists. "If she told you I did more than kiss her, she's lying."

White-hot anger nearly blinded Jeb at the thought of this man putting his hands on Anna Finch, kissing her. "Get out of here before I hurt you."

The Englishman only laughed. "I'm going to marry her, Sanders." He made a show of dusting the straw from his pants. "Pummel me if you wish, but that fact will not change. I'll not lose her to some ruffian."

Moving toward the untrained civilian was simple. Hauling him up by the neck, simpler still. Keeping his grip just shy of deadly, that was a struggle.

"No," Jeb said slowly, "you're *not* marrying Anna Finch because you're leaving. Today." Jeb relaxed his grip just enough to allow a bit more air into the man's lungs. "Your brother cares about you, though for the life of me I can't understand why. I want you to go in there and tell him you've been called back to London. Make up a good story so he thinks you're going to miss him, then take your things and go. Nod if you understand."

He did, and Jeb let him go.

And then Edwin Beck slugged him. Hard. Jeb reeled backward several steps before he recovered.

To his credit, Beck stood his ground. "As I said, I'll not lose Anna to any man unworthy of her."

Jeb reached for his weapon, but unfortunately, good sense prevailed. "You don't want to continue this, Beck," he managed. "It would be far too dangerous."

Beck seemed to consider the statement, but only for a moment. Then he smirked, gave Jeb a mocking bow, and left.

Some days being a Pinkerton had its benefits. Today, as he watched the sorry excuse for a man that was Edwin Beck strut toward the house as if he owned the place, Jeb had to admit the badge was a burden. Without the responsibility of carrying the Pinkerton name, he could have dealt with Daniel's brother in a far more convincing way.

He watched Beck disappear inside, then returned to the Finch home to resume his surveillance at a safe distance. No more losing his temper and giving in to stupidity. If he wanted to catch Doc Holliday and still keep his job, he'd have to make some adjustments to the plan.

Starting with taking due note of the fact that Anna Finch carried a Derringer in her pocket.

17

He was one of the finest, cleanest men in the
world, though, of course, he was a little handy
with his gun and had to kill a few fellows.
—*Wyatt Earp, regarding Doc Holliday*

Somehow the morning passed and the afternoon dwindled nearly to
evening. Anna pushed away from her desk to stretch. While the
unpleasantness with Edwin had sent her hurrying to her bedchamber, the thick packet of letters kept her there.

Most were of the hard-to-believe variety, while a few were trib-
utes to individuals whose names meant nothing. Letters of both
kinds were easily culled and returned to the packet, leaving half a
dozen choice leads that might make sensational stories.

Four gave addresses to which she could respond, an endeavor
that had kept Anna busy until well past lunchtime. Then came the
writing of tomorrow's column, an essay on a fellow known to locals
by the name of Soapy.

Perhaps, Anna thought as she folded the pages and prepared
them for delivery to Mr. Smith at the *Times,* the story's subject might
wish to refute her firsthand informants with a personal interview of
his own. For that, she'd certainly write a follow-up piece.

Anna rested her elbows on the desk, then cracked her knuckles, a horrid habit that, when she was a child, earned a swift reprimand. A knock at the door drew Anna's attention. A maid reminded her to dress for dinner.

"Dinner?" She gathered up the packet and held it behind her, then opened the door a crack. "Whatever for?"

The maid shrugged. "I'm sorry, miss, but your parents insist."

"My parents? My mother perhaps, but Papa's in Leadville until Thursday." Anna shook her head. "Surely Mother's much too tired from her journey to sit through dinner. Tell her she's not required to do so by me."

The maid gave another timid shrug followed by a curtsy. "Your father has returned. He said I should tell both you and your mother half past eight."

Anna covered her surprise. "Half past eight it is."

She closed the door and returned to her work. By the time she washed for dinner, true to her promise to Mr. Smith, Anna had managed to plan enough regular features to fill a month's worth of twice-weekly columns. Each would be added to the stories carefully clipped and resting atop the pile of Mae Winslow novels hiding in a locked trunk in the attic.

It all seemed so silly and clandestine, especially given her age and credentials. With the funds still languishing in the bank in Boston, she could live a quiet life elsewhere without any concern for what her parents thought. More than once she'd considered doing just that, finding some peaceful hamlet and focusing on her journalistic career without caring who knew.

For tonight, she was a daughter who would love nothing better than to speak with her father about the men who'd troubled her today. She wouldn't, of course, not in front of her mother. Later, perhaps, when Papa went to his library.

Anna greeted her parents as she entered the dining room and took her seat at the table. The meal was quiet, so quiet that Anna could hear occasional laughter from the kitchen, which told her the Pinkerton was on the premises.

"So, Papa, you've returned early."

Her father let the statement hang between them while he studied her mother. "Finished my business," he said. "Came home. Nothing else to tell."

A look passed between her parents, though Anna couldn't identify it.

"So, dear," her mother said, "did your father and I miss any social events? Anything you've done in our absence that warrants discussion?"

Become a well-received journalist? Exchanged letters with Doc Holliday? Threatened a British nobleman with a Derringer, perhaps?

"No," Anna said sweetly. "Nothing of any consequence."

This time the look was disappointment, and both her parents wore it. "No gentlemen callers?" her mother asked.

"Your Pinkerton tells me you took a carriage ride with Beck's brother."

Anna blinked, surprised her father had mentioned her hired gun. Mr. Sanders must have told him that she was aware of his presence and purpose. "Yes, a brief one," she admitted.

Mama exhaled a long breath. "Well, now," she said to Papa, "isn't that wonderful?" She lifted the bell. "Anna and I will take coffee in the parlor. Dear, will you join us?"

Her father waved away any response as he shoved back from the table and disappeared into the hall leading to the library. Anna considered joining him but instead dutifully followed her mother into the parlor, though what she might do to keep her eyes open and sleep at bay, she didn't know.

And then Mr. McMinn appeared at the parlor door carrying a large packet of what she knew must be yet another delivery of mail from the *Times*. Anna's heart sank. What was he doing? Always before the envelopes had been discreetly deposited on her desk. It was almost as if the driver wished her caught.

"Might I borrow your daughter, Mrs. Finch?" he asked.

"Of course."

If Mother was suspicious, she gave no indication. She went back to her embroidery work without further comment.

Anna followed Mr. McMinn through the kitchen, where she noted that the Pinkerton was nowhere to be found, and out to the stables.

"You'll want to be more careful with this." He handed the thick packet to her. "Not everyone's happy about this A. Bird fellow."

Grasping the envelope to her chest, Anna debated whether to respond at all. "Actually, I think the reporter is doing a fine job of making people aware of the injustice all around us."

Mr. McMinn shook his head. "I suppose." He turned his attention to the package in her hands. "But if I were you, I'd give some consideration as to how this Bird fellow gets his mail."

"I—that is, well…"

"Miss Finch," he said gently, "I won't ask how you know this reporter." He pointed to the envelope. "But might I suggest you stop this?"

"If I knew what you were talking about," she said slowly, "then I would have to tell you that A. Bird doesn't intend to stop."

"He's told you that, has he?" the driver asked with the beginnings of a grin.

"In a fashion, he has," she said.

"Well, might I offer some advice?" When she nodded, he continued. "I had this friend once with a similar situation. Important correspondence that needed to be kept strictly confidential."

"What did he do?"

Mr. McMinn held up his hand. "I'll show you."

He disappeared into a stall, then came back with a carpetbag, which he handed to Anna. She looked inside and found a slip of paper resting on a stack of boys' clothing.

Anna moved the paper, which had an address written on it, and pulled out a men's shirt of plain fabric. "I don't understand."

"There's a post office in Garrison. You know where that is?"

She did. The tiny town was practically on Denver's doorstep and an easy half-hour's ride away.

He shrugged. "I don't suppose you got any friends there."

"No," Anna said. "Why?"

"Easier for a stranger to ride in and out," he said. "Might not attract so much attention."

Anna grinned. "Mr. McMinn, you're brilliant." She looked around before leaning toward the driver. "How soon might this be arranged?"

It was Mr. McMinn's turn to grin. "Already done it," he said. "Figured you'd need another plan once I saw how many post office trips I'd have to explain to the boss."

"So my mail…" Anna paused. "That is, A. Bird's mail is already being collected in Garrison?"

"Should be." He rocked back on his heels. "You gonna need Maisie come daybreak on Monday?"

"Better make it at least an hour before," she said. "I figure I'll have to get up pretty early in the morning to slip away without the Pinkerton suspecting anything."

"Yes'm," he said with a tip of his hat. "I'll see to it."

&c.

True to Mr. McMinn's word, the horse was ready and waiting when Anna slipped into the stables that morning. Though she'd been provided garments for the ride, Anna elected to wear her own riding clothes. Somehow she felt better not intentionally appearing to deceive.

As the first orange rays lit the prairie, Anna allowed Maisie to set her own pace, heedless of her flying skirts. Soon the outline of the tiny hamlet of Garrison appeared on the horizon.

With the sun barely up, Anna realized she'd arrived far too early to do any business at the post office. Next time she would arrange her arrival to coincide with the proper hours, but today she found an open door at the lone eating establishment on the street and settled at a table with her saddlebag and the best cup of coffee she'd had in ages.

After taking a sip, she set the mug aside and hauled her saddle-bag into her lap. Beneath the Smith & Wesson, which she prayed never to have to use again, lay her stack of mail to be sent out. Some were notes of thanks to sources who didn't mind hearing from her, and others were letters of inquiry asking about subjects for future stories. All received some sort of clipping, either one in which they had participated or one she wished them to see to prove her skills as a writer.

Anna sometimes wondered why Mr. McMinn didn't go to her father with all he knew, but she tried not to dwell on the question. She preferred to believe that the driver shared her concern for the truth and didn't mind playing his part by fetching home each day more newspapers than the average citizen of Denver read in a week.

From the activity outside, it appeared the citizens of Garrison had finally decided to awaken and begin the day. She finished her coffee and hastened to the post office, where she found the postmaster sorting mail from a bag at his feet.

He looked up and offered a grin filled with more enthusiasm than teeth. "Might I help you, miss?"

Handing over the letters, she returned his grin. "Would you post these for me, please? And then I'll need to pick up my mail."

It took him only a moment to handle the outgoing pieces. "What's the name you're looking for?" he asked as he went to a back table filled with an assortment of mail in what appeared to be no particular order.

"Bird," she said, hoping the single name would be enough to achieve her purpose without drawing unwanted attention.

He gave her an appraising look from across the room. "Did you say Bird?"

Anna nodded.

The old man turned to face her. "First initial?"

"A."

"Is that so?" He shuffled back to the desk. "Well, it ain't gonna be back there, then."

Disappointment nudged her. "Perhaps next week." Anna cradled her saddlebag and turned to leave. At least she'd had a pleasant ride. Next time she'd leave after sunrise and likely not even need an overcoat.

"Miss," the postmaster called, "ain't you gonna take your mail?" He lifted the bag that had been at his feet. "Don't know what makes you so popular," he said, "but you sure do get a heap of letters."

`· ᏇᎧᏋ·`

Jeb watched Anna Finch step out of the Garrison post office with a saddlebag on one arm and a bag of mail on the other. Of all the women in Colorado, why had he been paid to protect this one?

A sombrero resting low on his head and a false mustache itching beneath his nose, Jeb pretended to worry himself with the reins to the borrowed wagon he'd brought along as cover. Any observers would think he'd arrived in Garrison for business purposes.

When his charge walked out of the post office, he'd been contemplating going in after her. Now he didn't have to, as her predicament offered ample opportunity for a knight in shining armor—or, rather, a dusty undercover Pinkerton turned Mexican wagon driver in a serape and hat courtesy of Mr. McMinn—to reveal himself and save her.

Anna Finch was nicely turned out in a dress fit for travel, and he wondered why she hadn't donned the boyish style she'd been wearing the last time she rode that heathen horse. It certainly would have been more appropriate for what she was attempting.

He climbed out of the wagon and moved toward her. "'Scuse me, señorita," he called as he got within speaking distance, careful to keep his hat low and his voice disguised. "You look like you've got a problem. Your horse, he don't fit your bag."

She didn't spare him a look. "To say the least," she responded, focused on her task.

Miss Finch wasn't much bigger than the bag she was hoisting, but she didn't appear to notice. It couldn't be heavy, or she'd have landed on her backside after trying to swing it across the saddle. As it was, she overshot her aim, and the bag landed on the street on the other side of her horse.

Jeb trotted over to retrieve the canvas mailbag. About half full of letters, from the way the contents shifted.

"Need some help?" he asked in a thickly accented version of English.

She gave him an odd look. "Do I know you?" Then came recognition. "Jeb Sanders."

He lifted the edge of his sombrero. *"Sí,"* he said. Before she could walk away, Jeb threw the bag over his shoulder. "Come on with me. I'll see you and all this gets home."

He ignored her protests and reached for the mare's reins, gently removing them from the post. He settled the mailbag on his shoulder and tugged on the horse's reins. The wagon was just across the way, and he moved that direction, hoping his cargo—human and animal—would comply.

18

Boys, you can't get out of this race. You are going
to run it.

—*Doc Holliday*

Anna watched the Pinkerton toss the mailbag into the back of a wagon across the dusty street. Then he leaned toward Maisie and patted her on the muzzle before offering her something from his pocket. An apple, perhaps? Or a carrot? Anna couldn't tell from this distance, but the traitorous horse was eating it—and the attention—up.

While Anna fumed, her hired gun led the skittish mare to the back of the wagon and knotted the reins around a plank of wood. With a grin, he loped across the street, his long strides kicking up dust on the thoroughfare.

"I'm going to Denver," he said. "I figure you are too."

"And if I'm not?" she asked without sparing him a glance.

"Oh," he said slowly, "you are."

Anna stood her ground. This man might be in the employ of her father, but she wouldn't take orders from him. "No, I don't think so."

"I'm taking your saddlebag to the wagon." He took the bag from her arms and slung it over his shoulder. His gaze swept the length of her. "Do I need to get you there the same way?"

Anna regretted her sharp intake of breath the moment it happened. "You wouldn't dare," she said.

"Miss Finch," he said in his false Mexican accent. "You do not want to test me on this." Mr. Sanders returned her icy stare, then had the nerve to offer her his free hand.

"I can manage, thank you." She stepped off the curb and followed him to the wagon where Maisie reached to nuzzle her. "Traitor," Anna said to the horse.

While Anna watched, the saddlebag joined the mail sack in the back of the wagon. Then Mr. Sanders turned to her. "Here, let me help you."

Arguing would serve no purpose, so Anna merely looked away while the lawman lifted her by the waist and settled her into the wagon seat. With a chuckle, he trotted around to the other side, climbed in, and took the reins of the most miserable pair of mules Anna had seen in ages.

"Where'd you find those two?" she asked. "Isn't my father paying you well enough to secure some decent horseflesh?"

"I figure it takes a mule to catch one," Mr. Sanders said. He glanced backward at Maisie and then slapped the reins to set the mule team in motion. "You being twice as mulish as most, I decided I'd need two."

Anna ignored the comment and slid him a sideways glance. "Must you continue with the ridiculous disguise?"

He shrugged and toyed with the mustache. "Didn't seem so ridiculous when you had no idea who I was."

Several responses came to mind. Anna kept them to herself.

They rode in silence for a few minutes. "Miss Finch, want to tell me why you're getting your mail in Garrison now?"

She ignored him.

He shrugged. "If you don't want to answer my questions, that's fine. You can answer your father's."

"You're not going to tell him about this," Anna said, trying not to plead.

The Pinkerton looked at her. "That's my job. Unless you want to tell me yourself…"

The wagon hit a rut, and Anna grasped the edge of the seat. "Watch where you're going, Mr. Sanders."

His only response was silence. Anna decided she much preferred silence to speaking.

The wagon clattered along until Garrison was behind them and nothing but prairie loomed ahead. The Pinkerton seemed absorbed in thought, so Anna gave up trying to keep her irritation going. Instead, she considered her next story. That thought led to whether Doc Holliday would ever give in to her request for an interview. Anna decided to give the outlaw two weeks to write before she began her own investigative piece without his input.

She'd begin by listing all the places Doc had supposedly been, including the one time she knew his whereabouts from personal knowledge. She decided that that fortuitous meeting at the Windsor would start the piece. Personal experience generally made for a stronger lead.

Anna gave her companion a sideways glance, caught him staring at her, and lost her train of thought. Planning her article would take more concentration than she could manage with the Pinkerton sitting beside her.

The sun's warmth basked her shoulders and gave Anna incentive to shed her overcoat. At their slow pace, it would take much longer to return to Denver than it took to make her trip this morning.

A look back at Maisie told her the horse's irritation level was rising along with her own. "Sorry, girl," she said to the mare. "No galloping on this trip." She turned to her companion. "Unless you can figure out how to make these animals pick up the pace."

"Believe me," he said, "if I could, I would. Only suggestion I can make is that you sit back and enjoy the ride. This is the nicest weather I've seen since last fall. You don't want to miss it while you're complaining."

"I have legitimate concerns about your threat to speak to my father, Mr. Sanders," she said. "What do you expect?"

He lifted the brim of his sombrero to scratch his head, then tossed it into the wagon bed and reached beneath the seat for his Stetson. "I owe Barnaby an explanation for your trip to Garrison today, seeing as I'm supposed to keep you out of trouble."

"How did you know where I'd be?" She shook her head. "Mr. McMinn told you, didn't he?"

The Pinkerton laughed. "A man never shares his sources." He gestured to the sky. "If I were you, I'd go ahead and get started on enjoying this day. Won't be much longer before we see Denver and you have to start pretending again."

She lifted a brow as she turned to look at her companion. "Pretending?"

"That you enjoy city life." He shook his head. "No one who rides a horse like you belongs in a gilded cage."

"You're funny," she said, "but that's not the first time I've heard the joke."

"I was serious," he said. "So get on about the business of enjoying the ride, and I'll see what I can do about getting us back safely."

Anna settled against the seat. Much as she hated to admit it, the hired gun was right. "It is lovely out today," she said as she closed her eyes and turned her face to the sun. "God does such wonderful work, doesn't He?"

Mr. Sanders chuckled. When she opened her eyes, Anna found him looking directly at her. "Yes, He does," he said.

"How long have you been a believer, Mr. Sanders?" she asked, surprising herself.

The question didn't seem to take Mr. Sanders aback, however. "I have been for a few years. Wasn't always, but the way I look at it, you've got to start somewhere. God, He doesn't stick a stopwatch on you, then change His mind when He thinks He's waited long enough." Mr. Sanders shrugged. "Leastwise that's my opinion on the matter."

"I think that's an interesting opinion. A good one," she added with haste. "I suppose we—"

Maisie let out an awful squeal. Anna turned in time to see the horse jerk backward and wrestle herself free of the wagon. In an instant she had broken into a gallop and headed at an angle away from them.

"Maisie!" Anna called, but the stubborn horse ignored her. "Maisie, come back here!" Maisie swished her tail and picked up her pace.

Mr. Sanders yanked on the reins and urged the mules off the road in the direction of Maisie's dust trail.

"You'll never catch her," Anna said. "She's impossible!"

He pulled back on the reins and watched the mare disappear. "She got a favorite watering hole?"

"Remember that place due southeast of here where you took a nap behind a log?"

The Pinkerton gave her a look. "You serious?"

"I am," she said.

He nodded and urged the reluctant animals forward once again. Without the smooth trail beneath them, the mules' pace was even slower. At times, Anna thought she might have to get out and push.

Finally she saw the stand of trees that marked the spring. "Over there," Anna said as Mr. Sanders urged the mules over yet another rocky patch of ground. She noticed the bouncing caused him to wince more than once.

"Where I shot you," she said, "it still pains you, doesn't it?"

"I'm fine," was his clipped response. He winced again.

"I'm sorry Maisie's such trouble."

"As much my fault as any," he said with a shrug. "I'm the one who did the tying."

She sighed. "Yes, but I'm the one who spoiled her rotten. Now Maisie thinks she can have anything she wants. She's like a willful child."

"Or a woman."

"I beg your pardon," she said with more than a little outrage. "What a thing to say."

His reaction was fast, his grin broad. For the first time, she noticed he had the loveliest dimples. "Come on now, Miss Finch," he said in a slow drawl that marked him for a southern man. "I'm trying to lighten the mood. Surely some man's spoiled you at some point."

My father, she thought. "Watch where you're going," she said.

Mr. Sanders gave her a long look before returning his attention to the ornery mules. "Well, in my opinion, you're definitely the kind of woman who ought to be spoiled." He yanked on the reins and looked at her. "And regularly."

"Oh my," she said under her breath.

He went back to the difficult task of convincing a pair of city mules that prairie grass was perfectly fine to trudge through. It worked until they reached a rutted path where neither animal seemed inclined to tread. The mule on the right stopped short, and the mule on the left stopped a half pace later.

"Get on," Mr. Sanders said. "Come on, mule."

Evidently neither spoke English, for they merely stood in place and stared straight ahead. Meanwhile, the spring was so close Anna could see the stand of trees swaying in what was suddenly quite a breeze. She glanced back at her companion.

"The wind's kicking up," he said, "which means we need to get this contraption off the prairie." He thrust the reins toward her. "Take hold of these and don't let go. I'm going to see if I can't convince these two which of us is boss."

Anna did as he instructed and held tight to the reins, but the mules ignored any attempt at coercion. Finally, Mr. Sanders threw his hat down and stormed away, taking long strides and no doubt biting his tongue in an effort to control his anger.

This sparked an interest in the mule on the right, who inched forward to sniff at the Stetson. The corresponding motion caused the wagon to roll forward.

"Mr. Sanders," Anna called.

He ceased his pacing and turned to look her direction. "What?"

"We've moved," she said.

"Now is not the time to joke."

"It isn't a joke," she said. "If you'll just come and fetch your hat, I'll demonstrate."

Retracing his steps, Mr. Sanders reached for his Stetson. "Now what?"

She gestured to a spot a few yards ahead, keeping her fingers firmly wrapped around the reins. "Throw it that way."

His skeptical look irritated her.

"If you'd like, I can do it, though you'll have to sit in the wagon." She adjusted her own hat, which had come loose in the breeze. "Either is fine by me, but I'd prefer not to argue about it."

After another long look, he gave the hat a toss. Both mules lurched forward. Before they could reach the hat, Mr. Sanders snatched it up and stuck it on his head. "Well, I'll be," he said.

"I told you."

Her long-legged companion easily climbed back into the wagon. She offered him the reins. "No, you go right on ahead," he said as he kicked back against the seat. "See if you can do anything with them."

"Get going, mules," she said. To her surprise, the mules complied. The wagon moved at a decent pace. "Good girls."

Mr. Sanders propped his boots on the buckboard and grinned, then crossed his arms over his midsection. His dimples really were quite nice.

"You've got a way with mules," he said.

"I find they're a lot like men." She noticed a suspicious-looking cloud in the westernmost edge of the sky.

He spared her a lazy glance. "Is that so?"

"It is." The animals in question halted again. "Your hat, please," she said.

Mr. Sanders shook his head. "I'll do it." He jumped to the ground and stood in front of the mules. "Tell me, how can you compare these ornery souls to men?"

She laughed in spite of herself. "You see what you're doing?"

He shrugged. "I'm showing them my hat."

"Waving something interesting in front of them to get their attention," she corrected.

"I suppose I am." He waved the hat and walked a few paces, but the mules refused to follow. "So what do you make of this, oh philosopher? I'm trying to give them what they want, but they won't take the bait." As if to prove his point, Mr. Sanders held out his hat and danced a jig in front of the mules. While they seemed completely unaffected, Anna nearly fell off the wagon laughing. A stronger reaction than she'd expected of herself.

"You can't just give a man—I mean, a mule—what he wants," she said. "That's far too simple. Throw the hat and let's get on with it."

He did, and the mules followed just as they had before. This time, Mr. Sanders had to jump on the wagon as it rolled past.

Landing askew, his knee brushed hers as he righted himself. "That was interesting," he said, "but you've not yet proven your point. If you have to get a man's attention by showing him what he wants but you can't just give it to him, then how does that all work?"

The wagon lurched over the edge of a dry creek bed. Mr. Sanders caught her before she slid to the floor.

"Watch out," he said. "When these mules are motivated, they don't see anything but moving forward. Give them a reason and they'll go every time."

"And that, Mr. Sanders," she said as she returned to her proper spot, "is exactly what I've been telling you." She paused for effect, eying their destination just ahead. "Just like a man."

"Is that so?" He leaned close. "Tell me, Miss Finch—that horse of yours. She's a mare, right?" He moved another notch closer. "A *female*."

"Well, yes, but…" Anna found his eyes, and the witty response she'd planned evaporated into a cloud of confused sensation.

"Thus, it was a woman who got us into this." He stood, bracing his boot on the buckboard. "And a man who will get us out."

Then Maisie bolted toward them, spooking the mules. The wagon shot forward, sending her protector tumbling backward into the bed of the wagon. They hurtled toward the creek.

As Anna dove for the reins while trying not to land under the wheels, she had the vague thought that she had once written a similar scene with Mae Winslow in the starring role.

And as she recalled, it hadn't ended well.

19

He was considered a handsome man. He was a
gentleman in manners to the ladies and everyone.
Being quiet, he never hunted for trouble.
—*Mary Cummings, a.k.a. "Big Nose" Kate, regarding Doc Holliday*

Jeb landed between the mail sack and the saddlebags. It took him a
moment to be certain he hadn't hurt something permanently, other
than his pride, which was deeply dented.

He tried to regain his feet, but the wagon bounced over a rock,
sending him back to bed of the wagon. He heard Miss Finch holler
something at the mules, followed by a lot of splashing, and then the
wagon lurched to a stop.

Miss Finch half climbed, half fell over the wagon seat and into
the bed. "Mr. Sanders. Get up." She yanked on his collar, and he
lifted up on his elbows.

"Where did the horse go?" he managed despite Anna Finch paw-
ing at him. Then he realized the wagon stood in the stream, not at its
edge. "Wait. Forget the horse. We've got to get out of the wagon."

Anna Finch stared at him as if she wanted to swat him. "Get out
of the wagon? Are you insane? Look at that current."

Far from the quiet tributary, the stream rushed past the wagon
and poured over boulders that had been far from the water a few

weeks earlier. The mules had plowed into the middle of the riverbed and stood up to their haunches in water.

Nothing about this looked good except her, and he couldn't give Anna Finch any more attention than he already was or they'd both drown.

Water lapped over the side of the wagon. Worse, as Jeb climbed to his knees, he noticed the dark cloud on the horizon was now fast bearing down on them.

He needed to free the mules. He wasn't sure how, but he'd been in worse scrapes. He'd figure it out.

The bank was a stone's throw away—or, in this case, a saddlebag's throw. As the bag flew toward the bank, he heard Miss Finch shout, "No!"

She dove into the back of the wagon and hauled him down with her. He landed too close for comfort but didn't dare scoot away. Not with her still clutching his wrist. An inch of water sloshed around them.

"What are we doing?" he asked.

A gunshot punctuated his sentence. He scrambled for his pistol.

"Mr. Sanders," his companion said.

"Not now." Jeb yanked his Colt out of its holster and raised his head just enough to look around. He turned to face her, his nose nearly brushing hers.

"No one's shooting at us," she said. "Remember the gun I keep in my saddlebag?"

"Intimately." Scanning the perimeter, Jeb turned to look behind him. The only trouble he saw was the mules quickly losing ground in the rushing water. "I suppose that's it. But now we've got a bigger problem."

A cracking sound split the air as a wheel broke and the wagon tilted, nearly spilling them both into the icy water.

"Hold on to me!" he shouted. Another wheel broke with a crack, and the wagon began floating downstream, dragging the mules with it.

He pulled Miss Finch toward him, and she tangled her arms around his waist. "Are we going to die?" she asked, staring up at him. "Because I'm not ready to die. I know I love Jesus, and someday when I do die, I'll see Him face to face and I know that's going to be the most wonderful thing ever, but today, right now, I just cannot imagine—"

Jeb pressed his finger across her lips as he struggled to hold on to the wagon. "Stop," he said, "or you'll panic and drown both of us." He paused. "Do you understand?"

She nodded, so he lifted his finger. "I don't want to drown us, I really don't. I wish I had learned to swim, but my father insisted that ladies should never—"

The only way he could stop her incessant talking was to kiss her. So he did.

He might have enjoyed it had the wagon not hit something and bounced, throwing them both to the side. Jeb braced one boot against the opposite side of the wagon bed and looked down at Miss Finch, who stared dazedly past his shoulder.

"Look at me," he demanded. When she didn't immediately comply, he placed his palm on her jaw and gently turned her face his direction. "We are not going to die. Do you understand?"

When she nodded, he took a deep breath and let it out slowly. The water in the wagon bed was getting deeper.

"Now," he said slowly, making sure to capture and hold her attention, "I want you to promise you will neither speak nor move."

"If I do, will you kiss me again?"

He almost laughed at the naive tone to her soft voice. "Would that be a punishment worse than death or an incentive to misbehave?"

Eyes fringed with thick lashes regarded him a moment. "Yes," she said.

"Yes?" This time he did chuckle despite the gravity of the situation. "Which one is it?"

She barely blinked as she said, "Both."

♋

Anna's heart lurched as something banged against the underside of the wagon. Until recently she had never in all her life been this close to a man.

Never.

A man who had kissed her.

She caught her breath with great effort, and her ability to speak abandoned her. The temptation to rest her forehead on the broad shoulder that blocked her view was bested only by her need to stop thinking about the situation.

And about the kiss.

By degrees, she became aware that he too seemed unable to do more than stare. Or perhaps he was merely amused by her.

Again she thought of Mae Winslow, the fearless woman who made both man and beast bend to her will. A woman more opposite to herself had never existed. Or rather, been created. Would Mae Winslow have been so incapacitated by a mere brushing of lips? Anna took a second look at the object of her thoughts. If Anna had written a hero who looked like this one and kissed as he did, even Mae would have felt a bit fluttery inside.

At another jarring hit to the wagon, she realized the fluttery feeling was more than stupidity. What in the world was a woman who might lose her life to this raging river doing mooning over the man who'd brought her nothing but aggravation and irritation?

On the second attempt, Anna found her voice. "Mr. Sanders? Release me."

The Pinkerton made the slightest nod in her direction, and yet his arm continued to hold her against him. "I can't be distracted by you while I see to the situation."

"I think it's too late to discuss distraction," she whispered even as she realized that statement was somewhat flattering.

He craned his neck to examine something over the side of the wagon, and she took advantage of his lack of attention to sit up and scoot away. Unfortunately, the movement tipped the wagon and sent him hurtling toward her. She attempted to stop him with her outstretched arms, but he rolled right into them.

Again they lay nose to nose. The temptation rose to experience just once more what it was like to be kissed and kissed well. Before she could say a word to induce such an event, Mr. Sanders wrestled her to the back of the wagon and held her prone beside him.

⚬⚬

Had he time to feel like a fool, Jeb might have indulged himself. Instead, he had more pressing problems. "Is there a gun in your mail sack too?" he asked.

When she shook her head, he tossed it toward the bank. It landed safely in the grass, and he turned his attention to Anna.

"You're not going to throw me, are you?" she asked.

"Hadn't considered it until now." When she opened her mouth to respond, he shook his head. "Don't move." He leaned toward the edge of the wagon. "And hang on to anything that floats."

"Where are you going?" Miss Finch's eyes widened. "Don't leave me back here."

"I've got to release the mules. If they stay yoked to the wagon, they'll drown."

Her nod was slow, her face pale.

"Do *not* move," he repeated, satisfied she would remain in place, then made his way to the front of the wagon.

He climbed over the buckboard and, despite the water, managed to manipulate the yoke and release the pair. As soon as they were free, the mules scrambled toward the bank.

Without the animals to weigh it down, the wagon picked up speed. While staying put until the makeshift vessel hit dry ground was tempting, the fact that Anna could not swim meant he needed to get her out of the water sooner rather than later.

They came to a sudden stop, and Jeb once again found himself face down in the wagon, this time up front where he'd been sitting a few short minutes ago. He could feel the wagon moving beneath him as the wind blew over his back. At least one of the wheels still remained in place, for it felt as though they spun in a circle.

Jeb rolled onto his back, and the wagon broke free. The last of the wheels was gone.

Not that anything else of this wagon could be salvaged. He didn't relish the walk back to Denver or the explanation that would be required on his expense report.

A glance at Anna Finch told Jeb that while she held tight to her assigned spot, she did not appear to have much left in the way of patience. Her eyes darted from one bank to the other, and when the wagon slammed against some sort of underwater obstacle, she looked as if she might bolt and try her hand at swimming.

Spotting a rocky outcropping nearby, he climbed to the back of the wagon and gauged the distance between where he stood and where he wanted to be. The bank was near enough to jump if he had only himself to be concerned with.

The wagon hit another rock, and he lost his footing. It was time to act.

He crawled toward Anna. "Hold on to me," he said as he wrapped his arm around her waist. "And no matter what, *do not* let go."

She nodded and buried her face in his chest.

Tightening his grip, Jeb plunged into the icy water. The shock of the temperature stole his breath, but the woman attached to his side kept him moving.

By the time his feet hit something hard, he was breathing again. Rock turned to sand or perhaps mud, which gave way under his weight. Jeb backtracked and pressed Anna closer to him as the water boiled around them.

The bank here was rocky and nearly impassable, so Jeb looked farther downstream to find a spot where he'd have more luck climbing out. Moving that direction was as simple as curling up his legs and allowing the current to carry them.

Then his boots caught in Anna's hem. The resulting tangle gave them both a good dunking, and in the process, Anna slipped from his grip.

He lunged after her as she slid downstream, reaching for her foot. He caught her shoe, which only slowed her down slightly before it came off, and she floated out of reach.

A boulder of decent girth loomed in her path. Jeb shouted a warning, causing her to turn around. He reached for her outstretched hands but missed. She hit the boulder hard and stopped, and from her expression and the sound she made upon impact, she'd likely have a headache.

A second later, Jeb slammed against her, pinning her between him and the rock.

He ended up nose to nose with her, and for a moment, the breath went out of him for reasons that had nothing to do with the coldness of the water or the force of his impact. With one hand, he braced himself against the rock while with the other he lifted the curtain of hair covering her face.

"You all right?" he managed as he fought to keep a respectable distance between them. The water wouldn't allow it, however, and Jeb ended up too close for comfort with the woman he was paid to protect. "Looks like you've landed between a rock and a hero."

"Funny," she said, though she clearly thought it anything but. "And I'll have the bump on my head to show for it."

Despite her ability to respond, Jeb knew he had to get her out of the water, and fast. "Can you hold on tight one more time? Here." He gently pried her hands off the rock and put them around his neck.

"This is exactly like *The Tale of the Terrible Tide*, only in that story it was the ocean and she fell in when the ship hit the rocks, but it was still wet. And had rushing water. And a handsome hero." Wide eyes met his. "Don't let go," she said. "No matter what, do not let me go."

A handsome hero? Jeb managed a grin. "I was about to tell *you* that. Now here we go."

"Wait!"

He froze. "What?"

Those eyes, wide as they could be, locked on to his. "Just once more. In case we drown…"

"What?" he demanded. Something hard slammed against his shoulders, and a piece of the wagon bobbed past.

When he turned back to her, Anna wrapped her arms around his neck and kissed him. Or made a valiant effort at it. Her lips landed just north of their intended spot and brushed his skin before she bounced backward and slammed against the boulder again. Jeb blinked.

"We could die," she seemed to offer as an excuse.

Realizing what she wanted, Jeb felt a surge of emotion he hadn't experienced in years. "Then I'll not have it on my conscience that you went to your reward with a deed left undone."

He fitted his lips over hers and forced himself to slowly and thoroughly kiss the woman who'd shot him even though everything in him told Jeb to get her out of the water.

Finally the need to escape won out, and he ended the kiss. "I'm going to get us out of here now," he said. "All you need to do is hold on tight. Can you do that?"

The word "yes" was a soft whisper against his neck that he couldn't afford to think on more than a second.

"I'll get us out of here, then. Long as you don't have any more hidden weapons."

20

There is scarcely one in the country who had
acquired a greater notoriety than Doc Holliday,
who enjoyed the reputation of being one of the
most fearless men on the frontier...

—*Eulogy of Doc Holliday,*
Leadville Carbonate Chronicle, November 14, 1887

"Weapons?" Anna's fingers tangled in Jeb's shirt, her other arm
wrapped around his waist. The water was cold. So very cold.

"I'm teasing," the Pinkerton said, his breath warm against her
neck. "Now, much as I'm enjoying this conversation, we've both got
to get out of this water."

"Mr. Sanders," she said as she clutched him tighter. "You kissed
me."

Her words hung in the air as the water swirled around them. The
Pinkerton appeared to be considering a response. "Miss Finch," he
finally said, "I'm afraid you're getting hypothermia. I kissed you
because you asked me to."

"That would explain it," she said.

"Would it?" He shook his head. "I'm glad you've got an explanation, because I certainly don't." He gathered her closer and studied

something on the bank. "Now, why don't you keep your talking to a minimum and follow my instructions instead?"

When she did not respond, the Pinkerton leaned down to brush her lips with his one more time. "Miss Finch, you'll not catch me doing this again, but if kissing you gets us out of this river, I'll suffer through it."

"If you insist." She leaned against him. "Perhaps having a Pinkerton in my father's employ isn't so awful after all."

"Now I know I've got to get you warm and dry. You're talking foolishness."

He started to move away, and Anna caught him. "Mr. Sanders, I'm in full possession of my faculties. I realize we're in quite a jam." Water splashed over his shoulder and hit her full in the face, causing Anna to gasp. When she recovered, the Pinkerton was holding her close.

"You were saying?"

"I was saying that I can barely feel my arms and legs. The water's rushing by at a dangerous speed. I'm not unaware of the danger." She bit her lip to keep it from trembling. "But your kisses, well…" Dare she continue?

"Miss Finch, I really must get you out of here before—"

She bobbed up on the next rush of water to capture his lips once again. "There," she said as warmth flooded her, "I won't freeze before we reach the bank now."

He lifted a dark brow. "Let me get this straight. You were using my kisses to keep warm?"

Anna nodded. The truth, in a way, but she'd not admit to anything more. How could she tell him that while she'd been kissed, she'd never been well and truly kissed by a man with his abilities?

"In that case," he said slowly, "we'd best get your temperature up before we take that swim."

And with that, he leaned down to kiss her. This time slowly. Heedless of the icy waters tangling her skirts and rendering her unable to move, Anna kissed him back, fully aware that once they were back on dry land, she'd be held to a higher standard of propriety.

"Miss Finch," he said, pulling away. "Now I believe we've both got something we'd prefer your father not hear about."

        ⌒⌒

Jeb pushed away from the rock. For a minute, maybe two, Jeb allowed the current to drag them along until they reached the spot where it looked the most favorable for escape. Jeb maneuvered himself between Anna and the bank, then lunged backward. If anyone ended up with a headache this time, it would be him.

In a matter of seconds, he was out of the stream and on the bank, though he still felt water against his skin. It was raining.

Anna was still tangled in his arms, and it took a moment to convince her to loosen her grip on his shoulders. She fell back on the grass.

"Anna?" Her gaze focused on him. "Nod if you're not harmed." She continued to stare, so Jeb grabbed her by the shoulders and lifted her into a sitting position. "Are you hurt?"

"No, I'm..." She barely blinked. "I'm fine. I think." Miss Finch lifted her hand to point. "But your hat...go get it."

"My what?" He looked the direction she pointed and spied his Stetson lodged in the brush a few feet away. It was an easy grab, but any minute it would likely be lost downstream.

"I can get another hat." When she protested, he shook his head. "All right, then. Don't move. No matter what, *do not move.* Promise me."

"Promise," she said as she swiped at the raindrops pelting her face. "Do be safe, please."

Jeb snagged his hat on the second try and stuffed it atop his head. Not the best-looking sight, he was certain, but at least his favorite hat was still his.

With a grin meant to keep her seated, Jeb made his way back to her. For a rich girl, she was handling the situation quite well.

He saw her lower lip tremble and looked up at the sky. "Not exactly walking weather," he said as casually as he could manage. "Why don't we get out of this before things get any worse?"

"The weather or the situation?" Anna said with a half-hearted chuckle.

"I do love a woman with a sense of humor." He grabbed her hand and pulled her to her feet. "I'm thinking if we head downstream we might have better luck."

She gestured upstream as thunder rumbled in the distance. "I have a favorite spot. It's small, but we might be able to stay out of the rain." Her voice was weaker than he expected. "That way."

"It's not a log, is it?"

"Stop teasing," she said.

Lightning zagged across the sky. "If I needed a sign, I'd say that's it." She wobbled backward, and Jeb tugged on her wrist. "But I don't think I'm going to let you walk."

He swept her off her feet.

While the feisty gal had nearly had the fight drowned out of her already—or kissed out of her—she still gave him trouble as he attempted to hold her against him and climb the muddy riverbank. Finally, he stopped.

"Miss Finch," he said as the rain pelted them, "I'm either going to carry you to safety or throw you back in the river. Which will it be?" He could see the indecision on her face, but all the fight went out of her. "All right, then. Be still and just maybe we'll get there. Now show me again where we're going."

"There," she said pointing to a spot up ahead. "See the rock that juts out?"

Up ahead, grass carpeted a spot under a rocky outcropping that looked like it might offer shelter from the storm. He moved toward it as the raindrops spattered around them.

When he set his delicate cargo on her feet, she slid inside a large cleft in the rocks and curled into the farthest corner of the makeshift shelter. It fit her perfectly.

"Looks like you've done that a few times," he said. "All you need now is a good book and a light to read by."

It was a poor attempt to take her attention off their circumstances, but it appeared to work, at least for a second. As Miss Finch ran her hand through soggy hair, the corners of her lips turned up in the beginnings of a smile.

And all he could think of was how well his lips fit over hers and how brazen she'd been to speak of her appreciation. It was a dangerous course of thought and one he knew better than to pursue, especially in the close confines of their refuge.

"Now, that's better," he said. "I was afraid your smile was drowned with your hat."

She affected what he hoped was only a teasing frown. "If my hat looks as poor as yours, then it's better off floating away. At least your mustache is still well stuck."

"Mustache?" He'd completely forgotten about the remainder of his disguise. "That must be why my kisses were so effective in warming you."

When she blushed, Jeb decided he'd gone too far. Removing the Stetson, he shook off the water. Miss Finch squealed as the dampness spattered her, though it did nothing that the rain and the river hadn't already done.

"You wound me," he said in his best imitation of the British upper crust. "A man's hat is a treasure to be revered and not to be cast aside."

"Are you a married man, Mr. Sanders?"

The question took him by surprise. "Would I kiss you if I were?" he snapped. Realizing the look on her face was not one of humor but of horror, he hurried to right the wrong. "Do you think my unmarried state might have something to do with my hat?"

There was a moment when she seemed unsure whether he was serious. Then, as he allowed the slightest beginnings of a grin, she did too.

"I do think that might be the cause." She seemed to be struggling not to laugh.

"Then," he said as he replaced the hat on his head and worried with it until he'd found just the right fit, "if I must choose between my Stetson and a bride, I'll remain happily without."

"Between a Stetson and a Bride, or the Story of a Love Gone Amiss,"

Anna said. "A story I'm not proud of, though it received many compliments. Are you a reader, Mr. Sanders?" She asked it as if it were a natural question under their less than natural circumstances.

It took a minute for his addled brain to catch up to the question. "On occasion," he said slowly. "Though I'll admit I've not read any of your—"

Lightning flashed too close for comfort, and Miss Finch screamed and lunged for his arms. He held her against him, her damp hair spilling across his shoulder and her face buried in his shirt.

He wasn't sure whether the true danger was outside with the weather or inside with Anna Finch.

"So," he said with what he hoped was a calm voice, "this isn't what I had in mind when I trailed you to Garrison this morning."

"Yes," she said slowly, her face still resting against his shoulder and her hands holding fistfuls of his shirt. "Certainly not how I thought I would be spending the day."

He waited for the tears. In Jeb's experience, there were always tears where women and unexpected events collided. Instead, she leaned away to stare past him at, he assumed, the foul weather. He followed her gaze and saw the mules had found them despite the thunder, lightning, and downpour.

"Oh no, you don't." He rose up on his knees to block the fool animal as one of the mules attempted to share their shelter. "Get your own place to hide out."

The mule kept trying to fit into the small space. As hard as Jeb pushed the critter back, he kept coming. The other one, soggy from his swim, ambled up and stuck his muzzle in as well.

From behind him, Jeb heard Miss Finch begin to giggle. At least this battle would have one winner, though it would be neither him nor the animal.

"You find this funny, do you?" he asked. "Why don't we trade places?"

He pretended to dart in her direction, and she squealed. When he rocked back on his heels, Jeb felt something bump his head.

And then his hat was gone.

"Hey, you." Jeb whirled around and reached for his hat, but the mule wouldn't let go. He realized he could either fight for his hat or get rid of the mule.

With a jerk of his hand he yanked the Stetson from the mule's mouth and tossed it outside. He watched the terrible twosome make a game of dividing the spoils. He might have given chase had a bolt of lightning not shattered the topmost section of a tree not thirty yards away.

As the rain quickly squelched the fire, Jeb dove back inside the tiny hideaway.

"Everything's all right." He swiveled to look at Anna. "And there's good news."

That seemed to get her attention. "Oh?"

Jeb settled back and got comfortable. "Yep. Those mules have taken my hat, which means I just might stand a chance of getting married someday."

Only then did he get what he'd expected earlier: a woman's tears.

21

That Doc Holliday had his faults none will
attempt to deny; but who among us has not, and
who shall be the judge of these things?
— *Glenwood Springs Ute Chief, November 12, 1887*

Anna felt like an idiot, crying now that she was safe. But the little
space was damp and smelled of earth and whatever animal had last
slept in it. Mud splotched her clothing, and one of her gloves was
gone. The other had torn and was completely useless. She peeled it
off and let what remained of it fall as the thunder rolled around them.
The back of her head throbbed, and when she checked, she found the
beginnings of a nasty bump.

And amongst all of this she'd had her second kiss in as many
days, and then her third. After that, she'd stopped counting.

To his credit, Mr. Sanders kept to his side of the space. Had he
attempted to console her, she might have allowed it, and that would
have been most improper.

Improper.

Anna began to chuckle. She certainly hadn't considered what was
proper when she behaved so horribly in the water.

"It's not funny," she said as she swiped at the last of her tears. "It
really isn't at all." Outside the little cave, one of the mules brayed

while the other chewed on the battered Stetson. "And your hat is ruined."

He shrugged. "Wagon's not in such good shape either."

"I'm terribly sorry about that. Please let me buy you another." He had the audacity to laugh. "What?" She swiped away the horrid tears. "Do you find my offer humorous?"

Mr. Sanders held up his palms. "No," he managed through his chuckles. "Not at all. I find it..."

"What?"

"I find it unnecessary." He shrugged. "Looks like we'll be in here awhile."

"Yes, it does." She sighed and leaned back against the damp grass while outside the mules moved on. The rain, however, did not.

"Puts me in mind of something I meant to ask before your horse caused all this commotion."

"About that," she said, wincing. "I'm very sorry. If it makes you feel any better, I haven't had much interest in riding her since our unfortunate first meeting, which, of course, I am also sorry about."

Mr. Sanders turned and shook his head. "Enough apologizing. Tell me about Doc Holliday. I know you have corresponded with him."

The breath went out of her. "How did you know?" she finally managed to inquire.

One of his shoulders lifted slightly. "I'm good at what I do, Miss Finch."

"I noticed." Anna shifted position to stretch out her legs and saw she wore only one shoe.

"And I noticed you haven't answered." He inched slightly closer, enough to cause his leg to touch hers. "So I will ask again. How is it you know Doc Holliday?"

"The rain seems to be letting up," she said, though nothing could be further from the truth.

He leaned toward her and pressed his palm against her cheek. His touch was gentle, his fingers calloused, and until she felt its warmth, she hadn't realized how chilled she was. Slowly he forced her to look at him. It was, under the circumstances, not an altogether unpleasant experience.

"You can trust me."

"No." Anna scooted out of his reach. "I think not. Though I don't mind answering your question." She paused to let her racing mind catch up to her words. "Mr. Sanders," she said carefully, "I'll admit I took delivery of a bag of mail. I also admit if there is a letter in that bag from Doc Holliday, I will be thrilled but also very surprised."

He lifted a dark brow. "So you admit you know him?"

Her temper rose. "No. As I said, I hope he's written to me." Anna narrowed her eyes. "You seem particularly interested in him. Has he wronged you in some way?"

That brought a reaction she hadn't expected. For a moment, she thought Mr. Sanders might answer in the affirmative. Then he looked away. "Miss Finch, it appears we are at the end of our discussion on this topic." He paused. "For now, at least."

"Mr. Sanders," she said, "don't you think under the circumstances you ought to call me Anna?"

As Mr. Sanders began to chuckle, a crash of thunder made Anna jump.

"You scared of bad weather?" he asked. "Because it's nothing to be ashamed off, though you're safe right where you are."

The rain came down so hard that it obscured everything beyond their little hideaway. Anna flinched as lightning slashed through the curtain of gray. "As many times as I've imagined it, I've never actually seen it from this perspective." She paused. "It's much different. Louder."

"I suppose."

"And there's a smell. A scent, actually. Earthy."

He gave her an appraising look. "I suppose," he said slowly. "I've never thought about how rain smelled or sounded."

Anna shifted positions, trying to find a spot where the rocks didn't cause her discomfort. She half hoped the Pinkerton would offer her a shoulder to lean on, but he didn't. "Does the rain make you sleepy? I'm exhausted."

"Sometimes." He began a story that had something to do with rain, and she tried to pay attention. Unfortunately, her eyelids refused to cooperate.

When she opened them again, the sun shone across her face, and Anna was alone.

Stretching as best she could, she gathered her wits and followed the sunshine out to the riverbank. She found Jeb Sanders hunched over something he held in his lap.

"Is that my mailbag?"

He jumped as if caught with his hand in the cookie jar. Then, slowly, he turned his attention to her. "Had to walk more than a quarter mile before I found it. I was checking to see if anything inside was salvageable." He handed the soggy bag to her. "It's not."

"I see." Indeed, the letters inside seemed to be a total loss. Any ink on the sodden pages was long washed away by the rain. She could only hope those who'd corresponded with her might try again.

Stretching out the soreness born from too much time in too cramped a space, she stepped past the mail to find her saddlebag, now with a single bullet hole decorating one side. This she would bring home. The mail sack, probably not.

At least not today, though perhaps she might return for it tomorrow when she no longer had company.

"It's a long walk back to Denver," Mr. Sanders said as he stood and moved toward the still-raging stream. He studied the remains of the wagon littering the bank.

"I don't suppose you could build a raft out of those pieces so we could float," she tossed over her shoulder as she climbed the bank and looked out over the prairie. There, grazing happily in the grass, was Maisie, the traitor that created this mess.

"Mr. Sanders," she called. "I think I've a solution to our problem. Or at least to mine."

"Oh no, you don't," he said as he caught up to her. "We're in this together."

When Maisie spied Anna, her ears perked up. The ornery horse nickered, then pawed at the muddy prairie before breaking into a trot. Anna called to the mare, and she came almost close enough to catch.

Almost but not quite. Apparently the mare had enjoyed her rain-soaked adventure much more than Anna and was ready to make merry at her expense. "Stupid horse," Anna muttered as she began walking toward Denver, ignoring the animal altogether.

"I agree you've not chosen the most trustworthy animal." Mr. Sanders fell into stride beside her. "And yet look over there."

Up ahead the mules waited. Anna laughed. "I never expected they'd be anywhere nearby."

He shrugged. "Guess they were too busy eating my hat to notice the weather and run from it. Though where would they run?"

"True," she said. "I wonder if they'll let us ride them." She looked up at Mr. Sanders. "Have you only used them to pull the wagon?"

He hesitated. "Well, yes. But I can't see why they wouldn't oblige."

Mr. Sanders inched toward the mules as if they were a pair of skittish horses. He got almost within reach before the pair of them bolted in different directions.

"Why didn't you move that fast when you were hitched to the wagon?" he shouted after them. He swiped at the mud on his trousers. "Miss Anna, how do you feel about a nice walk on a sunny afternoon?"

With a sigh, she turned toward Denver, which loomed in the distance. She couldn't just wait for some hero to save her. It was time to call on her years of writing Mae Winslow's story to find the courage to keep walking. If Mae, fictional as she was, could emerge from every disaster unscathed, then so could she. Anna squared her shoulders and turned her back on the river and Jeb Sanders.

"Hold up, there."

Anna ignored the man and picked up her pace. She'd only walked a few feet before she felt the saddlebag slip from her shoulder.

"I might not be able to control two mules, a mare, and a wagon, but I'm man enough to haul your bags for you."

He shrugged the saddlebag onto his shoulder, then swiped at his brow. Only then did she notice he also carried the mail sack. "In case something's readable," he said as he met her stare. "You never know. There might be something in there that the rain didn't ruin."

"I suppose."

Overhead the sun's brilliance matched the rainstorm's intensity. And on the horizon, the shimmering city of Denver seemed no closer, though she felt they'd been walking at least an hour. Other than occasional patches of mud to avoid, there was little to keep Anna's mind occupied.

"Mr. Sanders, I have a question."

He looked down at her and seemed slightly amused. "Fire away."

"Don't tempt me," she said, then regretted the poor choice of words. "It's about Doc Holliday. What if I told you I think there is more than one person claiming to be him?" She studied the lawman as he considered the question. "As you've said, you're good at what you do."

"I am."

She chose her words carefully. "Then you must consider the evidence I can present."

He met her stare. "Fair enough."

She shook her head. "You'll give me no argument on this? That's a first."

"I'm considering it." He toyed with the silly mustache. "Care to kiss me again before I take this off?"

Anna felt the heat rise in her face. "Mr. Sanders," she said, "I'll thank you not to mention my moment of foolishness again."

"Don't suppose I need this anymore, then." The mustache came off on the second tug. "Should you change your mind, I know where to find another on short notice."

"I assure you, Mr. Sanders," Anna said as she watched him toss the mustache over his shoulder, "I will not change my mind."

And yet with each step she took, Anna knew that forgetting his kisses would be as difficult as not changing her mind.

ఴ

Perhaps it was their indifference to the mare, or maybe it was the smell of the carrot in Anna's saddlebag, but just about the time Jeb decided they'd be walking until bedtime, Maisie loped past, then circled around to stop in front of Anna.

"Mr. Sanders," Anna said, "it appears our ride has arrived."

"Indeed it does, Miss Finch." He gestured to the horse. "Shall I catch the reins, or will that be your job?"

"I'll do it. Likely she won't let you."

Obviously Anna Finch had no idea she stood in the presence of a Texas man raised to court the affection of horses well before he learned to draw the attention of ladies. "Stand back and watch how it's done, darlin'."

"Darlin'?" She shook her head, though her amusement seemed to be tempered with something else.

"Don't worry," he said. "I won't hurt her."

"It's not her I'm worried about."

Jeb set his cargo aside and held the carrot in his palm but avoided looking directly at the mare. "I appreciate the sentiment," he said to Anna, "but I'll be—"

A searing pain halted his words. The mare had stolen the carrot and left on his hand to show for it a mark the size of her teeth.

Her mistake, however, was pausing to enjoy her treat. In that instant, Jeb snatched the reins and climbed into the saddle. She only bucked twice before settling down and continuing to chew on the carrot.

"And that," Jeb said as he took the saddlebag from Anna's outstretched hand, "is how a man tames a horse. Now hand me that mail sack so I can situate it, then I'll see if I can fit you up here too."

For a moment, Jeb knew the city girl considered he might leave her stranded in the prairie. To reassure her, he worked fast to attach the bags, then reached down to grasp her outstretched hand. As his fingers encircled her wrist, he realize she'd only fit in front of him. Where he'd have to look at her the whole ride back to Denver.

"Wait," he said, releasing her. "Let me see if we can't do better by moving these bags."

He tried. And he failed. And he realized Anna Finch would be riding sidesaddle in his arms. A glance at the horizon told him they had a much longer distance ahead of them than he'd like.

"Let's get this over with. Put your foot in the stirrup, and I'll give a good tug on three. One, two—" He hoisted her up without warning, hauling her against him. "Three," he breathed against the top of her head.

"That wasn't funny."

Jeb swallowed hard and held tight to the reins as the horse pranced and complained. "None of this is funny."

For all his faults, Jeb was a gentleman, and this female now tangled up in his shirt with her arms wrapped around him was the person he was sworn to protect.

And he had reason to suspect she could give him what he needed to bring down the great Doc Holliday. To bring Ella's killer to justice.

So he gritted his teeth and ignored the fact that Anna Finch felt like heaven in his arms. That the kisses he'd shared with her made him want another despite all the arguments against it.

Thankfully the mare settled down and pointed her nose toward Denver without any further complaint.

When they reached the bridge spanning the Platte, Jeb pulled back on the reins and aimed the mare for a stand of trees. His companion had slept against his chest for the last couple of miles, and she'd likely be horrified to learn of it.

On the other hand, he'd found an odd peace in riding that way, with a woman in his arms and the sun on his back. It was tricky, balancing a slumbering female and a high-strung horse, but he'd managed it.

Jeb took one last moment to look at her. Then, before he could change his mind, he began the process of waking her up.

"Miss Finch?" he whispered against the top of her head. When she didn't immediately respond, he slid his palm up her back to rest at the nape of her neck. "Miss Finch, you need to wake up now."

Her eyes flew open, and she nearly tumbled to the ground and took him with her. Only his feet in the stirrups kept them atop the mare.

Her sleep had been deep, as witnessed by her moment of confusion followed by a shake of her head. "What? Where..." She shook her head again, sweeping her hand through curls in sore need of taming.

"Are you awake enough to listen?" When she whispered a soft yes, Jeb gave her an appraising look. "I figure if you're seen riding back into Denver in this state, our friend Mr. Mitchell will hear of it before you reach home. I know you keep a Smith & Wesson in that saddlebag. You got any hairpins in there too?"

Anna felt her hair, then looked down at her rumpled dress. Her expression crumpled. "Oh, I'm a fright."

Jeb forced a chuckle. "Darlin', you don't frighten me in the least."

A lie for which he'd have to repent. The way she'd settled into his arms as if she'd been built to go there terrified him no end. Worse even than the kisses had.

He fumbled around in the saddlebag until he found a few hairpins and presented them to her. "I'd offer to help, but I'm not sure what I can do."

Anna took the pins, then promptly dropped half of them. "Oh no," she said, attempting to slip off the horse.

Jeb reached for her hand and covered her palm with his, steadying her on the saddle. "Turn your head that way," he said.

"Why?"

Jeb pretended exasperation. "As I said, I can't send you home like this."

She looked as if she might argue but then did as he asked.

"You'll have to hold the reins."

When he was certain Anna had the reins in her grip, he stuck the hairpins in his pocket and went to work turning her tangles into something resembling a braid. Her hair was soft, curling in places and waving in others, and was the color of soft burnished leather. It took him a minute to remember how, but once he recalled which strand went where, the braid began to take shape. That accomplished, he coiled the braid at the nape of her neck and stuck in the first hairpin. When she didn't flinch, he attempted another. Four pins later and the concoction held.

"There," he said. "Now give me the reins. I'm going to get us a little closer to Denver, then leave you to ride in alone. Can you manage to find home if I do that?"

"Of course I can," she said, regaining some of her spirit.

Jeb grinned over her head.

They made their way out of the trees and across the plains at a slow, steady pace. When Jeb felt they'd come as close to Denver as they could without being seen, he reined in the mare again.

"You're being awfully quiet for a talkative woman," he said. "I think I'll walk the rest of the way from here."

Before she could respond, he thrust the reins into her hand and hit the ground.

Her hand went to the back of her head, and she toyed with the mess Jeb had made of her curls. "Where did you learn how to do that?"

Jeb forced a grin. "Maybe someday I'll tell you. I'll hold on to the mare while you turn around and fit your feet in the stirrups." When she'd accomplished the feat, Jeb shook his head. "Now get on home before I change my mind and decide to ride into Denver with you in that state. Such a scandal we'd be."

She had begun to smile when he slapped the horse's haunches and sent it bolting forward.

22

Of course I couldn't let him murder me,
so I fired.

—*Doc Holliday*

By the time Anna reached the stables, she'd long given up any hope of arriving unseen. That her father and Edwin Beck happened to be leaving as she rode up might have horrified her under other circumstances. Today, however, she rode past as if it were normal for anyone to see Barnaby Finch's daughter in such a state.

When her feet touched the ground, Anna's knees threatened to buckle. Using Maisie to stand firm, she grasped the strings on the mail sack and hauled it over her shoulder. "Would you see to my saddlebag?" she asked the groom. "And be careful of my pistol."

The groom nodded and took Maisie's reins. As the horse trotted away, Anna slumped against the back of the stable and tried to muster the courage to move. What little bluster she'd managed in front of Papa and Edwin Beck had evaporated the moment her feet touched the ground.

"Anna," her father called. "Come here this instant."

So she did. With the mail sack over her shoulder and her hair exactly like her father's hired help had fashioned it. Though she didn't dare look down to see what her still-soggy dress looked like, she recalled as she reached the lawn that she'd lost one of her shoes. Kicking off the other, she held her head high and went to meet her father.

Intending to ask him why he'd wasted his money paying someone to follow her, she changed her mind when she came face to face with Edwin Beck. She'd hoped, if her father was summoning her in this state, that Mr. Beck had left.

"An interesting costume," he said to Anna. "Is this for next week's masquerade ball?"

Before Anna could speak, her father laughed. "Do tell Mr. Beck the joke you're playing on me." He glanced over at Mr. Beck, who waited by the Finches' buggy. "She's quite the prankster, my Anna."

Her father's eyes narrowed, obviously waiting for Anna to continue the farce. "I am, at that." She gave the neighbor's brother her broadest if not most sincere smile. "Quite the prankster. Do you like it?" Before either man could respond, Anna shrugged. "Yes, well, lovely to see you, Mr. Beck."

"And you, Miss Finch," the Englishman said. "You look beautiful as usual."

"Do I?"

"Indeed you do," he responded instantly.

Papa's eyes widened but he said nothing. The smile she gave him was a bit more sincere. "Are you leaving again?"

Her father looked surprised at the question, as did Mr. Beck. "We've a meeting to attend," Edwin Beck said.

"Very important," Papa added. "And possibly lengthy. Do see that your mother's entertained this evening."

"I hardly think…" Anna thought better of the shrewish remark and put back on her smile. "Of course, Papa. Now, if you'll excuse me, I've some letters to dry off."

With her newfound honesty lifting her spirits and propelling her toward the house, Anna turned her back on the two men and limped across the lawn on bare feet that hadn't expected the grass to contain burrs. Pride kept her from either slowing down or removing the thorns. Instead, she kept her pace, her back straight and head held high, until she reached the kitchen.

Two maids and Mr. McMinn greeted her. "Let me take that bag, miss," one of the maids said while Mr. McMinn's gaze traveled the length of her.

"Get caught out in the weather?" he asked.

"I did." She sank onto the nearest chair and inspected her feet for burrs. "I found a place upstream a few miles and hid out until it passed."

Only then did she allow herself to think of just who had been with her. And the kisses they had shared.

Humiliation flooded her as she recalled her behavior, both brazen and impetuous. Jeb Sanders was her father's employee. A Pinkerton paid to follow her. Certainly not a man with whom she should be sharing so much as a familiar moment, much less a kiss.

Or several.

Anna rose, trying to shake off the thought of what she'd done. Unlike Mae Winslow, who'd been more than willing to share the occasional embrace with her man, Anna would not be having any more such adventures.

At least not with Jeb Sanders.

It just would not do.

"If you'll 'scuse me, then," the driver said before tipping his cap and making a quick exit. Anna watched him hasten across the lawn to help her father into the buggy, then she turned and trudged up the stairs to her room.

There she found the maid had already delivered the mail sack. Beyond caring who found her or the evidence of this morning's trip to Garrison, Anna dumped the contents of the sack onto the floor and sat beside the soggy lump of correspondence. The only way to know if anything remained legible in any of the letters was to open each one.

She set to work one at a time, letter after letter. In each envelope she found a page or two, sometimes more than that. Occasionally she could read entire paragraphs or a name in a signature. Often, however, there was nothing left of the words. As she tossed each ruined letter back into the mail sack, her fingers stained from ink, Anna prayed the sender might make another attempt at reaching her. After a while she could tell almost immediately whether a letter might still be readable. The few that survived the rainstorm went into a stack beside her.

The pile on the floor had dwindled to almost nothing by the time a knock sounded at the door. Steeling herself for whichever parent desired to admonish her, Anna was pleasantly surprised to find a maid calling her to dinner.

"I'll take my meal here," she said. "I'm rather involved in this project."

"I'm sorry, Miss Finch, but Mr. Sanders wishes you to join him downstairs."

"Mr. Sanders?" Anna groaned. The last thing she could manage tonight was sitting across the table from the man she'd made a fool of herself with. "Please make my excuses," Anna said. "And if you'd not mind terribly, I would love a plate of whatever smells so wonderful."

When the maid returned, she carried a platter filled with enough food for two. In a move that would have horrified her mother, Anna set the platter on the floor beside her and reached for the next letter on the pile.

It was from J. H. Holliday.

She snatched it open and found the letter began with a note of thanks. "For what?" she asked. The remainder of the letter was completely smudged and unreadable, but Anna held the page up to the light and noticed the return address. "Altwood Springs."

Of course. The sulfur springs were reputed to help those whose lungs were scarred with the consumption.

What to do with the information? With an irritating hired gun following her and that awful Mr. Mitchell taunting her in the *Times*, Anna could hardly get on the train and make a trip to the springs. She could, however, bide her time and look for the right opportunity.

Anna rang for the maid, then waited while the tub was filled. As she sank into the fragrant water, she removed the hairpins holding her braid coiled in place.

Interesting that a man could manage such a thing, she thought as she tossed the pins to the floor. Even more interesting that she could feel so comfortable in his arms that she'd fallen asleep against his shoulder.

She sighed. She owed him another apology, for not only had she ruined his wagon and lost his mules—thanks to Maisie—she'd made him walk back to Denver while she rode home without so much as a backward glance.

A pounding at the door caused Anna to jump. "Who is it?" she called.

"So sorry, Miss Finch," the maid said, "but your father's asking for you to visit with him in his library." When Anna did not immediately answer, the maid pounded again. "So sorry," she repeated, "but I'm to fetch you immediately."

He was home already? So much for his long, important meeting. "That might be a bit difficult. I'm not dressed."

"Then get dressed," her father commanded. He must have been standing behind the maid the entire time. "I don't require formal clothing, Anna. Something simple and quick will suffice."

"Yes, Papa." She rose from the tub and toweled off, trying to shake the feeling of a soon-to-be chastised child on her way to meet her punishment.

Noticing the letter still on her desk, Anna retrieved the envelope and started to stuff the pages inside. Only then did she see what appeared to be a train ticket.

One good shake of the envelope and the slip of paper landed atop the desk. Anna reached for it and unfolded the page to find a note wrapped around the ticket.

"Perhaps I shall begin a tale," Anna read as she set the ticket aside. "And perhaps I shall merely spend a few hours in the company of a lovely woman. Unless you board the train tomorrow, you'll never know which."

She grinned. She giggled. She held the ticket to her chest and laughed out loud. Of course she would be on that train when it left the station the next morning. And thanks to Mr. McMinn, she had a carpetbag with exactly what she needed to make the trip undetected.

How she'd manage to leave without Jeb Sanders following her would require closer planning after she endured whatever lecture her father had planned.

She returned the letter and ticket to the envelope and hid it beneath her mattress. Anna then went to the wardrobe to choose a lilac frock and shoes to match. Papa might say he had no interest in seeing her well dressed, but she knew he would take note of her appearance the moment she stepped into the library.

Anna reached for her hair brush and yanked it through her curls until her scalp ached. In a moment of subtle rebelliousness, she fumbled her way through a braid and then coiled it at the nape of her neck. Holding it in place with one hand, she retrieved the hairpins and did a decent job of imitating the style Jeb Sanders had given her.

Making her way down the back stairs took Anna less time than convincing herself to open the library door. She stood in front of it long enough to find her courage, lifted her hand to knock, then decided against it and walked in unannounced.

Her father's library was an oversized space, as were most in the Finch home. Dark wood and darker carpeting kept the room tomb-like even on a day like today.

Papa grunted as she closed the door behind her. "Over here." He indicated the chair nearest him.

Arranging her skirts properly as she took the seat indicated, Anna met her father's stare without, she hoped, indicating her fear. He seemed busy, but then Papa always did. A check lay in front of him, though he quickly removed it to the drawer. A few notes jotted in a ledger, along with numbers added to the bottom of a lengthy column, and then Papa closed the book and put it too in the drawer.

Finally he seemed ready to speak to her. "I've taken the liberty of repairing the reputation you've cared nothing for."

"I don't understand."

He met her stare above his spectacles. "I think you do, Anna."

Her father pushed back from the desk and leaned against the back of his chair. "I'll allow you to explain your behavior this afternoon before we go any further with this conversation."

Anna swallowed hard. "What would you like to know?"

Papa's palms pressed against the desktop. "I would like to know why a properly raised and educated young woman from good parents would be riding a horse like a heathen in broad daylight."

Because I can't ride like a heathen in the dark, she longed to say. Instead, she remained silent.

"And why you've associated yourself with criminals and outlaws." His dark brows lifted. "Yes, Anna, I know of your luncheon with Mr. Earp. Many people in this town see things and report them to me, so don't look so surprised."

Like Jeb Sanders.

"I'm unsure as to what you're referring, Papa," she said gently.

And in truth, she was. Did he intend to ask about her brief lunch with the outlaw or the subsequent printing of his untold story that had given the man a measure of peace? Or perhaps it was her plea to him to intervene and request his friend Doc Holliday also place his trust in her ability to tell his story.

Surely he did not know of the train ticket beneath her mattress.

He continued to stare at her. "I'll refresh your memory, Anna. The Windsor Hotel. A very public place."

Anna thought for a moment, then began talking with the hopes the Lord would provide the words. "While waiting for Gennie, I did chance upon a lovely couple whose table was unsatisfactory. I offered mine so I might have a better view by the window." She shrugged. "That really is all there was to our supposed meeting. It was quite unplanned, though I found them to be interesting."

"Interesting," he echoed. "Quite." He rubbed his face and sighed. "You've a flair for the dramatic, as witnessed by that display on the lawn in front of Mr. Beck."

Anna tried not to cringe. At least he hadn't seen her riding sidesaddle in Jeb Sanders' arms.

"I'm very sorry to subject you and Mr. Beck to that," she said. And yet a very scandalous part of her dared to think, just for a moment, that at least Mr. Beck had found her display slightly pleasant.

"You need a husband, Anna." His pause barely gave her time for the statement to be felt. "And that is something you shall have."

"Papa, we've had this conversation." She paused to draw an unsteady breath. "I don't see how I can—"

"I'm not finished. I've humored you," he said. "For years I've made the mistake of allowing you great freedom to achieve an education that has, it appears, made you nearly unfit for marriage."

That statement took the bluster out of the protest she'd planned. "Unfit?" she said, all manner of disappointment evident in the word. "Is that how you feel about me, Papa? That I am unfit?"

Immediately his stern expression softened. "My sweet girl," he said, "you're the apple of your father's eye, and you know it. I've spared no expense to give you all you ever wanted. More, probably." He paused. "And now I'm giving you what you need. A husband. But first, I've got to remedy the condition that's causing this problem."

Anna shifted position. The chair had been chosen for appearance rather than comfort. "I don't understand, Papa. What condition?"

"You're a bit willful, Anna," he said. "And not nearly as pliable as your sisters. What man wants to marry a woman he cannot control?" He waved away any comment she might have made. "No need to answer, dear, for the correct response is none."

Tears stung her eyes, but she blinked them away.

"I'll be seeing to a few alliances that will prove profitable. Any one of these men would be lucky to get you." He looked quite satisfied with himself. "You'll know more of these suitors when the time is right. Until then, as you know, I've arranged for Mr. Sanders' presence as a more formal situation. A way of ensuring that you no longer run amuck on the streets of Denver."

Anna rose, outraged. "Run amuck? Papa, truly you exaggerate."

"Do I?" He shook his head. "Perhaps you could have convinced me of this before you arrived on that horse in garb that appeared to have been laundered with you in it. Imagine my humiliation when Edwin Beck asked if my youngest daughter was playing Paul Revere at next week's masquerade ball. My question," he said as he leaned forward, elbows on the desktop, "is where does one go in the predawn hours with only a saddlebag and a pistol?"

"Papa, I'm a grown woman," she said, "and I'm of no mind to

respond to questions that do not take that fact into consideration. And I do not run amuck."

"Sit down, Daughter." He waited until she did to continue. "Perhaps you're not clear as to what your role is in this endeavor."

Anna shook her head. "Must my life be characterized as an endeavor?"

He chuckled, though he was clearly not amused. "I'll make this simple for you."

Simple? She bit her tongue to keep from speaking what she thought.

"I am your father, and as such, I have been entrusted with the care and keeping of you until such a time as this responsibility is shouldered by your husband." Papa stifled a yawn. "I expect you to cooperate with this search."

"For a husband?" She shook her head. "As I asked you the last time we discussed this, how can I do that?"

"I'm glad you asked, Anna. It gives me hope you're actually coming to an understanding with me." He paused. "To begin with, I expect you to actively seek a spouse. Your mother or sisters can assist in this endeavor. And perhaps," he said, "you will give that nice man down at the *Times* a chance to help you as well."

"Nice man at the *Times*?" Her eyes narrowed. "Are you speaking of Mr. Mitchell?"

"I am," he said. "Other than his penchant for the dramatic, he seems to have a decent grasp of the language. And he certainly has taken notice of you."

"He is not a nice man, Papa."

"In any case, I want you to make yourself available for an appointment with him." He shrugged. "No, better than that. I'll have you speak to him at the next opportunity. The Millers are hosting a gathering tomorrow, so plan to have not only a conversation with Mitchell, but also with Mr. Beck—that is, Mr. Edwin Beck—to make him aware of the fact you've taken a strong interest in him."

"But I haven't," she protested. "Not a *strong* interest, anyway."

"You will." Papa rose and stepped around the desk to reach for Anna's hand. "I know this is difficult." Her inelegant snort caused him to raise an eyebrow. "But I am your father and I love you. Never forget that, Anna."

Again traitorous tears threatened. She could only nod before managing a quick, "Yes, Papa, I shall recall this even on those times when I wonder if it is true."

Her words were meant to sting, but they obviously did not meet their mark. Her father lifted her to her feet with a gentle tug of her hand. "You're special, Anna, and you always have been. A bright, special young lady. You're not like your sisters."

"I'm not sure that's a compliment, Papa," she said, "for my sisters had no trouble fulfilling your marital dreams for them. It is I who seem to be the problem."

"I've never backed down from a challenge, Anna," Papa said, "and if the care and marriage of my youngest is to be a challenge, I shall meet it and beat it."

He grinned. Anna, however, could only cringe and consider what this statement might actually mean when carried out.

"So you'll be kind to Mr. Beck and to any other prospective suitor?" When she nodded, he continued. "And you'll not go riding off to who knows where like some heathen? And wherever you go, you shall have Mr. Sanders in attendance. I'm paying top dollar for his services, and I expect him to earn his pay."

"Mr. Sanders," she said as casually as she could manage. "Surely he has more interesting employment opportunities than to be following me about like an oversized nursemaid. And what about traveling? What would people say if I'm seen in his company leaving Denver unchaperoned?"

"Anna," her father said gently, "Mr. Sanders is your escort. People will say your father has taken great measures to see to your safety."

The butler entered and whispered in her father's ear. When the servant left, Papa looked directly at Anna.

"You're dismissed," he said to her. "Remember we've struck an agreement here that's not to be breached."

"We have?" She shook her head. "I fail to recall what we've agreed to."

"We agreed you're to be married. In the interim, Mr. Sanders will see that your reputation suffers no further tarnishing."

Not if I'm tempted to kiss him again. If only she could say the words rather than think them, Papa would understand how very unsuitable Jeb Sanders was for the job of protecting her.

Anna held her head high and her back straight. "I do hope you're paying my hired gun enough to buy new mules. And a wagon." She paused at the library door to look back at her father over her shoulder. "He's going to need them."

Her words chased her as far as the stairs, where she realized the folly of taunting her father on this topic. She'd only guaranteed that Jeb Sanders would follow her everywhere she went. Including the post office in Garrison or the train to Altwood Springs. With him on the job, she could not do hers. And then what would happen to the people whose stories needed to be told?

Perhaps there was another way.

She hurried back to the library and knocked before slipping inside again. This time she walked directly to her father. When he rose, she slid into his embrace. Tears beckoned, and this time she let them slide down her face. "Papa," she said when she could manage it, "will you forgive me? I do want to keep you happy."

And she did. With Papa happy, she could continue her journalistic endeavors without interruption. Or matrimony.

He patted her back for a moment, then held her at arm's length. "You're a good girl, Anna. A bit high strung and misguided, but a good girl. Still, I would be remiss in my duties as a father if I knew you needed protection and did not provide it."

Anna looked up into eyes that matched her own. "What can I do to keep from being shadowed by a stranger?"

His smile dawned. "That's simple. Find a husband and you'll have no need for a hired gun."

23

It wasn't considered policy to draw a gun on Wyatt
unless you got the drop and meant to burn powder without any preliminary talk.
—*Dodge City Times, July 7, 1877*

Anna sat by the window, watching the prairie turn to mountains and
Denver become smaller and smaller. Midway between Denver and
Altwood Springs, she threw away caution and a lovely traveling frock
of emerald green. It and the bag that had contained the male garb she
now wore went out the window of the narrow-gauge train over the
Platte River. Likely some poor fisherman would be the recipient of a
soggy surprise come morning.

She'd miss the green dress, but Anna had little time to prepare.
Perhaps next time, if there was a next time, she might have a better
plan. In either case, she certainly couldn't take the chance of being
followed, and she hoped the change in clothing would help her go
unnoticed.

Sighing, Anna clutched her satchel to her chest. If recent reports
of the outlaw's health were true, there might be no more hastily
planned meetings. No more stories shared. No more letters to mail.

And unless she convinced him otherwise, no ending to the story
she hoped to tell.

Perhaps this dire prognosis was the product of an active imagination. After all, Anna wasn't completely sure the man she was meeting was actually the real Doc Holliday.

But then that was part of her reason for accepting the ticket he'd sent. To get at the truth.

As the train ground to a halt and the population of the rail car spilled out onto the platform, Anna glanced behind her. None but the average collection of citizenry surrounded her. It was too late in the season for the crowds who thronged the hot springs, and too early for the next. This was a blessing, she decided, as she skirted the sheriff's office and headed for the place she'd been told she could find Doc Holliday.

The fewer people she passed, the less chance someone would recall the oddly dressed youth with the oversized hat and undersized shoulders. Anna let out a long breath and adjusted the cap she had pulled over her braid lest the breeze coming off the mountain give her away as the woman she was rather than the male she pretended to be. The bandages binding her chest chafed and had begun to itch despite the cool temperature, and yet she forgot all her discomfort as she gave the man behind the front desk of the hotel a disinterested shrug and made for the stairs.

Finding the room proved simple. Anna knocked, and a slow, southern voice called for her to enter. Inside, the air hung thick behind shutters that did a poor job of keeping out the dust and sulfuric smell of Altwood Springs. Thin slats of sunlight slanted across rough floor boards, though the man in the corner appeared not to notice.

"Ah, Miss Bird." John Henry Holliday's eyes took in her garb and he smiled. "Or perhaps I should say A. Bird? You came." He rose halfway from his chair before sinking back into it. "Forgive me. This isn't one of my better days."

"Of course I came. You'll not regret this, Mr. Holliday," she said, moving into the room.

"That remains to be seen." He paused. "Despite my lack of enthusiasm for your writing project, I seem to have no trouble with my own." He gestured to the writing table, which held a stack of letters. "There are others, though I'd be much obliged if you could see to addressing them for me."

"Of course," Anna said softly as she moved toward the table. "I hope to change your mind about my project. Our project," she corrected.

"Indeed," he responded drily. His chuckle held no humor. "Won't you be disappointed if I brought you all this way to play secretary for me?"

Anna gave him an even stare. "But you haven't," she challenged.

Silence filled the space between them. "No," he finally said, "I haven't. Now, for that address."

By the second letter, Anna already knew the name and address by heart. She recognized it as the same Georgia address that had been on the first set of letters she'd mailed for him. Though she did not read the letters she folded and slipped inside the envelopes, two things were hard to miss: the thickness of the missives—never less than three pages by her estimation, but often a half dozen or more—and the greeting with which each began.

My dearest.

As she heard Holliday cough and watched him dab at the corner of his mouth, those two words strung together created an image of unrequited passion. Of lost opportunities. Of a man and woman whose circumstances conspired to keep their love from finding its way.

All conjecture, of course, for the last thing Holliday seemed to want to talk about was the woman who would open the letters. Anna glanced at the silver-haired man of thirty-five and wondered how many more times she might have the opportunity to speak with him.

She swallowed hard and put on her best smile as she snatched the ridiculous cap from her head and set it on the nearest flat surface, a worn but serviceable sideboard that held a pitcher of water, two cracked mugs, and a dime novel her friend Gennie would have loved.

"Are you reading this?" Anna set her satchel down and turned the cover toward her. "Well, how about that?" she said. "This one's about you."

His response was not in keeping with the man she'd expected from the newspapers. "Hardly," he said. "Though I fear many will think so."

She drew nearer, leaving the volume where it lay. "What does it matter? It's just a storybook."

His stare met hers, blue eyes barely blinking. "Stories have power, Miss Bird. Don't you know that?"

She fetched her satchel, which held her writing materials. As an afterthought, she gestured to the pitcher. "Some water before we start?"

When he shrugged, Anna filled a mug and held it toward him

until she realized he wasn't going to take it. After setting it within reach on the braided rug, Anna backed away. Fear, pure and simple, kept her from standing too close or offering to bring the mug to his parched lips.

I was thirsty, and ye gave me no drink.

The consumption was contagious, and an awful, slow death. Any fool knew this.

Verily I say unto you, Inasmuch as ye did it not to one of the least of these, ye did it not to me.

She rose. "Have some before we begin," she insisted as she fetched the mug and straightened to bring it within reach.

Again he ignored it.

"All right, then," she said. "I suppose you'd prefer to wear it." She lifted the mug and pretended to consider dumping its contents in his lap.

Ever so slowly, a grin worked its way onto his face until the gunman's scowl was replaced by what might have been quite a handsome smile in a less ravaged face. "I think you're going to be more trouble than you're worth," he said with something resembling fondness. He allowed her to place the cup against his lips.

"She is, at that," came a familiar and unwanted voice from the door. The statement was punctuated by the unmistakable click of a gun being cocked.

Wonderful.

"Leave us be, Jeb Sanders," Anna said with more bravado than she felt. She straightened without turning toward the door. "You're not supposed to be here."

"Neither are you, Anna. Though I doubt *my* pa's wondering where I am." He paused. "Get yourself out of that indecent get-up and into something more ladylike, and I'll see if I can't talk your father out of locking you up and throwing away the key."

"Don't bother," she said. "Then he'd have no further need for you to torment me with your constant attention."

A low chuckle was his only response.

A glance told her the outlaw also took some measure of amusement at the exchange. Anna, however, could only try to keep her irritation from blossoming into something more akin to full-fledged anger.

Slowly she turned, mindful of the fact that Jeb had not only called her indecently dressed but also ordered her home like some errant pup gone missing. Somewhere along the way she must have made the unfortunate mistake of praying for patience. That could be the only explanation for how the Lord had allowed the exasperating Pinkerton to remain in her life despite all her heavenly petitions to the contrary.

"Surely you've misspoken," she offered in her sweetest voice as she closed her eyes. "A gentleman, especially one in the employ of my father, wouldn't dare request that I step out of my clothing right here in front of him."

"Well, of course not," he blustered. "I meant for you to give those clothes back to whatever miner you stole them from and put on a dress."

"I don't have a dress handy, so I suppose I'll have to stay right here while you trot on back to Denver without me." Anna opened her eyes.

When their gazes met, something shifted inside her, and she had to work to maintain her outrage. Of all the hired guns in Colorado, why had Papa chosen this one?

Jeb lowered the gun but kept his finger on the trigger. His jaw clenched. Were she a betting woman, she'd offer even odds that the Pinkerton would hoist her over his shoulder and haul her out of Altwood Springs kicking and screaming.

"Then," he said slowly, "you can purchase a new frock at the local mercantile on your way back to the train." Jeb offered Mr. Holliday a look that would have quailed a lesser man. "Mighty kind of you to meet the reporter in a town where there's a decent dress supply."

Holliday responded with a tip of his head.

"How did you find me?" Anna asked. "I had no idea you had followed."

His gaze was direct. "That was the point, Anna. I'm good at what I do."

Indeed. Anna swallowed hard and looked away. With no good response handy, she decided to deflect the statement by addressing the obvious. "Put that gun away. There's no danger here." She cast a quick glance behind her, noting that Mr. Holliday's amusement had turned to something else. Defiance, perhaps?

"Doc Holliday." Jeb managed to turn the name into a threat. "I ought to take you back to Arizona and let them be done with you."

Pale blue eyes narrowed even as the outlaw chuckled. "Been a warrant out for me and Wyatt for years. Nobody cares about that anymore. Any questions in that regard were answered in Leadville." He turned his attention to Anna. "An unfortunate acquaintance of mine chose to cause some trouble in a public place and—"

"That was Hyman's Saloon," Jeb said, "and if you'd been given the choice, you would have killed Billy Allen right there on the floor where he lay."

Holliday refused to spare Jeb a glance. "An unfortunate rumor that persists even now."

"The truth, and we both know it."

Mr. Holliday turned to Jeb. "Who are you that you think you'll be the one to deliver me?"

It was as if the air went out of the room. Slowly, Jeb shook his head. "Don't guess you remember me."

"Should I?" No trace of the disease ravaging the thin man's lungs showed in the question. He rose.

The door slammed shut, and Anna jumped. Jeb had entered the room. "I've been your shadow for years, Doc Holliday, though I made a point of not letting you know." He shrugged. "I'm decent at hiding in plain sight."

The gunfighter gave an almost imperceptible nod of his head. "If you're so good at it, why don't you tell me when we last met so I can reminisce with you?"

"Remember that miner who pulled your arm back as you were about to unload on Allen? The one you said ought to be next in line to be shot?"

An unreadable expression crossed the older man's face. "Liar," he finally said. "He looked nothing like you."

Jeb's smile held no humor. "I told you I was good. And by the way, your hand would have lost. Hiram Powell's flush had you beat." A pause, deadly in its promise. "Until they let you off, I always figured I'd let my revenge be the fact you'd someday rot in jail."

"Revenge. It is a powerful motive," Holliday said. "Enough to make a man do most anything."

"You ought to know. You never did like Johnny Ringo, did you?"

Holliday barely blinked as he returned to his chair. "If ever a man believed God made mistakes—which I do not—Ringo would have been proof of that theory."

"So you're a God-fearin' man now?" Jeb said with a sneer. "I'm sure your good friend the devil will be sorry to hear that."

"Jeb Sanders," Anna blurted. "Take that back this instant. For your information, he's been writing letters to a convent—"

Holliday's sharp expression stalled her speech midsentence. He lifted his hand as if shooing flies, then set it back in his lap, seemingly exhausted.

"Let the man speak as he believes, Miss Bird, no matter how misguided he might be." He returned his attention to Jeb. "I'll not respond to any allegations of where or to whom my letters are going, but I will admit the Lord has been good to me even when I've not appreciated His extraordinary efforts on my behalf."

Anna saw Jeb's shoulders slump. The admission seemed to momentarily take the bluster out of the hired gun.

"And as for my association or lack thereof with Mr. Ringo and his band of thieves and liars—rest their souls—well, perhaps you don't read the papers," he said. "Four months after my acquittal on those unfortunate charges you've mentioned, my esteemed colleague Mr. Earp unburdened himself to a reporter of some renown regarding the truth behind many of the lies being told on their behalf. And ours."

"Lies." Jeb seemed to roll the word around before unleashing it. "I'm a man of proof. An article in the paper, no matter who wrote it, will not change the truth. And the truth is you're a cold-blooded murderer."

"As you said, it is the truth of the matter that tells the tale. So, if you're to call me a murderer, you would need proof of this." Holliday's eyes sparkled and color flooded his gaunt face. Anna wondered if interest in the topic or a fever caused it. "So tell me," he continued. "Can you offer such proof? For we are in agreement that much of what is written in today's newspapers is conjecture and outright fabrication."

Anna watched the scene unfold between the men with a mixture of interest and shock. The Jeb Sanders she knew might be a lot of things, but a man so bent on revenge—or whatever drove him to hate Doc Holliday—was not one of them.

"Leadville. Fourth of July." Jeb moved to put himself between Anna and Holliday. "Back in '77."

Anna peered around the Pinkerton's broad back to watch the outlaw square his shoulders. "Seventy-seven?" he asked, slow and ponderous. "That was a long time ago. You must've been just a kid."

"I was old enough," Jeb snapped.

"Years run together nowadays." Holliday raked his surprisingly steady hand through pale hair, then caught Anna staring and winked. "Unless there's a pretty lady involved."

"Oh, she was pretty, all right. Her name," Jeb said slowly as he lifted the pistol and took aim, "was Ella."

24

I'm your huckleberry. That's just my game.

—*Doc Holliday to Johnny Ringo, as reported by Tombstone bystanders on January 17, 1882*

Sunlight slanted over the angles of the hired gun's face as Anna watched a muscle in his jaw twitch. Anna knew she must intervene somehow or the outlaw would meet his Maker.

She set her writing case down and placed herself between the Pinkerton and the subject of what she hoped would be a headline-worthy piece of journalism. "Mr. Sanders, I insist you put that gun away."

"Move," he said, deadly calm.

"Do you have a warrant for this man's capture?" Anna asked in what she hoped was a strong voice. "I thought not. Nor do you have any legal recourse should I have to testify that you shot him."

Silence. Thankfully, Mr. Holliday said nothing.

Anna affected a pose she hoped would indicate to the Pinkerton that she was considering her options. "So tell me, does a man sworn to protect me discharge his duties when he discharges his weapon into an innocent man?"

"This is no innocent man," Jeb said.

"Never claimed to be," Mr. Holliday replied.

"Then let the Lord judge him." She paused. "Notice he's not drawn his weapon. Do you intend to shoot a man who's not drawn his weapon and call it justice?"

Silence once again fell between them, and Anna allowed it. Perhaps something she said had caught Jeb's attention. Or perhaps he was merely deciding how to put a bullet into Doc Holliday without injuring her.

"I assure you, Miss Bird, I am unworthy of your efforts," Mr. Holliday finally said, "though I applaud the enthusiasm of your husband in this endeavor."

Anna did not dare look away from Jeb. "And I assure you, sir," she said to the outlaw, "were I foolish enough to take this man on as a husband, I would deserve to be shot."

A poor attempt at humor, and yet it did cause one of the men in the room to laugh. Unfortunately, it was not the Pinkerton.

The look on Jeb Sanders' face when she placed her hand over his reminded her of the expression he wore when he first emerged from behind the log a couple of weeks ago.

"Move," he repeated through clenched jaw. "Now."

She stared up into eyes narrowed by the same anger that held his mouth in a tight line. To argue with a man in this state would do no good, so she did what Mae Winslow would do and placed her fingertips against the lips she'd so recently kissed. This caught his attention quicker than any exchange of retorts.

"Enough of this. You may stay, Mr. Sanders," she said as calmly as she could manage, "but if you do, I would thank you to remain silent so Mr. Holliday and I can conduct our business. As you know from the agenda my maid delivered to you this morning, I must return to Denver in time to attend a function this evening. A shooting would only put us off schedule."

For a moment, Anna feared she'd gone too far. Then, slowly, her hired gun lowered his revolver.

"Thank you," she whispered. Behind her, the Georgia dentist begin to clap.

"Well done," Holliday said when Anna turned to face him. "Had I any questions as to your qualifications in this endeavor, they were just answered. Now, what do you require to begin?"

Anna ignored the Pinkerton's response, but she did not allow her attention to stray from his gun until he finally put it away. "Only your story," she said to Holliday. "I thought to compare your recollections to what has been written in order to find a trail of false claims."

Mr. Holliday remained still, his gaze studying her. "Yours is not the first interview I've given, Miss Bird. Did you not consult your *Rocky Mountain News* for my statement? May of '82, it would have been." He crossed his arms over his chest to affect a casual pose, emphasizing the leanness of his frame. "Or was it June? Then there were the various papers in Tombstone and beyond. Had a decent write-up in one of the San Francisco periodicals. Apparently I am well liked in that part of the country." He toyed with his mustache. "So, which was it? June of '82 serves my recollection."

Piercing blue eyes stared into her as he awaited her response. Or perhaps to see if she would pass this test.

"It was May, Mr. Holliday, and the paper was the *Denver Republican,* though given my premise that not all words in print are the truth, I'm sure you will understand if I prefer to conduct my own interview. I will need more light in order to work." Anna gestured to the window. "May I?"

When he nodded, she picked up her writing case and set it on the table, then went to the window. When her second attempt at raising the sash failed, Jeb Sanders nudged her out of the way and opened it for her, allowing a sulfuric-tinged breeze to blow through. Beyond the Pinkerton's broad shoulders, the view was a poor one, the brick wall of a building and a meager back alley one floor below, but sunlight glinted off Jeb Sanders' badge and spilled across the simple wooden table.

Anna gave Mr. Sanders one last firm look, then seated herself and opened the case to remove pencil and paper. Only then did she turn her attention to the legendary gunman. "How would you like to begin, Mr. Holliday? Or should I call you Dr. Holliday?"

"That you've called on me at all is sufficient, dear lady." He rose, an effort that caused a coughing fit. Recovering, he removed a handkerchief from his pocket and mopped his brow. "Mr. Bird," he said, taking two shuffling steps toward Jeb.

"Sanders," the Pinkerton corrected as his hand went back to his gun.

"Rest easy, Mr. Sanders." Holliday paused as if to study Jeb. "I mean you no ill will. Tell me, who is Ella?"

Anna set down her pencil. She didn't intend to miss this answer. The contrast between the Pinkerton and the gunfighter was striking.

Where Jeb stood tall and broad shouldered, John Henry Holliday looked old beyond his years and pale, his hair already graying. Anna could only guess at Jeb's age, though she assumed the pair weren't as far apart in years as their appearances showed.

"She was your woman." Holliday dipped his head. "My condolences for your loss."

For a moment, Anna thought Mr. Sanders might actually respond. Instead, he adjusted his new Stetson and turned his attention to Anna.

"I'll be outside this door," he said, "and I won't take kindly to foolishness. Get your story and get out of here." He consulted his watch. "You've got an hour." Then he focused on the outlaw. "You even *think* of touching her and I'll kill you, warrant or not. Understand?"

A slow smile spread across Holliday's face. "I do indeed."

"Mr. Sanders," Anna said, "how dare you berate the subject of my interview. Do apologize."

"Apologize?" His expression turned dangerous. "I should have put an end to this foolishness back in Denver instead of letting you get on that train."

"Letting me get on that train? Of all the nerve." Anna's eyes narrowed. "You were completely flummoxed that I managed to sneak away."

Jeb moved between Anna and the outlaw. His gaze scorched her as it swept down the length of her, then collided with her stare. "Do I look like a man who would ever be flummoxed?" He leaned closer. "Ever?"

Had Anna been in the mood to be honest, she might have admitted he did not. Instead she rocked back on her heels and nearly collided with the wall. Only the Pinkerton's hands on her waist kept her from tumbling. His grasp was unnecessarily firm.

"Just outside the door," he said, his voice a low rumble in the otherwise silent room.

"I am not a child in need of a nursemaid," Anna said to his retreating back.

The Pinkerton stopped, one hand on the polished brass door-knob. "Were you a child," he said slowly, "I'd have a remedy for your behavior that would make you think twice before attempting to cross me again. Don't suppose there's any hope of finding a woodshed in this town, is there, Doc?"

Sanders looked past her, and Anna followed his gaze. Doc Holliday appeared more than a little amused.

"Get out." Pressing both palms to Jeb's back, she gave him a gentle but firm shove. "I'm terribly sorry," Anna said to Holliday when the door slammed behind the Pinkerton. "I had no idea he would follow me, nor do I appreciate it."

"Miss Bird," Holliday said with a grin, "you cannot accept responsibility for a man determined to follow." He paused to allow his gaze to travel the length of her. "Despite his primitive behavior, he is obviously a man of refined tastes."

"What?" She shook her head as understanding dawned. "Oh, no, you've misunderstood. Mr. Sanders and I do not have that sort of relationship."

He chuckled. "Of course you don't. Yet."

She considered protesting, then decided to leave the insinuation unaddressed. "So," Anna said as she retrieved her pencil, "have you an expectation for this interview?"

He studied her a moment. "Should I?"

"Well," Anna said, "I had hoped to make your innocence the focus of this article."

His laughter echoed in the tiny room as he settled back onto his chair. "Then, my dear, I fear this shall be a short interview. I am far from an innocent man." Her surprise must have shown, for the gunman's grin faded. "Miss Bird, your letter indicated an interesting theory. Might we begin by discussing just why you think there are two of me?"

"There are at least two of you," she corrected, "possibly more. You could not have been in all the places where you're charged with crimes. It's impossible." She reached into her case and pulled out a stack of newspapers, then began spreading them across the table. "Come and look at this. You're accused of shooting a man during a card game in Tombstone on the same day you were with me and the Earps in Denver."

While he read the article, Anna found another paper. "And see," she said as she pointed to the front page of the *Aspen Daily Times,* "this man doesn't even look like you."

He set down the papers and joined her at the table. "My friend Wyatt has vouched for you, and that is why I've allowed this," he said as he settled himself. "That there are men using my name is an old theory long discarded." Holliday gestured to the stack of newspapers. "Forgive my impertinence, but what assurance can you offer that this is not yet another colossal waste of time?"

"None," Anna responded hastily. "Perhaps it will be just that." She paused to point her pencil at him. "But what if it is not? What if there is but one man carrying on this ruse? And what if my story…*your* story," she corrected, "is exactly what gets that man caught?"

"Is that why you've brought a Pinkerton with you?"

The question hung in the sulfur-tinged air for a moment before Anna set down her pencil. "How did you know he's a Pinkerton?"

The legendary gunman shook his head. "A man with a badge carries himself differently than other men. I know," he said slowly. "I wore one a time or two."

"Well, though it may appear otherwise, Mr. Sanders is assigned to me, not you," Anna said. "Courtesy of my father."

He laughed and toyed with the diamond stickpin on his lapel. "Because you accept invitations for clandestine meetings with outlaws?"

"Because I refuse invitations from potential grooms." She reached for her pencil. "Now, about that story."

"Do not judge your father for his concern," Mr. Holliday said. "I only recently visited with mine. In New Orleans, and in the midst of a dental convention, no less. I'd not trade for anything the trouble it took to accomplish that."

For a moment, he seemed lost to her, his attention transported away from the small hotel room. Imagining Doc Holliday at a New Orleans dental convention was impossible, even though he truly was a dentist himself. So far removed from the normal, the mundane, was this man.

"Miss Bird," he said, "I fear I must strike a bargain with you. Between the law and the Lord, my time grows short. There is much untold. Triumph and mischief are often regaled, but who is left to chronicle the rest?"

Anna leaned back against her chair to consider the question. "What are you asking, Mr. Holliday?"

"Should I decide you're the one to tell my tale, I will be asking for more of your time than you'll likely wish to offer, and certainly more than the scope of this interview would require. I wish to tell my story, Miss Bird. All of it. Beginning to end." He reached for his handkerchief and dabbed at his forehead. "Or at least as much of it as I can recall. I will arrange the meetings, which may come at times you consider inconvenient. Compensation is negotiable, for I am not without means, but confidentiality is required. Even your Pinkerton cannot know what transpires between us. What say you to this?"

"Yes, of course," she said before she had time to count the cost of secret meetings and slipping away from one particularly cranky Pinkerton. The details she would manage as she must, but the idea of being the one to chronicle "the rest" won over any concern.

Anna set her pencil to the paper. "Absolutely. Let's get started."

◈

Jeb checked his watch, then stuffed the contraption back into his pocket. She was late.

"Figures," he said under his breath, and he rose from his post at the bottom of the stairs. If he wasted another minute trying to fill the time by untangling memories best left tied up, he'd lose what was left of his patience. According to the schedule at the train station, the only train to Denver left the station in a half hour.

Missing that train meant staying a night in the only hotel this little town had to offer—the same hotel where Holliday would sleep as well—and somehow protecting Anna Finch from herself without compromising her reputation in the process.

Jeb's traitorous thoughts tumbled back to the river and the woman whose skirts wrapped around his legs just as her arms wrapped around his back. Part of what made Anna Finch so irritating to be around could be traced right back to that river. To those kisses.

A lesser man might have owned up to the fact that no woman since Ella had stopped him in his tracks like Anna Finch. But he was not a lesser man, and she'd never know. He'd learned the hard way all those years ago that a Pinkerton's woman might as well have a target on her back.

He wouldn't lose another love to a bullet.

The fact that Anna Finch couldn't stand him made things much easier. Didn't change how he was beginning to feel, but it did give him a good reason to ignore it.

Jeb cleared his throat and put his rambling thoughts back where they belonged. His boots hit the third step at the same time a door opened and closed upstairs. Jeb paused and waited, his weapon handy.

"One stop and we'll be off," Anna Finch said before breezing past as if she hadn't just spent one hour and twelve minutes alone with the notorious Doc Holliday.

"That's it?" Jeb called.

Miss Finch reached the street before he caught up to her. As Jeb shortened his steps to match hers, he lost her once more to a dress shop conveniently located two doors down from the hotel.

"I'll just be a minute," she said as the door closed behind her.

Jeb looked up at the sign above the door. Spicers' Emporium. Purveyors of Fine Ladies' Clothing Since 1872.

"You take more than five and I'm coming in after you," he called through the door. "Five minutes. I'll not miss that train."

Several passersby gave him a wide berth, but Jeb didn't care. Two buildings away, the man who killed Ella waited, and Jeb only had to walk over and pull the trigger. Without Anna in the room, there was nothing stopping him.

Nothing except a Bible verse warning that vengeance was for the Lord and not Jeb Sanders. A verse he hated so much he'd once torn an entire page out of the Bible just so he didn't have to look at it.

But it stuck fast in his mind long after the ruined Bible was replaced, and every time he thought about Doc Holliday, he had to step around it. Today, he'd almost managed to forget that if he pulled the trigger, he'd be going it alone, something he hadn't done on purpose since the Lord got hold of him. Something that might happen again if he didn't get Anna Finch to the train station soon.

Jeb shrugged off the irritation building inside him and stepped into the store to find a world of ruffles, satins, and feminine garments that made him dizzier than the Finch parlor. What he did not find was Anna Finch, though several other women stood about admiring the goods.

Two or three seemed to be admiring him as well.

"Miss Finch," he called. "You in here?"

Every head in the place turned his direction. He ignored them.

An elderly female with a no-nonsense expression and a pair of thick spectacles headed his way. "I'm Mrs. Spicer. May I help you?"

"Looking for a woman," he said. "Name's Finch. She came in dressed up like a boy." He held his hand up to just below shoulder height. "About that tall."

"You need to leave," she said.

"I mean you no disrespect, ma'am, but I'll be glad to do that soon as I find her." Jeb pressed past the woman. "Anna Finch," he called as he spied a back exit to this torture trap. Making his way toward the door meant negotiating an obstacle course of frilly frocks and womenfolk, but he managed it without too many missteps. Just a few downed dresses and a display of bonnets that got in the way of his elbow.

"I'll pay for 'em," Jeb called as he jerked open the back door and stepped out.

Or rather, in. He hadn't found an exit at all. Instead he'd found a dressing room.

"Mr. Sanders," said Anna Finch, who wore a new dress and perched on a cushioned bench, "do wait outside while I slip on my shoes."

The floor looked like a dress factory had exploded around them, in contrast to the row of neatly arranged shoes in the corner. Mirrors on three walls added to the chaos and reflected the face of a man who wished to be anywhere but here.

"Miss Finch," he said as he slowly backed out of the room, "we've got a train to catch."

The cause of his discomfort looked up from buttoning her shoe. "Do be patient," she said.

Patient? Well, that did it.

"Miss Finch, I have *been* patient. Now I'm *done* with it." Reaching for her case with one hand and her wrist with the other, Jeb hauled Anna Finch to her feet.

"I'm not finished," she said as she lifted her foot to show the as-yet-unbuttoned shoe.

Jeb reached down to slip the shoe off her foot, then stuffed it inside the writing case. "Can you walk with just one?"

Her face turned as red as the roses climbing the wallpaper in the Finch parlor. "Of course I cannot walk with just one." She made a grab for her case.

He lifted the case out of her reach. He had two choices to diffuse the situation: react or retreat.

Retreat was not an option. Not with the train to Denver leaving the station in less than ten minutes.

He gestured to the case. "You want this?"

"Don't be ridiculous. Of course I do."

He gave it to her. Distracted by the unwieldy box, she couldn't stop him from hauling her into his arms. He might have made it to the door, despite her kicking and complaining, had Mrs. Spicer not stepped between him and freedom.

"Nobody leaves here without paying," she said. "Them clothes are expensive."

"All right." Jeb marched to the center of the store, where he set Anna and her writing case on the counter. He gave her a don't-dare-move look, then pulled out enough money to purchase half the inventory. "Much obliged, ma'am," Jeb said to Mrs. Spicer. He tipped his Stetson, then reached for Anna.

"I've changed my mind." She scooted off the counter and landed on her feet. "I can manage just fine with one shoe. Now, shall we catch the train?"

The Finch woman walked with her back straight and her head held high all the way to the train station. Only those looking closely would have noticed her stride wasn't quite right.

When they reached their seats, Anna Finch turned toward the window and ignored every statement he made, including the apologies.

Another reason not to fall in love with the woman. She was as bullheaded as he was.

By the time the whistle blew and the train lurched out of the station, Jeb figured he could do no more than catch a few hours of sleep before their arrival back in Denver. He took one last glance at Miss Finch, then pulled his hat low over his eyes and did exactly that.

When he woke up at the station in Denver, she was gone.

25

Precautions were immediately taken to preserve
law and order, even if they had to fight for it.
—*Tombstone Daily Epitaph, October 27, 1881*

Any questions Anna had about whether she'd completely lost her wits
when she'd kissed Jeb Sanders were now answered. Oh, he was handsome enough and quite skilled, but as she gathered her writing case
and slipped past him down the aisle and out onto the platform, Anna
knew the sooner she was rid of him, the better.

Not only was he insufferable, overbearing, and cared nothing for
embarrassing her over the slightest thing, he also snored. And he had
a mysterious past involving some woman named Ella who made him
heedless of crossing the line between lawman and murderer.

It might have been interesting had Anna not needed to find Mr.
Sanders someone else to protect. The last thing she intended to do
the next time she met with Mr. Holliday was bring the Pinkerton
along.

Making her way through the crowded station, Anna emerged
into the early afternoon sunlight. Her father's bank was only a few
blocks away, so she headed that direction. Likely he'd have a carriage
she could borrow to get home. She'd claim she came shopping for a

new frock should Papa ask, though she'd not offer that she'd pur-
chased that frock in Altwood Springs.

Or rather, Mr. Sanders had. She'd have to pay him back as soon
as she saw him again.

The sound of the train's whistle and the lack of a Pinkerton shadowing her made Anna wonder just how long that might be. The
thought of the hired gun waking to find her gone made her grin.

"Now that's a lovely smile."

Anna turned toward the voice and saw Edwin Beck. She picked
up her pace.

"Miss Finch, you wound me," he said when he caught up to her.
He glanced down at her skirt. "Dare I ask whether you're still in possession of the pistol you mentioned at our last meeting?"

On any other day she might have been able to act the polite,
well-bred girl her parents expected her to be. But with notes on
Doc Holliday's story vying with her irritation over Jeb Sanders'
behavior, her ability to tolerate the younger Beck brother was
severely compromised.

Thus, Anna kept her mouth shut and her eyes on the sidewalk
ahead.

"Fine," Edwin Beck said. "I deserve no less for my abominable
behavior. It's just that, well, I am hopelessly smitten."

To laugh aloud at the ridiculous statement seemed rude, so Anna
picked up her pace.

"And I was led to believe you were amenable to my advances," he
continued. From the stunned faces of the trio of matrons exiting
Simon's Apothecary, the comment did not go unheard.

Anna stopped short. "You were led to believe this by whom? Certainly not me."

He looked sheepish as he toyed with the watch chain on his waistcoat. "I'd prefer not to answer that. A gentleman takes his promises seriously."

"I see."

"Miss Finch." He removed his hat and held it against his chest, his expression passably contrite, his features more than passably handsome. "If I thought it would affect your opinion of me, I would kneel right here in the middle of downtown Denver and beg your forgiveness. Shall I?"

"Truly, Mr. Beck, I've had enough embarrassment for one day."

The source of which apparently had gotten off the train in time, for a block away Anna spied Jeb Sanders making his way toward them. When their gazes met, the hired gun had the audacity to wave. She suppressed a groan.

Holding her writing case against her side, Anna refused to acknowledge the Pinkerton. "If you will excuse me, Mr. Beck, I must get to the bank to see my father."

Before she took three steps, Daniel's brother stood in front of her. "That's impossible. I just left the bank, and your father's not in the office today."

"I see. Well, thank you for that information."

Now what? She could take public transport, at least to within a few blocks of home. Not ideal, but better than walking all that way.

She moved away from Edwin, hoping he would leave her to her thoughts. He did not.

"It was that Pinkerton fellow."

Anna slid him a sideways glance. "Excuse me?"

Daniel's brother shrugged. "A vow can be broken when to keep it is dishonorable. The man who told me you were amenable to my advances was the Pinkerton. What's his name?"

She glanced behind her and found Jeb Sanders had paused and now had company. Hank Thompson had joined him, and both men watched her.

"Thompson?" she offered. "Hank Thompson?"

"No, that's not it." Edwin snapped his fingers. "Sanders. That fellow my brother's so fond of. He's the one."

Anna shook her head. "Are you telling me that Jeb Sanders…"

"Indicated you had an interest in me?" His smile broadened. "Don't be angry with the chap. I'm sure he only had your best interests in mind."

She turned to look past Edwin at the man in question. Jeb had the audacity to grin. "And why would you think that?" she snapped.

"Because a union of the Beck and Finch families could only be beneficial to both of us." He moved a strand of hair that had escaped her bonnet. "And my understanding is that once you are securely wed, he is no longer in your father's employ."

"Mr. Beck," Anna said. "Surely you're not proposing that…well, surely you're not proposing. I barely know you."

Features that reminded her so much of Daniel softened. "Of course not, Miss Finch," he said. "What sort of suitor would make such a crass offer to the one whose hand he seeks?"

It was too much, this talk. The Pinkerton watching. The story awaiting her attention in the writing case. Anna began moving away, taking a step backward.

"Are you unwell, Miss Finch?"

"I—" Anna's foot landed on an unstable board and her balance faltered.

Jeb watched Daniel's brother talk to Anna Finch while Hank Thompson yammered on.

"A plum assignment, Jeb," Hank said. "A real plum assignment."

He forced himself to look at Hank. "Sorry," he said. "What were we talking about?"

Hank's smile didn't quite fit the rest of his expression. "I said that while I'm dividing my time between Denver and Leadville, you're following Anna Finch. Some men get all the luck."

"I don't know about that," was the best response Jeb could manage.

"Do you think she'll marry Beck?" Hank asked. "Much as we try to keep it from happening, if she wants to marry him, you know her pa'll encourage it."

Jeb could only nod. A thought occurred to him. "Hank, what's stopping you from giving Daniel's brother a challenge? You'd make Anna Finch a fine husband."

"That society gal's got no interest in the likes of me." He shrugged. "I can't get close enough to kiss her hand."

Guilt slammed Jeb between the eyes. He'd certainly done more than kiss her hand.

Before he could respond, Hank slapped him on the back. "Hate to do this, but I've got business to attend to." He cast another long look at Anna Finch, then returned his attention to Jeb.

"What?" Jeb asked when his friend continued to stare at him.

"Just figuring."

"That so?" While Jeb didn't much care for the former Pinkerton using witness interrogation techniques on him, he cared even less to reveal what Hank was looking for.

Hank scratched his head, then shoved his fists into his pockets. Then, slowly, he began to shake his head. "Take care of her," he finally said.

"I am." Jeb glanced in their subject's direction and found her far too interested in the Englishman.

"She's something special," Hank said. "Now go handle that problem she's having."

Jeb looked up sharply. "What problem?"

"The problem of spending time with the wrong man." Again Hank shook his head as he walked away. "A special one, for sure."

"Too special for Edwin Beck," Jeb muttered under his breath as he aimed his boots toward the couple now engaged in what appeared to be a serious conversation. Just as he came up behind Anna Finch, she stumbled backward.

Jeb caught her and turned her around to face him. Her face was pale. "I'm taking you home now," he said. "No argument." He spied Isak, Daniel's driver, and waved to him, then guided Anna that direction. "Your carriage awaits."

Isak greeted them, and Jeb helped Anna inside and climbed in with her. Only then did he notice that Daniel's brother had followed.

"Sorry," he said as he exchanged a look with Isak. "If you don't mind, I'm paid to see to her safety."

"But that's my carriage," Beck said.

"It's your brother's carriage." Jeb paused. "I'll see that it's returned to you as soon as we're done." He stared down at Edwin Beck. If the man wanted trouble, he'd find it right here. Nothing would make Jeb happier than an excuse to wipe the smirk off the Englishman's face.

When Daniel's brother stepped back from the carriage, Jeb nodded to Isak. A crack of the whip and the horse lurched forward.

Inside the close confines of the Beck carriage, Jeb became uncomfortably aware of the woman seated beside him. "Miss Finch, there won't be a repeat of today's adventure."

"Of course not," she said, her face suspiciously innocent.

"Why don't I believe you?"

She smoothed her skirt and didn't answer.

"Fine. Make all the plans you want. They won't work. You're not going to run off and do anything foolish again. He's a cold-blooded murderer, and you're a woman of quality. What possible reason would you have for saving his skin?"

Anna Finch turned to face him with fight in her eyes. "Mr. Sanders, I recall that you are a believing man, yes?"

"I am," he said, wary of what might come next.

"Then surely as the book of John says, the truth will set a man free. Or, should Mr. Holliday prove to be all that you've alleged, have you considered that the truth might bring justice where it has been lacking?"

He hadn't. Her look of satisfaction goaded him.

"It's settled, then," she said as she leaned back against the seat.

And yet as he studied her, Jeb had the strong suspicion nothing had been settled at all. That in fact, quite the opposite had just occurred.

He spied the Finch home ahead and forced himself to relax. Once the carriage stopped, Jeb jumped out and reached for Anna to help her down. Best to steer the topic to safer ground, he decided. "According to the schedule, I should be ready for tonight's event by eight."

She shook her head. "Actually, I think I'll beg off for tonight's event. I doubt the governor will miss me if I stay home."

"Tomorrow, then," Jeb said. "I'll just wait for the schedule."

Anna turned without so much as a wave and walked toward the house, leaving Jeb to stare. "I'd miss her. Wouldn't you, Isak?"

The driver grinned but kept his silence, though Jeb swore he heard Isak laughing as the gate closed behind him. It was enough to send Jeb off in pursuit of Anna.

"Miss Finch, a minute of your time," he called, taking the steps to the front door two at a time.

"Not now," she said.

"Now." He stepped between Anna and the door and linked arms with her. She seemed about to protest, but her expression changed and Jeb knew he'd won. "Let's take a walk away from prying eyes."

To his surprise, she handed off her case to the maid who'd met her at the door and joined him without complaint. Jeb led her away from the house and down a path that curved into a stand of trees at the back of the property.

Satisfied they would not be overheard, Jeb paused. "I'm going to make this simple, Miss Finch. All verbal sparring and Bible quotes aside, I want your word that what happened today will not happen again."

She looked up at him, eyes wide beneath her bonnet's brim. "You have my word."

Her quick agreement took him by surprise. "Simple as that?"

Anna nodded. "Simple as that."

"All right, then." He rocked back on his heels, reluctant to leave though he knew spending time alone with Anna Finch was a bad idea.

"It's lovely here." She walked a few steps down the path, then paused. "Over there," she said, her voice wistful, "I once had a playhouse. A castle, actually."

"For a princess," Jeb supplied.

She looked back at him. "Yes, I suppose."

His companion seemed content to enjoy the afternoon, and her inattention gave Jeb time to study her. Much as he hated to admit it, she was a lovely woman. A woman who could shoot and ride like a man.

A woman he wouldn't mind kissing again.

"Mr. Sanders, may I ask you a question?"

He smiled. "I'm sure I'll regret this, but go ahead."

She moved toward him. "How badly do you wish to be finished with this assignment?" When he did not respond, she stepped past him. "Your silence speaks for itself."

"Wait." He caught up to her and saw she'd begun to cry. "What's this?"

"Mr. Sanders, if it were within my power to discharge you from your duties, I would certainly do so." She straightened her shoulders and swiped at her cheeks. "Although I admit it would be easier to find a husband and be relieved of not only the burden of a hired gun shadowing my every move but also that awful Mr. Mitchell."

Evidently Mitchell needed another reminder of their agreement to keep Anna Finch out of the papers. He made a note to pay the man a visit as soon as possible.

Jeb reached into his pocket and pulled out his handkerchief, then dabbed at Anna's cheeks. "It's clean, I promise."

Her smile was brief, her gaze intense. "I'm sure another man can be hired should you require a release of duties. You do not have to arrange my matrimony to achieve this."

"Arrange matrimony? Me?" When he stopped laughing, Anna Finch started walking again. "I'm sorry," he called. "Why would you think that I'm arranging a marriage? Me, of all people?"

She froze, then turned slowly to return to the place where he stood. "Who am I to believe, then?"

"Believe?" Jeb shook his head. "What are you talking about?"

Miss Finch seemed to consider the question a moment. "I'll not marry Edwin Beck."

"No," he said without hesitation. "I refuse to allow it."

"You refuse?" The words came out like a whisper. "But he said…"

It took all he had for Jeb not to pull her into his arms. "Who said?"

"So you're not…" She paused to snatch the handkerchief from him.

"No, Miss Finch," he said as gently as he could, "much as I enjoy a cold bedroll and bad campfire coffee, I'm making do just fine here at your humble home."

She smiled and held out his handkerchief.

"You keep it," he said. "Now tell me how you came to think this."

"Well, I was speaking with…" She seemed reluctant to continue, so Jeb decided to help.

"With Edwin Beck?"

Fresh tears began, and this time he ignored good sense and gathered Anna to him. Resting her head against his chest, she gathered two handfuls of his shirt. "He said you'd encouraged him to pursue my hand. That you told him I would be amenable to his advances."

Jeb bit back what he wanted to say and gathered Anna tighter to him. "I'm sorry he upset you. I know what he did on that carriage ride you took with him. Likely he's not happy that I set him straight on how to treat a lady."

This time she looked up to meet his stare. "You confronted him?"

"I did."

Her lip trembled. "But how did you know?"

"I told you, I'm good at what I do." He grinned.

"You are, aren't you?" Anna released her grip on his shirt and smoothed the wrinkles with her palms. Jeb grasped her wrists and stilled the motion.

"Miss Finch," he said slowly, "I'm not saying that some man ought not snatch you up and marry you. Any fellow would be lucky to have you."

"Do you think so?" she whispered.

"I do."

Kissing her bore hard on his mind, but Jeb knew better than to try it. Nothing good would come of it, and as before, there would be plenty of regret afterward.

Anna, however, obviously had no such reservations.

"Miss Finch," he said as she lifted herself onto her toes, "I'm not sure this is a good idea."

"Mr. Sanders," she said, her breath warm against his neck, "must we always disagree?"

"Yes," he whispered against her lips and then surrendered the last of his good sense. His lips fitted against hers just as well as he remembered, and the soft sigh she made when he pulled away was nearly his undoing.

"And to think I was going to apologize for kissing you in the river," she said.

"Actually, I was going to apologize, but I think I'll blame it all on those mules."

Her smile was radiant. "I think you're remembering incorrectly, Mr. Sanders. The real trouble began with your Stetson."

"Did it?" Any memory he had of that day focused on her and not any farm animals or hats. "Well, today it's your hat I find troublesome." Jeb tugged on the ribbon holding her bonnet in place. The bow gave way, and the frilled finery came with it. Curls tumbled around her shoulders, and Jeb reached to wrap a chestnut strand around his finger. "There," he said. "You're lovely without it."

"Scandalous," she whispered. "I now see why my father decided I needed supervision."

Her joke, harmless and yet close to the point, kept him from act-ing on feelings that had begun to take hold.

"Miss Finch," he said as he moved her to arm's length, "I fear we've overstayed our time here. Likely someone will question why you've not returned."

She seemed oblivious to his warning. "Mr. Sanders, I'm a grown woman. Far too old for caring what the help gossip about."

"And yet," he said gently, "I am the help."

A breeze rustled the tree limbs, and Jeb looked up, glad for some-thing to focus on besides Anna Finch.

"Mr. Sanders," she finally said, "I regret causing you to kiss me."

Jeb returned his attention to Anna. "Do you?"

Moving away to retrieve her bonnet, she gave him a quick grin. "No," she said as she started on the path toward her home. "Not in the least."

"Nor do I," he called. "Though there is some debate as to who caused what."

"Must we always disagree?" floated to him through the trees.

"Yes," he shouted, though he doubted she heard. "If we ever find something to agree on, I'll be sunk."

26

The public sentiment, which has nothing to do
with the law, is largely in favor of Holliday.
—*The Leadville Daily Democrat, August 26, 1884*

Mr. Sanders saw to it that the weekly mailbag from Garrison was delivered without incident. Though Anna had enjoyed riding Maisie to the picturesque town, she couldn't afford the risk of being seen each week. Not with her column hugely popular and Mr. Mitchell looking for any opportunity to mention her name in the paper.

Then there was the problem of having a hired gun in tow no matter where she went. It was much simpler to do things his way, at least when it came to receiving mail.

For one full week she managed to avoid any social event where she might be required to have an escort. As much as she enjoyed the company of Mr. Sanders when he was kissing her, she could find no enthusiasm for occasions where Papa might play matchmaker and send her into the arms of another man.

Crazy as it seemed, Anna had begun to understand the feelings the fictional Mae Winslow had for her Henry Darling. While she wouldn't call her situation anything near love, she'd certainly begun to anticipate the next time she might be caught alone with Jeb Sanders.

It was at once scandalous and innocent. They'd only shared a few clandestine kisses, and as the week drew to a close and another began, Anna wondered if she might have an opportunity for more.

Writing the Holliday piece filled most of her days, and the dread of seeing Edwin Beck filled her nights and kept her home. She debated having a discussion with Daniel but decided against it. Daniel had enough reason to dislike his brother without adding yet another.

She turned in her article and waited for a letter that contained train tickets.

On Monday night, she sat at her desk and pieced together a chart of dates and times she could take to Mr. Holliday when he summoned her. And he would, of this she had no doubt.

Tuesday morning she awoke to a knock at her door. "There's a delivery for you, miss," the maid called.

Anna sat up in bed. "Bring it in, please."

"Yes'm," the maid said. The door opened and she entered, dragging an oversized mailbag behind her. "Where shall I put this?"

Gesturing to her bedside, Anna felt her hopes soar. Surely this was the week that Doc would invite her back.

And it was.

When she found the note, Anna nearly squealed for joy. The seal had not been broken, giving Anna hope that the Pinkerton had not discovered the letter. This time, the ticket inside sent her to Carleton, a much smaller town. She placed the ticket and the letter under her mattress, then went to work sorting the other mail.

By midday Anna had finished. Only her hunger drove her from her room to seek something to eat in the kitchen. There she found

Jeb Sanders reading the latest edition of the *Denver Times*. "Quite the article by this Bird fellow," he said as he lowered the paper. "Wonder how he gets these stories."

Anna ignored him and found an apple and a slice of bread, which she slathered with a bit of fresh butter and sprinkled with sugar. She turned to leave, but the Pinkerton rose to place himself between her and the kitchen door.

"So," he said as he took the fruit from her hand. "Any news from your friend?"

He pulled a rather lethal-looking knife from his pocket and began to peel the apple. Anna watched the red spiral stretch toward the floor.

"Mr. Sanders, I have many friends, and some correspond more often than others. For example, Gennie has written to inform me of a lovely garden party she and Charlotte attended in Newport. Glover Cottage was the place, and the Howes were hosts. Care to hear the details?"

He lifted a dark brow before shaking his head. The apple skin fell onto the tabletop.

In response, Anna took a bite of bread, then had to remind herself to chew.

"Your apple, Eve." He handed the peeled fruit back to her, allowing his fingers to graze her palm.

"Thank you." Anna curled her fingers around the apple. "Now if you'll excuse me, I've correspondence to handle."

"I'm sure you do," he said.

"I do." Anna skittered past only to have the Pinkerton once again halt her progress. She looked down at the hand grasping her wrist.

Her hired gun reached up with his free hand to swipe at the corner of her mouth. "Sugar and spice and all that's nice," he whispered. "That's what Anna Finch is made of."

Anna's traitorous heart did a flip in her chest. What was it about this man that turned her thoughts to kissing?

Without further comment, he went back to the table and resumed reading the *Times*.

After hurrying back up to her room, she set the lock and took a bite out of the apple, though her fingers shook. "Concentrate on the task at hand," she whispered before setting the sugared bread on her desk.

Tomorrow's trip to Carleton would require more than a little planning. She took another bite of the apple. "I have all day to figure it out," she said as she went back to her work. "And Jeb Sanders won't catch me this time."

ひひ

The next morning Anna climbed down the back stairs a full two hours before her train's departure time. The night was black as pitch and the chickens were still asleep as she stuck to the shadows and made her way down the driveway to the street. From there, Anna walked the rest of the way into town.

With no sign of the Pinkerton, Anna boarded the train and took a seat near the back of the first car. At the stop before her destination, she slipped out to change into the clothing stashed in her bag. Once the train finished taking on water, a new—or rather different— passenger sat in Anna's seat. If the conductor recognized the change from woman to boy, he did not comment.

The directions were simple, the hotel sparse. In the lobby she found only two settees and a chair occupied by a man who appeared to be losing his battle with good health.

"So the famous A. Bird is not done with me after all." He gave her an appraising look. "So this is what a Wellesley education purchases? A newspaper career playing truth or dare?"

"How do you know of my education, Mr. Holliday?"

He shook his head. "I am not without my sources."

So it would be like this? *Fine,* she decided. She returned his stare.

"Train was late," he said abruptly. "Usually arrives well before now."

Ignoring his statement, Anna pulled her notebook from her case. It was stuffed with notes and clippings, research done in the hopes of reaching this day and speaking to this man again. "I wonder if there might be a place where we could talk in private."

He led her upstairs to a suite that appeared to take up a good portion of the second level. "Do make yourself at home."

She took her place on the settee nearest him and placed her satchel on the floor beside her. "Might I speak first?"

"Please," he said as he leaned back against the chair.

She handed him the chart she'd created and laid out the papers so that he could see for himself what she'd figured out. When she came to the end of her story, Anna sat back and waited for his reaction.

He shrugged. "I always thought the photo that keeps ending up in the papers was just some stupid mistake that couldn't be corrected."

"No," Anna said. "I think that is the actual photograph of the man pretending he is you." She pointed to the pages scattered across the table. "And as you can see, he's been at it for quite some time. At least ten years."

"Ten years." He let out a low whistle. "I am confounded. I don't like being me most days, so it baffles me that anyone else would want the job."

She shared a smile with him. "All I know is the dates do not match. And there are places where you are reported to be in one state but documented in another."

He rose. "I would ask for your documentation, but I assume it's not for me to keep."

"No," Anna said, "but I did take the liberty of making this for you." She handed him a detailed explanation of what she'd just gone over. "It has all the basic information."

Rather than look at it, Doc folded it into thirds and tucked it into his vest pocket. "Much appreciated," he said. "Now get on along with you, or you'll miss your train back to Denver." He patted his vest as if recalling something he'd almost forgotten. "Might I trouble you to post these for me when you get back to the city?"

She didn't have to look to know they were addressed to a convent in Georgia. "Of course." Anna tried not to allow her disappointment to show as she nodded and gathered up her valise.

When she got to the door, he called her name.

"Yes?" She turned to face him.

"Thank you," he said.

"You're welcome." Then she stopped. "You didn't call me here to send me away. Are you ready to tell me your story?"

The aging outlaw paused. "Yes," he finally said, "though I'd decided to let you go on back to Denver if you didn't put up a fight for the privilege."

She set her satchel aside and watched as the gunfighter seemed to contemplate his words.

"I'm going to give you the story you've never expected." His smile dawned. "Though you're quite good at what you do, so perhaps I won't surprise you as much as I think."

Anna fumbled through her things for pencil and paper.

"Not so fast," he said. "There are a few stipulations."

"Such as?"

"What I'm about to tell you is not for your readers in Denver." He held up his hand to stop her protest. "You got your story last week, and that will have to suffice. I fancy a broader audience for this. Perhaps a national appeal."

"Perhaps," she echoed.

He leaned forward. "I want you to write a book. A book that actually tells the real story of Doc Holliday. Are you up for it, A. Bird?"

Anna's grin was quick and genuine. "I am."

Doc shrugged. "Of course you are, given your pedigree. But this will be no dime novel." His smile was quick. "I told you I have connections, Miss Finch."

"I welcome the truth," she said, "and will answer any questions you might have about my qualifications. I would ask the same of you."

"Of course." He steepled his hands. "Then we shall start."

Jeb paced outside the door of the outlaw's hotel room. Anna was inside. The letter from Holliday had been easy to find.

This time the anger he felt was tempered by other less understandable feelings. After their kiss in the woods, Jeb knew he must choose. Either he continued as her protector or he bowed out in favor of a Pinkerton who would actually do the job.

Right now he was all but useless where it concerned Anna Finch.

He could hear laughter through the door, and it nearly killed him not to kick his way into the room. Doc Holliday was not the safe man Anna thought. Far from it.

If he harmed her...

The silence was worse than the laughter. Finally Jeb could bear it no more. The door opened on the second push, and he spilled into the room, landing on his feet. Holliday looked up from a table filled with papers while Anna rose to greet him.

"What are you doing here?" she demanded, hands on her hips.

"He's protecting you, Miss Finch," Holliday said. "That's what Pinkertons do. They protect. Isn't that right, Mr. Sanders?" Before Jeb could respond, Holliday snapped his fingers. "Help me with something. On our last visit, you mentioned an occasion when we spent time together. Did you say Fourth of July of '77?"

"I did," Jeb replied, not bothering to temper his curt tone.

"Your accent marks you for a Texan." When Jeb ignored the statement, Holliday continued. "Ever been to Breckenridge, Texas?"

"I've heard of it."

Holliday shrugged. "On the Fourth of July, 1877, I was a guest of their detention facility." He directed a look at Jeb that was almost a dare. "Look it up."

Anna slid between Jeb and Holliday. "He doesn't have to. I have it right here." She reached into the case and thrust a report toward Jeb. "He's right. See?"

Jeb took the page and read it. Then he read it again. Slowly he lowered it and handed the paper back to Anna.

"So you couldn't have…" He paused, unable to continue.

"Killed your woman? No, it's quite impossible." Holliday turned to Anna. "That's the story you need to tell. Catch that man, Anna."

Jeb shook his head, anger still pounding at his temples. "That's my job, and I'll do it without her."

Holliday nodded. "Surely you could, but you'll be sorry if you don't let her help."

He looked at Anna. "What is he talking about?"

"Research. Weeks of it." She gestured to the table. "I tried to tell you before. I have proof."

While Jeb gathered up the pages, Anna turned to Holliday. "About the book—perhaps I could contact my editors at—"

"Not yet. There's something more important today."

Anna shook her head. "All right," she said. "What do you want?"

"Two things." He paused to take another sip of the water she'd given him. "First, I want you to help this man find out who's been impersonating me and see that justice is done."

Jeb looked up from the various papers. "I'll see what I can do about that."

"Now, wouldn't that be a fine change? The law on my side for once." Holliday's smile was weak. "I do like it. Now the second thing, that's going to be a bit more difficult." He turned his attention to Anna. "I'm going to extract a promise you're not going to like."

"All right."

"Those letters you've been mailing for me, you know they've all been going to the same person at the same address." When she nodded, he continued. "When you hear I'm gone, I want you to take your copy of that story and send it off to her."

"I prefer not to." She gathered up her research. "But I will."

Holliday looked past Anna to stare at Jeb. "I know you've wanted to kill me for a long time. It's going to take some work to transfer all that desire for revenge to the man who did the killing. I trust you'll manage it."

"Let's go," Jeb said to Anna, the last of his patience wearing thin. "You've spent enough time here."

To her credit, she did not argue. At least not until they were seated on the train back to Denver.

"You had no right to follow me," she said, though the lack of fight in her voice showed she knew it was a weak argument.

"We had an agreement," Jeb said when he'd bit back enough anger to manage it. "And I had to come find you. You lied to me."

"I did not," she said. "I…"

"Exactly."

"I wanted the story," she said.

He let out a long breath. She wasn't making this easy. "Enough to lie?"

"I only promised that what happened last time wouldn't happen again. And it didn't, not exactly. We're in a completely different town, for one."

Jeb swiveled in his seat. "You just don't understand, do you? I've cared about you since—well, I can't even tell you when I fell for you. I did, though, and sure as you shot me, I will bear the scars of it. And I don't mean the one on my belly."

"You care about me?"

Her surprise twisted in his gut. "You're the reporter, Miss Finch," he said, "did you miss the clues?"

"Clues?"

Outside, the landscape rolled past. Jeb knew he'd waded into dangerous territory. Silence was the best answer right now, but he had to keep going.

"I kissed you," he said loud enough for anyone in the car to hear. "Regularly."

"Yes," she said softly. "You did."

"And contrary to what you may think of me, I am not a man given to kissing a woman unless there are some pretty strong feelings tied to it." He paused to take a breath. "Do you understand what I'm saying to you, Miss Finch?"

"I do," she said softly as she reached to entwine her fingers with his, "and under the circumstances, I wonder if you might call me Anna."

"Anna," he said with the last of his ire, "you need to promise me you will not sneak off to visit that man again."

"Jeb," she said. "Kiss me."

So, weak man that he was, Jeb did. But he didn't miss the fact that her answer was no answer at all.

27

I said to him one day, "Doctor, don't your
conscience ever trouble you?"

"No," he replied, with that peculiar cough of
his, "I coughed that up with my lungs long ago."
—*Colonel Deweese,*
attorney for Doc Holliday, in The Denver Republican

When Anna returned home, she discovered that one of the letters
tucked into her writing case was addressed to her instead of the
Atlanta nun. She opened it with a smile, knowing her next set of train
tickets was inside.

While she hadn't exactly promised Jeb she wouldn't meet Holliday again, she also hadn't said she would. Thus, when she left home
three mornings later and watched the sun rise from a train car headed
for Bender's Creek, her excitement was tinged with more than a little guilt.

This time Doc met her at the station, his health such that he
appeared to suffer none of the effects of the consumption. "Lovely to
see you," he said as he led her past the few buildings that made up
the town and into the hotel. "I hope your reputation's not suffering
from our meetings, Miss Finch," he said as he closed the door behind

him. "Or should I leave this open so the Pinkerton doesn't have to make such a dramatic entrance this time?"

"If you wish," she said, "though I'm fairly certain he's not followed this time."

And he hadn't, though he did meet her at the train station in Denver that evening, mad as a hornet and ready for a fight.

"Before you say anything, I made no promises to you, Jeb," she said as she allowed him to hand her into the buggy. "I will not be put into a position of choosing between you and a story."

"It's a story now? I thought you and Holliday were collaborating on a book."

She studied the toe of her shoe rather than look at the anger so evident on his face. "We are, actually," she said. "Though I don't see what difference it makes if—"

"You see what you want to see, Anna Finch," he snapped. "That's the problem with you."

"Is it, now?" She took a deep breath and let it out slowly. "Tell me about Ella."

Jeb slapped the reins and the horse shot forward, throwing Anna back against the seat. Instead of turning toward home, Jeb aimed the horse for the prairie, neither stopping nor answering her questions until they reached the scene of their first kiss.

There by the river, with the water lapping almost benignly against the rocks, Jeb brought the buggy to a halt. For a long time they sat in silence. Then he cleared his throat, his attention still focused on the river.

"Ella was my wife. Doc, or whoever that man was, shot her."

"I'm sorry."

He turned to face her, his hands still holding the reins. "I am too, Anna," he said. "She was a good woman, and she's dead because a man who wanted to kill a Pinkerton killed his wife instead."

Anna leaned over to place her hand over his.

"I gave it all up after that. Liquor and the law. Didn't want any part of the Pinks." He paused, and Anna felt his hand move slightly beneath hers. "Hank Thompson's the reason I'm back with the Pinkertons. He came and got me. Told me about Jesus and made me see that to lay back and let a murderer get away wasn't how a man behaved."

He took in a ragged breath and, with his free hand, swiped at his cheek. Anna reached into his vest pocket and pulled out his handkerchief.

His smile disappeared almost as soon as she offered it. "I'll never put another woman in harm's way again."

"Jeb," she said, "I'm going to have to disagree with you."

"Of course," he said. "That's what you do, after all."

"Loving you doesn't mean I'm being put in harm's way."

He stared at her. "Are you saying you…"

"I'd prefer you to say it first, actually," Anna said. "Hurts a girl's pride if she has to be the one."

"But what if…"

"Jeb, stop stalling," she said. "And if I might ask, I'd like a kiss as well."

He obliged, and when he'd kissed her thoroughly, Jeb lifted his hand to caress her cheek. "Anna Finch, I can't believe I'm telling you this, but I've gone and fallen in love with you."

In love. Her heart sang and she felt an inexplicable giggle rising in her throat. "Jeb Sanders, that is not the kind of declaration that gives a woman goose bumps. Can't you do better than that?"

"Not with words," he said, his voice husky. He kissed her again.

This time when he moved away, he held tight to her hand. "I will have a promise, Anna Finch, and I won't allow any evasion. You will not see that man, Doc Holliday, alone again."

She thought only a moment. "Then come with me. Would you do that?"

Two kisses later, he finally agreed.

⊙⊙

Anna almost floated down to breakfast. She expected to find Jeb at the table, but instead only Mama and the familiar stack of papers awaited. The *Denver Times* sat atop the pile, so after she'd completed the required small talk with her mother, she quickly turned to the horrid Mr. Mitchell's column. Satisfied no mention had been made of Saturday's trip to Bender's Creek or the buggy ride to the river, Anna set that paper aside and reached for the next.

"Will you be going out again today?" her mother asked.

Anna picked up her coffee cup and shook her head. "I hadn't intended to," she said as innocently as she could. Thus far her mother hadn't inquired as to the cause of her extended absences. As for her father, likely he either did not know or assumed the hired gun was worrying enough for the both of them.

"Then if you will excuse me, I'll go and prepare for my morning."

"Of course," Anna said as she watched her mother leave. Finally alone, Anna reached for the rest of her newspapers. On the third one, a headline that spread the width of the page caused her breath to catch in her throat.

Man Murdered in Cold Blood by Doc Holliday

She glanced at the name of the paper and her heart sank. "The *Bender's Creek Standard.* Oh no." She began to read the article.

"What's got you looking so serious?" Jeb asked as he took the chair across from her and began filling his plate from the platters of food Anna had yet to touch.

"Read this." She thrust the paper toward Jeb. "The imposter. He did this."

Jeb stuffed a slice of bacon in his mouth, then turned his attention to the newspaper. "But this is impossible," he said. "The man was killed at noon in the saloon beside the rail station. Your train arrived at eleven-thirty. Holliday had to have been with you when the shooting happened."

"He was."

Another slice of bacon disappeared while Jeb considered things. "That was just Saturday. Likely he hasn't gone far."

Anna's stomach growled, and she reached for the platter of scrambled eggs. "What do you have in mind?"

"I have to do some figuring on this." He accepted the platter of eggs from her and heaped them in the center of his plate. "Might even have to do a little traveling. And since I'm sworn to protect you, I'm afraid you're going to have to—"

"I won't stay here," she said. "I refuse and I'm a grown woman. You cannot make me."

Jeb chuckled. "I was going to say that I'm afraid you're going to have to come with me."

"Oh," she replied meekly.

After three more bites, Jeb pushed away from the table. "Pack a bag and be prepared to stay overnight." He paused. "Or is that inappropriate to expect? You have my word as a gentleman that I'll not attempt to compromise—"

Anna laughed. "While I appreciate your concern for my reputation, I'll be fine. My goal is to learn the end of Mr. Holliday's story, and catching this man is certainly an ending I'd like to see in print."

Jeb gave her a quick kiss on the cheek. "Do me the favor of spending today working on that story. Or doing something that keeps you home. Would you, please? I can't prepare for tomorrow and worry about you too."

This promise Anna kept, spending the day in her father's study, working on her book. When Jeb returned that evening, he found her bent over her father's desk, her fingers stained with ink. His attitude had changed.

"What's wrong?" she asked.

"The trip is off," he said. "My sources don't agree with what's printed in the paper."

"What?"

"There was a misprint," he said. "It should have read midnight, not noon."

Anna set down her pen. "You don't think he might be guilty, do you?"

"No, Anna," Jeb said. "I believe he *is* guilty. And as of right now, I forbid you to have anything more to do with that murderer."

"But he didn't kill your wife!"

The Pinkerton folded his arms over his chest. "He's killed plenty of other people."

Anna rose to move toward him. "Likely he has," she said carefully.

If Jeb was surprised by her admission, he didn't show it. "Now that we've got eyewitnesses placing him at the scene, I have ample reason to arrest him."

Jeb's ample reason to think the worst of Doc Holliday merely gave Anna ample reason to hide her continued association with the gunfighter. The next time he sent her a letter, this time by regular mail to her home address with no return identification, she opened it with anticipation. The fact that Jeb's past blinded him would not keep her from helping Doc Holliday complete the book about his life. This she assured Doc when she stepped off the train in Colorado Springs and found him waiting at the Antlers Hotel.

"I heard of the murder same as you," Doc said. "From the papers. Trouble is, I was already here and thus unable to defend myself."

"I can swear out an affidavit," Anna said.

"Saying what? That I was with you twelve hours after the shooting?" He shook his head. "Better we continue to work on our project. Time's running short."

She looked him over and found no evidence of it. "Your health appears better than ever," she said.

"Then the ruse is working." He gestured to her writing case. "Get out your papers. I fear we'll be working twice as long now."

When she was ready, Doc continued his tale exactly from where he'd left off at their last visit. As she'd expected, the story's twists and turns were fascinating, especially when the topic turned to women. He'd found trouble in places where none was thought to exist, but he'd also found love in the name of a woman named Kate.

"Or rather what passed for love, given I was denied the real thing as a youth."

"Denied?" Anna asked. "How so?"

"We were cousins," Doc said, "and the church refused to marry us." His expression took on a faraway look. "But then, wondering what might have been isn't a worthy use of a man's time."

Anna remained silent. A man of declining health ought to spend his time doing whatever he pleased, though she'd not interrupt his thoughts to say so.

"Ah, but Kate, now she was something," he finally said. "And if I do say so, most of the time she thought I was something as well."

After a while, Doc ceased his recollections and began coughing so hard that he couldn't continue.

"I can fetch water and perhaps some lunch," Anna said, "if you want to keep going." He nodded, and Anna stood. "Anything special I can bring back?"

"Yourself will suffice, though I understand the restaurant downstairs serves an excellent larded beef."

"Larded beef it is," she echoed as she hurried from the room. She returned twenty minutes later with a double portion of the delicacy—both for him.

"Come sit here," Anna said. "Let me pour some water for you."

The outlaw rose as obediently as a child and seated himself at the table. But as Anna set the food before him, his face hardened. "Miss Bird," he said, his voice icy, "I am no invalid."

"Of course not," she hastened to say.

"I'm also no saint," he continued. "So I ask that no matter what I tell you, you not portray me as one."

Anna had no idea how to respond, so she remained silent. He allowed her to attend to him, but when the meal failed to restore him, she sent him to bed and packed up her case for the trip home. Before she closed the door behind her, Doc's soft snores assured her he had found a fitful rest.

She made notes and arranged information on the trip back to Denver so that when she arrived home, she might immediately begin work on the next chapters. Mr. McMinn met her at the station, and she half expected Jeb to be with him. When he wasn't, Anna figured she'd escaped without detection. She carried this hope all the way home, then promptly gave it up when she saw the expression on Jeb's face.

Mr. McMinn scurried away without helping Anna from the carriage, leaving her at the mercy of an angry Pinkerton.

"Where was he this time, Anna? Fort Collins? Aspen?"

She gathered up her dignity and her writing case and climbed out of the carriage herself. She swept past Jeb and moved as quickly as she could toward the house. "Colorado Springs," she called as the door slammed behind her.

When Jeb did not follow, relief set in. Then, by degrees, disappointment replaced it. He was angry, and rightly so, but Anna knew she'd done nothing wrong.

To prove it, rather than dismiss the invitation to the soiree at the Miller home that evening, she made her preparations to go out. Her sapphire dress, newly arrived from Paris and in the latest fashion, was chosen with more care than usual. Fitted just right and paired with a smart hat and gloves, the dress was created to catch a man's eye.

Or make him forget his anger.

Anna pinched her cheeks, then reached for her bottle of Fleur d'Italie and dabbed it on her wrists and behind each ear. She took one last look in the mirror and pronounced herself passable.

At the bottom of the stairs, her escort waited, though Jeb barely spared her a glance.

"Good evening," she said and received a grunt in return. When he turned to lead her outside, Anna froze. "Mama and Papa," she said. "Won't they be joining us?"

"Unfortunately not." He handed her into the carriage, then climbed in beside her. His arm brushed hers and he leaned away. Anna felt disappointment settle in her stomach but took some satisfaction at the sideways looks he surely thought she did not see.

A moonlit ride, romantic under any other circumstances, quickly became the staging ground for a war of silence that spilled over onto the walkway leading to the Miller home. Stars dusted the evening sky, and the cool night air sent Anna burrowing into her wrap as the carriage drew to a halt. Jeb lifted her to the ground, then waved away Mr. McMinn and the carriage. Before Anna could escape, the Pinkerton caught her elbow.

She gave him a disdainful look even as her traitorous heart jolted at his touch. Up ahead, the Millers' door opened, spilling light down the path toward them.

"You gave me your word," Jeb said abruptly.

"And I kept my word," she responded, ignoring the twinge of her conscience.

"No, you did not."

Anna dared a look at him. Even with shadows slanted across his features, there was no missing his stubborn expression.

"You did not, Anna," he repeated. "Admit it."

She opened her mouth to do just that, but someone called her name, and Anna found herself in the midst of a tight knot of party-goers moving toward the door.

The Pinkerton hung back and watched while Anna allowed herself to be propelled forward. As much as she tried to ignore his stare while she exchanged greetings with those around her, Anna found her attention returning to the dark-haired hired gun.

The man who'd admitted to more than protective feelings for her.

"Anna, darling!" She turned to see Mrs. Miller reaching to embrace her. "Don't you look lovely? That shade of blue has always been so beautiful on…" Her hostess looked past Anna, and her eyes widened.

"You know Mr. Sanders, of course," Anna said to the Millers by way of introduction before slipping away to blend into the crowd. Only when Edwin Beck found her did Anna regret not remaining at Jeb's side.

"I fear I shall never find the words to end the trouble between us," he said. "Though I shall not cease until I do."

"You are lovely company," she said, and she meant it. "But I don't trust you."

His smile broadened. "Must you trust me in order to dance with me?"

Anna saw the Pinkerton watching her as he carried on a conversation with one of Papa's more talkative business partners. Satisfied

Jeb was sufficiently occupied, she smiled at Edwin Beck and moved toward the dancers.

As she reached the dance floor, she felt Edwin's hand press against the small of her back. She turned to say one of the banal things appropriate for dance conversation but found it was Jeb, not Edwin, who'd joined her.

His gaze scorched the length of her as he gestured behind him. "Your friend was delayed."

Anna saw Daniel's brother a few yards away, his attention held by the same gentleman who'd only just been speaking to Jeb. The orchestra struck up a waltz, and Jeb led her into the group of dancers.

"What have you done with my dance partner?" she asked.

"I'm sure he'll be here soon enough." Jeb led her effortlessly through the crowd. "I'll just go over the rules before he finds his good sense and stops talking to that banker about money when he can speak to you about…well, you know what he wants."

"Actually, I am more interested in knowing what you want, Jeb."

He almost stumbled. "What I want, Anna, is for you to stop making things so difficult."

"About that." Anna followed Jeb's lead as the room turned around them. "I wasn't exactly forthcoming with you."

"Forthcoming?" His dark brow rose.

She gave him what she hoped was a sincere look. "I've been awful. Will you forgive me?"

The Pinkerton stopped and dancers swirled around them. "Don't toy with me, Anna Finch."

"I humbly apologize for misrepresenting my appointment with my previous interviewee. Do you accept my apology or must I continue?"

"I'll think about it. In the meantime, I—"

She pressed her finger to his lips, and her hired gun began to grin. "Do you want to dance or talk, Jeb Sanders?"

He shook his head and led her off the dance floor. "I want you to enjoy yourself tonight. And then we'll have our conversation on the way home."

"All right."

Out of the corner of her eye, Anna saw Edwin approach. She expected Jeb to intercept the Englishman and was stunned when the Pinkerton stepped away.

"A dance, Miss Finch?" Edwin Beck asked, ignoring Jeb's presence completely.

She stepped into his arms as much to irritate Jeb Sanders as to avoid any deep conversations with Daniel's brother. But as the orchestra struck up the next tune, Edwin struck up a conversation.

On marriage.

"As my wife you'd enjoy a lovely home and all the travel you wish," he said.

"I have those things now, Mr. Beck." Anna sighed. "Let's do change the subject."

"I refuse." His expression immediately became penitent. "Forgive me," he said quickly. "It's just that your father is most happy I've made this offer to you. He is, in fact, quite pleased to become a member of our family." He paused. "Through you, of course."

"I'm sure my father would take great pleasure in seeing me wed," Anna said. "I am not, however, interested in having that groom be you." She shook her head to stop his response. "You'll make some woman quite happy. You're most pleasant to look at and your charm is obvious."

"I suppose I should thank you for the compliment." Edwin met her stare. "But you must understand that arrangements have already begun for our union."

"Arrangements?" Anna kept her tone light, her attention focused on the man guiding her across the floor. Where was Jeb Sanders when she actually needed him?

"Miss Finch." He paused. "Anna. You must understand my visit was not a random appointment to become reacquainted with my brother. I've known of you and your plight for quite some time through correspondence with your father."

"Correspondence with my father?" Anna attempted to pull away from him, but Edwin refused to allow it. "And no one thought to inform *me*?"

Her dancing partner looked baffled. "Why? Your father made a compelling case for you. Nothing further was needed to pique my interest. All that remains is to formalize our union with a wedding. In Britain, of course. While your little town is quite charming, certain persons of quality would be unable to attend."

"Mr. Beck," Anna said as firmly as she could manage, "I do not wish to marry you."

"Anna, dear, you are an absolute delight, but there's no need to play the coquette." He leaned toward her. "I am entranced by you and will give you anything you wish."

She gave Edwin her best version of a flirtatious expression. "Truly? Anything?"

"Anything."

"Then there is but one thing I desire." Crooking her finger, Anna drew the Englishman near. "That you look elsewhere for your bride. I shall neither marry you nor entertain any thoughts of keeping even so much as a social acquaintance with you, Mr. Beck."

Edwin reared back, surprise and anger flashing across his face, and her hired gun finally arrived. Jeb Sanders cut in and whirled her away from the Englishman before he could say a word in response.

"It's time to go home, Anna," he said.

She smiled at an acquaintance, then returned her attention to Jeb, bursting with pride at her ability to stand up to Edwin Beck.

Jeb spun her, taking her breath away in the process. When he pulled her back to him, he dipped his head. "Well done," he said in a low voice into her ear. He straightened. "Get your wrap. I'll wait."

"Why? I'd like to stay." The song ended. She moved away, but he caught her arm.

"Anna, must we always be at odds?"

"If you continue to be so unreasonable, then I fear we must." She walked away, caring very much whether he followed.

ॐ

She'd stood up to the Englishman, judging by the direction their conversation had taken and the expression of surprise on Edwin Beck's face. Allowing himself a satisfied smile, Jeb skirted around more than one obstacle to reach the woman he'd been hired to protect, placed his palm against her back, and moved her toward the door.

"Your carriage awaits, m'lady," he said in a mock English accent.

She frowned. "How much did you overhear?"

"Enough." He gestured to the door. "It's midnight, Cinderella. Time to leave the ball."

Strangely, she put up no further protest as Jeb led her outside. Emerging into the chill of the evening, Anna shrugged out of Jeb's grasp.

"I know I'm going to wish I hadn't asked," Jeb said as he lifted her into the carriage, "but what's got you riled up now? You were practically glowing a few minutes ago."

She fell back against the seat, her arms crossed. "My father has attempted to barter me off like a piece of prized horseflesh."

"To Beck?"

"Yes."

They rode in silence until the Finch gates closed behind them and the carriage stopped. Anna allowed him to help her out of the carriage, though only because her fancy gown did little to aid her in climbing down from such a height.

He thought about following her inside, then decided against it. She was wrong about Doc Holliday, and any attempt on his part to convince her of that tonight would not end well. He adjusted his Stetson and turned toward the stables and his meager bunk.

"Mr. Sanders."

Jeb turned at the sound of her voice but said nothing. To his surprise, she stormed toward him like a woman on a mission. That mission, as it turned out, was to kiss him goodnight.

Truly and soundly kiss him.

"That, Anna Finch," he said as he held her against him and savored the warmth of her breath against his neck, "was a memorable way to end an evening."

"I hate fighting."

"As do I."

"Then apologize, and we shall not speak of it again."

He looked down at her wide, brown eyes. "Apologize? For what?"

There the memorable evening ended. Anna stormed away, slamming the door as she went inside.

"Women," McMinn said from the other side of the carriage. "Who can understand 'em?"

"Surely not me," Jeb said. He walked toward the bunkhouse.

28

No man can have a more loyal friend than Wyatt
Earp, nor a more dangerous enemy.

—*Bat Masterson*

"Wake up, Pinkerton man."

"Anna?" Jeb drew the blanket up to his chin to hide his bare
chest. "What are you doing here?"

Something dropped onto the blanket. He blinked until his
eyes adjusted to the light. It was a newspaper. A Colorado Springs
newspaper.

"Read the headlines."

"'Faro dealer murdered in cold blood by notorious Doc Holliday.'"

She snatched it from him and read the article aloud. When she
got to the time of the incident, Anna paused. "Doc was with me at
the Antlers Hotel at that hour. A dozen people will testify to it."

"You're sure?" Jeb leaned up on one elbow. "Absolutely sure?"

"There's no doubt." Her attention strayed to his midsection.

"Looking for another spot to shoot me?" he asked, gathering the
blankets higher.

The prettiest color of pink rose in Anna's face, and she let the
newspaper drop once more. "What are you going to do, Jeb?"

He gave her a sideways look. "So it's my plan now? I figured you weren't going to speak to me until I apologized for whatever it is I did."

"You're good at what you do," she said, "and I want this man caught. I'm willing to forgive your tendency to order me around."

He stood up, the blanket wrapped around his waist, and she backed into the doorway. "No, you don't, Anna Finch. I'm not going to do a thing for you until the two of us come to an understanding, so you might as well come back here."

She didn't move.

"All right," he said. "I guess you can find another hired gun to do your investigating for you."

"Really, Jeb." She fiddled with her hair as her eyes once again found his middle. "This is important. A man's life is at stake."

"Yes, it is." He moved an inch toward her. "Mine."

"What are you talking about?"

"I'm trying to make a point, Anna. You and I are dancing in circles when we ought to be waltzing together."

Her attention came up to his face. "What? We just waltzed last night."

"Look, woman, I'm trying to be poetic." He shrugged. "I swore I'd never let another woman get hold of me, and long as I live I'll never figure out how you did it. But you have."

The source of his discomfort furrowed her brow. "What are you talking about?

"I'm talking about how infuriating it is to fall in love with a woman when that's the last thing a man needs or wants."

She leaned against the door frame, arms crossed in front of her. "*I'm* infuriating?"

"You could come over here and argue the point, but that's probably a bad idea." He paused. "About that murder, give me some time to formulate my plan. I'll let you know as soon as I've decided how to go about this."

She slipped out the door without another word, and Jeb reached for his shirt, his mind already running through possible leads.

⊙⊙

Anna spent the day alternately pacing her room and attempting to concentrate on what she'd begun to call her Holliday project. The fact that she might actually help bring a guilty man to justice was more than Anna could fathom. Was this how Jeb Sanders felt when he concluded a case? If so, perhaps her next job should be as a Pinkerton.

The sun was firmly in the western sky before Jeb finally sent up a note. "We leave at half past six," she read. "That's all? No details?"

She got nothing further from him on the ride to the train station or, for that matter, on the trip to Colorado Springs. "Are you just going to ignore me?" she finally asked.

He shook his head. "I'm working, Anna."

"So am I, Jeb Sanders, and if you don't tell me what you're up to, I'm going to make a real fuss. You don't want every eye in the place on you when you're trying to fit in, do you?" She pointed to the bag in his hand. "You can start by telling me what's in there."

"Keep quiet until we get to Holliday." He paused. "If you'd like to play the spoiled society girl, go right ahead. But know it will be you who ruined this opportunity, not me."

How she hated it when he was right. Or rather, when she was wrong. "Sorry," Anna muttered.

They left the train station and walked to the Antlers Hotel, and Anna showed him to Doc's door.

Doc answered their knock promptly. "I'm glad you could come on short notice," he said to Jeb. "My understanding is the man's still here."

"My contacts tell me the same thing," Jeb said.

"Forgive me," Doc told Anna, "I've not so much as greeted you. It's charming to see you back so soon." He glanced at her empty hands. "You've not brought your writing instruments."

Her smile was quick. "I'm sure I can purchase something that will suffice."

"Yes, do that," he said. "If, of course, your Pinkerton friend doesn't mind."

Jeb nodded his approval, and Anna reluctantly left them to fetch what she needed. She hurried toward the mercantile a block from the hotel. While her surroundings were the height of small town charm, Anna could barely take in what she saw for wondering what was going on between Jeb and Doc. She paid for the items then nearly ran back to the Antlers.

Two Doc Hollidays waited for her in the hotel room. One, however, outweighed the other by a good fifty pounds.

"Truly, you could fool my dear departed mother," the real Doc said, "for there was a time when I could have passed for a man of your breadth." He seemed to shake off the memory as his expression sharpened. "You'll need the stickpin." He handed Jeb the diamond pin from his lapel.

Jeb allowed Anna to put it into place, then stepped back to look in the mirror. "If I'm not back by eleven, go to the sheriff."

"Wait!" she cried. "Please tell me what you're going to do."

"I'm going to catch a killer, Anna," he said. "So come over here and give me a proper send-off."

He held out his arms, and she moved into them. He kissed her.

Long after he was gone, Anna stared at the door. Finally, she turned her attention to Doc, who watched her intently, a hint of a smile on his face.

"Shall we get back to it?" she asked.

ര

Smoke and the sounds of what used to pass for fun swirled around Jeb as he stepped into the Wagon Wheel Saloon and went straight for the faro tables. Halfway there, a woman's laugh made him freeze.

Ella. He hadn't thought her presence would ride so high in his mind today.

If he closed his eyes, he knew he'd hear the crack of the pistol. See the blood. Watch a good woman die.

And yet as he prepared to confront the man who murdered his wife, he knew he also needed to put to rest the belief that killing the man who shot Ella would even the score. Nothing on this side of heaven would atone for his loss, and yet the Lord had somehow seen fit to let him love again.

It was a mystery he knew he'd never solve.

He didn't deserve Anna Finch, but he'd be a fool to let her get away. And while he was a lot of things, a fool wasn't generally one of them. So he kept his eyes open and his mind on the job at hand.

Though the crowd stood shoulder to shoulder in some places, it didn't take but a few minutes to find the person he sought. In the far corner of the room sat the man whose face matched the picture in that day's paper and Jeb's memory of that night in Leadville so long ago. His mustache was thick in the middle and tapered down on each side, his jaw square and prominent. With brown eyes and a sturdy build, he couldn't possibly be the ailing dentist from Georgia.

Jeb marveled that he'd ever believed they were the same person. But then, how many people really knew what Doc Holliday looked like? If a man claimed to be a legendary gunfighter, it was usually in a body's best interest to believe him.

Moving closer, Jeb kept his attention on the suspect. The suspect, however, had his attention focused on a fetching blonde. When Jeb reached them, the blonde took one look at him and scampered away. The imposter turned.

"You Doc Holliday?" Jeb asked, one hand on his pistol.

The imposter rose. "Who wants to know?"

Jeb stepped into the light, and the color drained from the other man's face. "Who do you think?"

The man's hand went to his gun, but Jeb was faster. With the man who murdered Ella Sanders in his sights, Jeb's finger found the familiar spot on the trigger. One move and the man was dead. Sent straight to the One who would judge his reprehensible actions.

It would be so easy to justify it all.

"Go ahead," Jeb said. "Give me a reason to kill you."

But the stranger just stared, his weapon drawn but his expression showing only fear. "I didn't mean no disrespect," he said. "The opposite, you know? It's just—havin' a *name,* it gets you places."

"Leadville. Eighteen seventy-seven." Jeb watched for any recognition on the stranger's face. "Her name was Ella and she was my wife."

"Was she pretty?"

"Until you shot her, she was the prettiest gal in Leadville," Jeb said, his voice deadly even. His finger pressed a notch harder on the trigger. Any excuse and this man was dead. Any.

The man stared at him. Then, by degrees, he began to smile. And then he had the audacity to laugh. "You're no more Doc Holliday than I am!"

Jeb's shot, aimed at a spot just above the man's head, took the bluster out of the criminal and caused him to drop his weapon. When he came up from behind the table, Jeb's revolver was aimed at his forehead.

And so was Doc Holliday's pistol.

"You're right, he's not Holliday," Doc said, cocking his gun. "But I am."

"I thought you were staying back at the Antlers," Jeb said.

"When there was justice to be had?" Holliday lifted his lapel with his free hand to expose the badge pinned to his chest. "Last time I wore this, courtesy of my friend Wyatt Earp, I sent more than one cowboy to meet his Maker." He focused on the imposter. "How would you like to join them?"

The imposter fell to his knees and began to beg, and Doc rolled his eyes.

"This one's not worth shooting," he said as he put away his pistol. "Give the sheriff my best. I've got a pretty gal back at my hotel room who can't wait for my return. She's hanging on my every word these days."

When Doc winked as he walked away, Jeb shook his head. He never thought he'd share a joke with Doc Holliday.

The sheriff arrived in a mere five minutes as reports of the ruckus had quickly reached the lawman's office.

"Ain't that something? Heard tell Doc was here," the sheriff said. "I wouldn't have figured to have one of them in town, so two's a surprise."

Jeb handed over the prisoner, then adjusted his Stetson. "Wouldn't know about that," he said. "Must've been talking about me, though I'd be glad to show you a badge I've got showing I'm a Pinkerton."

After providing his credentials, Jeb walked out of the saloon. A few blocks away he stopped and looked up at the Colorado sky, diamond stars scattered across its surface.

He'd done it at last—put Ella's killer behind bars. He thought he'd feel lighter somehow, or happy or satisfied. Instead he just felt quiet, like some voice that had been whispering in his ear for years had finally fallen silent.

Suddenly he wanted nothing more than to see Anna Finch.

∞

In the Antlers Hotel, Jeb found Anna scribbling while Doc Holliday rambled on about some trip to New Orleans to see his father. He crossed the room and pulled her into a hug. Despite her small noise of surprise, she embraced him with a pleasing amount of enthusiasm.

"Doc says you got him," she said, pulling back and looking up into his face.

Jeb nodded. "We need to go now, Anna. Our job here is done."

"Yours might be," she said, "but if you don't mind, I'd like to continue with what we're doing."

Doc gestured to the door behind him. "Got a nice bed in there. Get yourself some sleep."

"You'll see she doesn't do anything foolish, like run off?" Jeb asked.

"Where would she go?" Holliday asked with a grin. "Apparently I'm the only one she leaves town to see."

"You've got a point." Jeb glanced at Anna. "First thing tomorrow morning, and there will be no argument."

"Promise," she said.

When morning came, Jeb found Anna still working at the table where he'd left her. Sometime during the night, Doc had fallen asleep in the chair and sprawled there, snoring softly.

"How bad off is he?" Jeb asked as he found his hat.

"Just tired," Anna said. "But I've got what I came for." She stacked her papers, then folded them in half. "He's asked me to do something. I'm not certain I can."

Jeb raised one brow. "What's that?"

"The book. He doesn't want me to publish it. He wants it mailed to the woman in Georgia."

"The nun?"

Anna nodded.

"If that's what he wants, then that's what you'll do," Jeb said. "I heard tell he had a wife, though I didn't realize she'd checked herself into a convent."

A rustling sound told them that Doc had awakened.

"The thought of Kate in such circumstances is enough to entertain me for quite some time. I regret, however, that this is not the person to whom I've requested the book be sent." Doc sat up. "I take it you're leaving now." He rose and stretched. "Miss Finch, it has been a delight. My friend Wyatt was correct in his assessment of you. And I stand corrected on what a Wellesley education can offer."

"Thank you." Anna moved past Jeb and into the arms of Doc Holliday. "I shall miss you terribly."

"No, you won't," Doc responded. "I've been considering a move to Denver. For my health, of course."

"Of course," Anna said with a giggle. "Do think harder on that. I'd relish another lunch with Mr. Bonney and his friends at the Windsor."

When Anna stepped aside, Jeb reached to shake Doc's hand. For a moment, their eyes met.

"Don't lose this woman," Doc said. "She's something special."

Jeb nodded. "She is indeed."

66

Anna slept in his arms all the way back to Denver, her curls spilling over his shoulder and one arm resting beneath his. At the station, Jeb gently woke her, then tucked her hair beneath her bonnet and helped her stand.

"We did it," she said.

"You did it," he replied. "Now let's get you home and into bed so you can rest. I believe you've got a book to write."

"I do," she said, "though I wonder if you might give A. Bird an exclusive interview, considering recent events."

He grinned but didn't respond. Any tale he might tell wouldn't see newsprint, that much he knew for sure.

Anna smiled and rested her head against his arm as they made their way onto the platform. "Do you still love me, Jeb Sanders?" she asked, half asleep.

He paused to gather her into his arms. "Yes, Anna Finch, I still love you."

"Well, now, isn't this cozy."

Jeb looked over Anna's head to find Winston Mitchell staring at them with a nasty look on his face. "Been out all night, kids?" he asked. "Or rather, *in* all night?"

This worm of a man questioning Anna's reputation made Jeb's blood boil. "What are you insinuating, Mitchell?" he asked as calmly as he could manage.

He laughed. "Me, insinuate? Perish the thought!"

Beside him, Anna looked ready to faint. "You'll not write a word of this," Jeb told Mitchell. "Not one word."

"Are you asking me to ignore a valid news item?" Mitchell gave Anna an even stare. "You know I cannot."

Anna swayed, and Jeb lifted her into his arms. "Is she ill?" Mitchell asked as he trotted alongside Jeb.

"She's exhausted," Jeb replied. Mitchell, of course, wrote this in his notepad.

Jeb spied a carriage for hire and waved to the driver. Setting Anna inside, he climbed up to join her. "Not a word," Jeb told Mitchell. "Else you will regret it."

29

That nothing's so sacred as honor, and nothing
so loyal as love!
—*Wyatt Earp's epitaph*

Anna slept until well past the dinner hour. After the maid told her
Mr. Sanders had left on Pinkerton business, she fell back into bed,
despite the fact that both Mama and Papa sent word they wished to
see her. Pleading exhaustion, she put off the inevitable and didn't
open her eyes again until morning.

The next morning she prepared to answer whatever questions
her parents might have. Fortunately, the maid who awakened her also
informed her that Mama and Papa had taken the early train to
Leadville. With their return at least a day away, Anna hoped she
might enjoy breakfast with Jeb Sanders. Taking special care with her
hair and in the choosing of her frock, she was disappointed to find
that she would be dining alone.

"Mr. Sanders is away on Pinkerton business," Mr. McMinn
recited when she went out to the stable, looking for Jeb. He would
say nothing more. Nor did the stable hands or the maids know where
to find him.

Anna returned to her room and stayed hard at work until curios-
ity made her wonder exactly what sort of Pinkerton work Jeb might

be doing. No longer able to focus on her writing once this thought took hold, she decided to do something about it. She went directly to the one man who might be able to help her: Hank Thompson.

Finding him behind the desk in Daniel's office suite, Anna made quick work of exchanging pleasantries before getting to the point of her visit. "I want to know where he is," she said. "It's not like him to disappear."

Hank laughed. "It's exactly like him, especially considering the write-up in the paper today."

Anna spied an open copy of the *Denver Times* on Hank's desk. The pages had been folded back to reveal Winston Mitchell's latest column. She snatched up the page, allowing her eyes to scan the scathing lines.

What birdie's scandalous behavior is the talk of the nest?
Why, our favorite little bird, of course. Finding someone to
clip her wings might be evading Papa Bird, but filling the nest
with little chickadees? That might happen soon enough given
recent activities. This reporter witnessed firsthand our little
bird's shockingly ruffled return from an all-night tête-à-tête.
Did I say that? Perish the thought!

"Filling the nest with chickadees? All-night tête-à-tête?" Hank leveled an even stare at her. "Only one thing that could mean, Miss Finch."

Anna squared her shoulders and turned on her heel, leaving Hank's allegations unanswered. She could feel tears burning her eyes, but she forced them back. She'd brought this on herself. That she might have caused Jeb to leave was the only part she regretted. At least until she had to explain the situation to her parents.

As she walked from the Beck office to her carriage, she noticed the stares of several of Denver's finest. The word had spread. "I'm ruined," she said as Mr. McMinn helped her inside.

"You're a tart, that's what you are," said the all-too-familiar voice of Winston Mitchell.

"How dare you!" She swiveled to see the awful man coming toward her. "What have you done?"

"Done?" He shrugged. "Only reported the truth. Shame on you, breaking the heart of visiting royalty and spending the night cavorting with your hired gun." He shook his head. "Oh, and then there was the disheveled state in which you presented yourself at the train station. Why, who knows what sort of wild carousing you'd been up to? Your poor father and mother. I'm sure they're horrified."

Anna closed her eyes, envisioning her father's face.

Then another voice joined the conversation. "Mr. Mitchell— or is that truly your name?" She opened her eyes to see Jeb walking toward them. He stopped next to the carriage. "It's not, is it, Henriech?"

"Henriech?" Anna echoed.

Jeb nodded and crossed his arms. "From New Jersey."

The journalist's face turned red. "Look, Pinkerton, I—"

Jeb shook his head. "You will print a retraction. In the next edition."

"Based on what?" Mitchell had the audacity to ask.

"Based on the fact that the woman whose reputation you are attempting to ruin is my wife. Or will be, once she's been properly asked and ushered to the parson."

"Wife?" Anna and Mr. Mitchell said at the same time.

"Wife," Jeb responded as he reached into the carriage to take Anna's hand. "Unless you've got an objection to marrying up with me."

"Well," she said, "I do need to convince my father to get rid of that hired gun he paid to follow me around. He's become quite a nuisance. Papa says getting married is the only way."

"Is that so?" Jeb reached toward her, then seemed to recall they were not alone. "Mr. Mitchell? I'm going to give you exactly one minute to leave my presence. You will return to whatever hole you crawl out of each morning and write a column refuting every word you've written against Miss Finch. Do you understand?"

"And if I don't?"

"If you don't, then I'll turn the truth about you over to an intimate friend of mine for publication. You've heard of A. Bird, I suspect."

"But that's…"

Jeb pulled his watch from his pocket. "Thirty seconds," he said.

Mitchell scampered away.

"Now," Jeb said. "About that marriage proposal."

"You'll have to ask my father." Anna paused. "But I'd appreciate it if you let me speak to him first."

He bristled. "I'd rather handle this man to man, Anna. I won't have you doing my job for me. I've got my own ranch and money enough to take care of you. I don't need your help convincing him—"

She touched her finger to his lips. "Please."

Jeb visibly relented, the stubbornness fading from his shoulders. "On one condition," he said. "You've not been properly proposed to until I—not you—have spoken to your pa. Understand?"

"Yes," she said, and pulled him into the carriage.

ᘒᘓ

When her father finally returned from his trip to Leadville the next morning, Anna followed him to his library, knowing he would seek a few minutes of peace and quiet before being called for lunch.

"My daughter," he said when he'd settled behind the desk. "Aren't you the talk of the town?"

Anna refused to take the bait. "Papa, I must speak to you about Edwin Beck. I will not marry him, and there's nothing you can say to force me to. As I am a grown woman with a means of providing for myself that does not include an inheritance from you, I am fully prepared for you to disown me."

Her father listened attentively. "And you would find this preferable to wedding Edwin Beck?"

She let out the breath she'd been holding. "I would."

"Well, fortunately for you, Mr. Beck has withdrawn his offer for your hand due to new facts he's uncovered about your virtue." Papa pressed away from the desk and rose. "Might I inquire as to the validity of his allegations?"

"Why, I don't know what..." The article. Mr. Mitchell. Anna sighed. "There were veiled statements besmirching my reputation in one of yesterday's newspaper columns. Lies. Most of them," she amended.

Papa nodded. "So you've not taken up with some fellow and gone on wild train rides out of town with him while your mother and I thought you were visiting friends?"

Anna suppressed a groan. "I wouldn't exactly say wild, though there was a man nearly shot in Colorado Springs, but only in self-defense. And then there was the arrest, which was a shared endeavor between myself and two Doc Hollidays."

Her father looked as if he were having a bit of trouble breathing. He sagged against the edge of the desk and grappled to loosen his tie. "Anna," he said, "have you shot another fellow?"

"I have not," she answered quickly.

He seemed a bit less flustered as he took a gulp of air. "All right, then have you allowed your virtue to be compromised in any way?"

She thought for a moment. "Actually, or in appearance?"

His eyes narrowed. "Actually."

Anna smiled. "Then my response is no."

Papa looked relieved. "Then there is hope I may still marry you off."

"More than you know, Papa," she said, "and when he comes to call on you, I'd like you to remember one thing."

"What is that, dear?" her father said as he reached for the carafe of water on the desk beside him.

"I love him."

With that statement, Anna left her father to his sudden thirst. She headed for the stables but found only Mr. McMinn, brushing out Maisie.

"She's lovely," Anna said, "though more willful than any filly ought to be." She looked beyond the horse to the quarters where it seemed like she'd only just awakened a sleeping Pinkerton.

"He ain't in there," Mr. McMinn said.

"I don't suppose you know where he went."

"Actually, I do, but you ain't gonna get it out of me."

"Then allow me to finish that." Anna reached for the brush and took over the driver's job of combing out the horse's coat. When she was done, she set the brush aside and called for a stable boy. "Saddle her, please," Anna said. "I've a mind to ride."

While the boy hurried off, Anna raced upstairs to the trunk where she kept her favorite riding attire. Pulling the rough shirt and trousers from the trunk made her smile, though donning the clothes made her itch.

She returned to the stable smiling, any thought of dignity tossed to the wind along with her reputation in Denver. When she slid into the saddle atop Maisie, she didn't bother pulling her hat low over her face. *Let them stare,* she decided. *No more hiding.*

She considered heading toward Garrison and the post office that might have a bag or two for A. Bird, but decided that could wait, as could the letter to her readers she would be printing soon. Unless Jeb disagreed, Anna planned to let Mr. Smith at the *Times* know that A. Bird needed a change of name.

A. Sanders had a much nicer ring to it.

As Maisie settled into a languid, relaxed pace, Anna reached up to release the first of her hairpins and contemplated what sort of conversation Jeb might have with Papa. She prayed it would go well.

Giving Maisie free rein meant the horse meandered about then eventually headed toward her favorite watering hole, which Anna decided was a fine way to spend a nervous afternoon. At the rise above the stream, the horse's ears pricked and she slowed.

"What is it, girl?" Anna asked as she leaned forward to scratch the horse's ear. "You haven't been here in a while, have you?"

Gone was the raging river in which she and Jeb had nearly lost their lives, and in its place flowed the swift stream that would likely remain until the winter freeze. Once the horse cleared the rise, Anna dismounted and allowed Maisie to wander toward the water's edge to drink.

"Taste good?" she whispered. "I bet it does."

She knelt beside the stream a few yards ahead of the horse and cupped her hands in the icy water. It was good, cold as the dead of winter, but good. Sitting back on her heels, Anna sighed. The only thing missing from this glorious day was an official proposal from Jeb Sanders.

"Please, Lord, let Papa say yes."

She rose and dusted off her pants, then spied a familiar landmark. The log. She grinned. How long it seemed since she'd last taken aim and shot at it. Perhaps it was a good day to try again. Anna giggled as she caught Maisie and hobbled her, then pulled out the Smith & Wesson.

What were the odds she'd shoot a man this time around? Negligible, she knew, but as soon as the thought occurred to her, Anna lowered the gun.

"Surely not," she whispered as she edged nearer the log. "What sort of fool would be hiding behind a log in the middle of the—"

A pair of arms reached up to grab her, and Anna tumbled forward to land in Jeb's embrace. The gun slid away and landed with a plop in the stream.

"You scared the life out of me," Anna said as she swatted the Pinkerton. "I could have shot you."

"I told you I'd never let you sneak up on me again," Jeb said. "And I meant it."

"But how did you know…"

He touched his finger to her lips. "I'm good at what I do, Anna."

She smiled. "You owe me a pistol."

Jeb sat Anna upright, then rolled into a sitting position and reached into his shirt pocket to produce a tiny box. "Would you settle for a ring?"

Anna's gaze went from the exquisite ruby and diamond creation to the face of the man she loved. "You promised you'd ask my father first."

"Already have." He shrugged. "As soon as you left on that heathen horse of yours, I went straight to his library and had a talk with him. He wasn't too keen on marrying you off to a common hired gun, and I wasn't too keen on taking no for an answer. Lets just say I convinced him I could tame you."

"You'll do no such thing."

He grinned. "Wouldn't dream of it."

"But how did you beat me out here?"

"I've a very fast horse."

"But—"

He silenced her with a kiss. "Anna, I'm going to ask you to marry me, so don't interrupt."

She giggled, then forced herself to find a somewhat serious expression. "All right," she managed.

Jeb rose onto one knee and reached for her hand. "Anna Finch, you've left scars on me that'll never heal, so the least I can do is brand you with my last name. Will you marry me?"

"Charming," she said as she fell into his embrace. "Truly charming."

He held her at arms length. "You didn't answer."

"Yes, of course," she said. "Why would I answer anything else?"

He grinned at her. "According to Daniel, his brother's packing to leave on the afternoon train. Thus, if you wish Gennie to be in attendance at the wedding, that can be arranged."

"And Doc too?"

The hired gun wrapped one of her curls around his finger. "Yes, of course, if he's well enough."

Anna made a face. "My mother will insist on a big wedding. The plans could take months."

"There's a way around that, you know." Jeb's grin took a wicked turn. "I admit to being impatient when it comes to claiming my bride, so I wouldn't mind cheating a bit. All we need is a parson and a couple witnesses."

Anna thought about that, and a smile slowly spread across her face. "Then there's only one thing left."

Jeb lifted a brow. "What's that?"

"You need to kiss the bride-to-be."

And so he did.

ANNA FINCH MARRIES HIRED GUN

**A special report by Winston Mitchell,
columnist and close friend of the bride**

THE DENVER TIMES

September 5, 1885—An event of memorable and epic proportions was held Friday at the home of Barnaby Finch, banker and man of some means, and his wife, the former Miss Harriahan of New York and Baltimore. Their daughter Anna Mathilde Honorée Finch was wed in an afternoon ceremony befitting royalty to one Mr. J. E. Sanders, a Texan in the employ of the Pinkerton Agency.

Dressed in a silk and lace confection of exquisite construction and elaborate design, rumored to have been provided by House of Worth, Miss Finch descended the staircase at the Finch mansion looking every inch the princess to join her princely groom and three hundred fifty onlookers consisting of family, friends, and close business associates. Her mother's tiara and grandmother's triple strand of pearls were among the adornments this darling of Denver society wore. Guests were invited to attend a sit-down supper at the Windsor Hotel followed by entertainment provided by the Winburn String Orchestra, Mildred Winburn, accompanist, and Minnie Winburn, vocalist.

The event was a splendid success with only the slightest issue of trouble revealing itself. Sadly, this reporter was informed that the new Mrs. Sanders, upon being served a particularly aromatic second course of cheeses, became quite ill and excused herself from the festivities for a time. Relieved of her duress, the bride returned to her groom and made merry until such an hour as she was escorted to the honeymoon suite for the night.

Those who know the couple say the match was truly one made in heaven. As for this reporter, he can fully and confidently report that Mr. and Mrs. Sanders seemed very much in love. Why, it was as if they'd been married for quite some time and not only wed just that afternoon.

Did I say that? Perish the thought!

MAY DAY BRINGS BABY MAE

A special report by Winston Mitchell,
columnist and close friend of Anna Finch Sanders

THE DENVER TIMES

May 5, 1886—This reporter takes great joy in announcing that the lovely Anna Finch Sanders, formerly of this city, has provided her husband, the noted rancher, investor, and Pinkerton agent, J. E. Sanders, with his first child, a daughter called Mae. Her arrival into the world, occurring as it did on the auspicious May Day after which it is supposed that she was named, caused family and friends some level of concern as the darling bundle was not said to be due for at least another month. I have it on the authority of the happy and doting grandparents that both mother and daughter are doing exceedingly well.

Though this reporter has not yet had the privilege of paying a visit to the Sanders family, those who have indicate little Mae is a lovely child with her mother's eyes and her father's even temper. Or perhaps 'tis the other way around. Likely she will be tall like her father rather than possess the petite and feminine stature of her mother, given that mention has been made of the strapping heft and size of the dark-haired newborn.

Did I say that? Perish the thought!

Historical Facts

A journalist's facts are the mainstay of any article. Consider the following:

- John Henry "Doc" Holliday graduated from the Pennsylvania College of Dental Surgery in 1872. He opened a dental practice in Dallas shortly thereafter. He later took up the practice of dentistry in Tombstone, Arizona, though in both cases ill health caused him to give it up.

- The legendary gunfight at the OK Corral was over in just under thirty seconds, and more than thirty shots were fired.

- The last known meeting of Wyatt Earp and Doc Holliday took place at the Windsor Hotel on May 1, 1885 (other sources claim 1886) and was documented by Earp's wife, who was also in attendance at this historic meeting.

- Wyatt Earp lived well into the twentieth century, moving to California, where he befriended many in the movie business. Two cowboy stars of the time, William S. Hart and Tom Mix, were pallbearers at his 1929 funeral.

- The Pinkerton Detective Agency's logo was a large eye, and their motto was "We never sleep." Alan Pinkerton earned fame as the man who foiled an early assassination attempt on Abraham Lincoln.

- The first book in Beadle & Adams' Beadle's Dime Novel series, *Maleaska, the Indian Wife of the White Hunter* by Ann S. Stephens, dated June 9, 1860, is widely considered to be the first dime novel.

- The *Denver Times* was an actual newspaper published from 1872 through 1926. Winston Mitchell, however, is completely fictional and never wrote a column for the paper.
- Nineteenth-century journalist Nelly Bly, born Elizabeth Cochran but who wrote under a pseudonym taken from a Stephen Foster song, blazed for female reporters a trail that included a stint in an insane asylum playing the part of an actual inmate. She had only one year of formal education, and that was at home under her father's tutelage.

Acknowledgments

Research is the backbone of any historical novel, and in my search to make Anna's story as authentic as possible, I found several exceptional sources. While I relied on multiple books on the topic, *Doc Holliday, The Life and Legend* (John Wiley & Sons, ISBN 978-0-470-12822-0) by Gary L. Roberts gave me incredible insight into the person and history of the Georgia dentist. I urge any reader who wishes to know more about the real Doc to pick up this wonderful resource.

In addition, microfiche and online editions of newspapers such as the *Rocky Mountain News,* the *New York Times,* and other historical newspapers, provided excellent first hand information on the time, location, and subject matter of this book.

In some cases liberties were taken with details such as train schedules and weather. Wherever possible, however, I have endeavored to give the reader an enjoyable story set against a background based in fact. Any mistakes made in the telling of this tale are mine alone.

I would like to acknowledge Jessica Barnes for bringing out the story that wanted to be told and Amy Partain for asking the tough questions and catching my mistakes during the copy editing stage.

Many thanks to Wendy Lawton of Books & Such Literary Agency, friend, cheerleader and agent extraordinaire, for her wisdom and encouragement during the course of completing this novel.

Finally, my deepest gratitude goes out to the dear friends who were an integral part of praying this book into existence. You are my village!

Author's Note

I've been a fan of all things western for as long as I can recall. However, my fascination with John Henry "Doc" Holliday began in 2007 when longtime friend and fellow WaterBrook author Tracey Bateman convinced me to slip away from the International Christian Retail Show and visit the Margaret Mitchell House Museum.

There I first heard the details of the story behind *Gone With the Wind*. The tale of Ashley and Melanie becomes more poignant in light of the real-life family members Mitchell used as models. According to docents at the museum, Ashley Wilkes was inspired by Doc Holliday, Mitchell's cousin by marriage, while Melanie was based on Margaret's third cousin (and Doc's first cousin) Mattie "Sister Melanie" Holliday.

Because the church refused marriage to first cousins, Doc and Mattie's love was denied them. Doc went west, some say as much to heal his heart as to heal lungs scarred by tuberculosis, known as consumption. Word reached Doc that Mattie had joined a convent. Throughout his life, Doc wrote letters to Mattie. Upon her death, those letters were burned, so no record of what Doc and Mattie shared remains.

It is in this void of information that I set Anna's story. While I made every attempt to check details against the known history of the outlaw dentist, there are also gaps in time where Doc is unaccounted for. In addition, there are instances where only a second (or possibly third) man could have committed the crimes for which Doc Holliday was accused.

Like Anna Finch, I hope you find Doc Holliday unforgettable.